ACADIAN WALTZ

By

ALEXANDREA WEIS

World Castle Publishing

WCP

World Castle Publishing
Pensacola, Florida

Smashwords Edition
ISBN: 9781938961786
First Edition World Castle Publishing January 15, 2013
http://www.worldcastlepublishing.com

Cover: Karen Fuller
Photos: Shutterstock
Editor: Maxine Bringenberg

For My Mom
Wish You Were Here

CHAPTER 1

For many, the course of an entire lifetime could be summed up in a few defining moments, but moments do not choose your path. There was always an indescribable force lurking inside of us that shaped our destiny. Whether this motivation was the result of fear, longing, or in my case, guilt, it haunted our being and oversaw our every action. Like a constant voice inside our heads, this energy gave each of our lives direction.

My inner voice was hugely influenced by the city where I was born. Built at the bend in the Mississippi River and tucked behind protective levees, New Orleans nurtured a peculiar world infatuated with the Catholic rituals of sin and penance. Therefore, it should be no surprise that those of us who endured in this swamp-ridden land below the level of the sea had mastered the art of sin. In fact, we turned it into something of a tourist industry. It was the penance part that many of us had not quite gotten a handle on. But God, in his infinite wisdom, wanted to make sure that we were always reminded of our heavy feelings of culpability. That was why he created the greatest guilt-making machine of them all—the mother.

Mine was named Claire Mouton Gaspard Kehoe Schuller. My mother's first husband, Etienne Gaspard, had been her high school sweetheart. Etienne was known for running touchdowns, shrimp boats, and little else. Their marriage ended the day my mother first laid eyes on Clayton Kehoe at the criminal court house, where she had gone, yet again, to bail her drunk husband out of jail.

Her second husband, the late Clayton Kehoe, had been a prominent attorney in the city of New Orleans. Mother's current husband was a Jewish jewelry maker named Lou Schuller. Lou was not as influential as Kehoe had been, but infinitely more skilled with gold and diamonds, which invariably pleased my mother to no end. But my mother had always insisted that it was Clayton Kehoe who had swept her off her feet from the first moment their eyes met.

"Your father," Mother would always say. "Had the sweetest way of talking, and he always knew how to treat a lady like a queen."

My mother was nineteen and my father was thirty-two when they married. It was a happy marriage, with lots of parties, many friends, and eventually the arrival of me, Nora Theresa Kehoe. I was named after my mother's favorite saint and my father's favorite movie star.

Marriage to my father must have agreed with Claire. She enjoyed being the wife of a well-connected New Orleans attorney, and thrived on the social circuit of parties and political gatherings. Even after my father died when I was fourteen, she would still meet with her old friends from the various political groups around the city, and pound the pavement for many of my father's former colleagues who were running for office. But that all ended when she married Lou Schuller.

At fifty-five, Lou was dumpy, chubby, bald, and had the personality of a matzo ball. But Lou had the money to keep Claire in the lifestyle to which she had made herself accustomed, even after all the insurance money my father had left ran out. In the beginning of their marriage, Lou tolerated my mother's love for the social scene, but he soon grew tired of the endless cocktail parties and political fundraisers, and reined in Claire's activities. Now, after fifteen years of marriage, middle-aged, and trying to cope with the passage of her youth, my mother had found a new venture in which to place all of her efforts; me. Or more to the point, my marriage to some man, preferably wealthy, in the hopes of attaining the beat all and end all of middle age—grandchildren.

"You're thirty now, Nora. It's time to meet a man and settle down. Why haven't you found someone? It can't be all bad out there," my mother began one Sunday morning in March.

I had returned home to join Mother and Lou for our weekly brunch at their large home off St. Charles Avenue.

"Mother, the worth of a woman is not measured by the size of the diamond she wears on the third finger of her left hand. Maybe I don't want to get married," I griped as I buttered a piece of toast at the grand mahogany table we were forced to dine at for every meal.

"Not get married!" Mother roared, making the fine blue veins on her forehead pop out. "I knew I shouldn't have sent you off to college. Those professors fill young girls' heads with ideas, like women's rights and global éclairs."

"Global affairs, Mother." I rolled my eyes, mortally embarrassed that she could confuse a pastry with equal rights. "I didn't learn about women's rights by going off to college. I studied it in high school, along with all the other—"

Mother put her hand dramatically to her chest. "Oh, my God, you're a lesbian!"

"Now, Claire," Lou chimed in, giving my mother a critical gaze over his thick, black-rimmed glasses.

"Well, I can't tell, Lou." Mother's puppy-like brown eyes looked from me to my stepfather. "You know how kids are today; all that experimenting they do. She probably hung out with lesbians in high school. That's how it starts. I saw a television show on lesbians once. That's why she never brings over any men to meet us, and why I never see her with any girlfriends." She paused and her lower lip quivered ever so slightly. "Do you have friends, Nora? You know, the normal kind?"

"Mother, stop it." I pounded my fist on the brightly polished mahogany table. "I work fifty hours a week at the hospital running the total joint program for the orthopedic department. I don't have time for friends. I don't bring any of my dates here because you would scare them to death." I shook my head as the tremble of her lower lip became more pronounced. "Mother, I'm thirty years old.

I'm well past experimenting and no, I'm not a lesbian." My mother's shoulders sagged with relief. "Why should I want to marry anyway? I already own a house. I make great money as a physical therapist. I'm working my way up the corporate ladder and have lots of opportunity to further my career in management. What in the hell do I need a husband for?"

Mother rolled her large eyes, accentuating the wrinkles beneath them. Her bright red hair shimmered under the dining hall imported Irish crystal chandelier. "Nora, a husband can't be out of fashion. How do you expect to have children?"

"I don't have to get married to have children, Mother. Conception has been known to happen outside of the marriage bed." I winked at Lou.

Lou, turning a light shade of red, tried to shrink further down in his chair.

"No daughter of mine is going to have a child without a wedding. Can you imagine what all of my friends would say? What would Father Delacroix say? What would the Women's League of St. Rita's Church say?" Mother pulled at the pale cream lapels on her perfectly pressed Chanel suit. "Lou, say something!" she shouted.

He peered over at my mother with his pale hazel eyes "Claire, you're overreacting." He stabbed a thick piece of ham on his plate with his fork. "Give the kid a break. She'll marry when she's ready."

My mother stood from her chair and dropped her linen napkin on her untouched plate of ham and grits. "When will that be? I'll be dead before she's married, and I'll never get to see my grandchildren."

"Grandchildren?" I chuckled with profound amusement.

She balled her hands into fists and her pale complexion began to boil over red as she glared at me. "I want grandchildren!" she hollered, while pumping her diamond and gold-encrusted fists up and down for added effect.

"Mother, please," I begged as I sat back in my chair, stifling my desire to bolt from the room.

"If you don't give me grandchildren before I'm old, you will have broken the first cardinal rule of being a daughter."

"What rule?" Lou asked, and then stuffed his piece of ham into his mouth.

"That daughters are obligated to provide grandchildren for the pleasure of their parents, and the betterment of mankind," Claire barked as her voice broke under the strain of her rage.

"The betterment of mankind…really, Mother! Eliminating all politicians I can see being for the betterment of mankind, but children?"

"Since when do you want to be a grandmother?" Lou inquired as he eyed my mother, half-laughing. "You had a panic attack last year when your daughter turned thirty. Cost me fifteen-grand in plastic surgery, that did."

"Shut up, Lou!" she yelled. "This is not about age, it's about duty. Every generation is obligated to the one that went before it. Grandchildren are part of that duty."

"Duty? For goodness sake, Claire, it's the not the invasion of Normandy." Lou slammed his napkin down on the table and stood up. "Children should be born out of love, not because of some silly sense of duty. Let Nora find someone to love first, then you can pester the poor girl about grandchildren," he argued, giving Mother one last scolding with his eyes. He turned from the table and marched out of the mahogany-paneled dining room.

Mother scowled at me. "Now look what you've done."

"Me? You yelled at him." I picked up my plate. "You can't make me do something I don't want to do, Mother. I'll marry and have children when I'm damned good and ready." I turned from my mother and carried my plate into the kitchen, signifying that the conversation, as far as I was concerned, was over.

But little did I realize on that Sunday morning that the full impact of a mother's guilt had been passed on to me. The heavy mantle of parental expectations had been thrown over my shoulders, because after that day, something inside of me changed, and my life would never be the same.

* * *

I left Mother and Lou later that morning and headed out of the city. I drove past the swamps that surround the metropolitan area as I made my way toward the small town of Manchac. The community was on the outskirts of Lake Pontchartrain, and was made up of old Cajun families who had always made their living on the freshwater fish and shellfish found in the Louisiana bayous.

I veered off the interstate and down a shell-covered road leading to one of the harbors located along the edge of the lake, where many of the best shrimpers and fishermen in the state did their business. Setting out well before sunrise, these intrepid men with rough, callused hands and worn out souls scoured the bayous of southeast Louisiana to catch their living. They worked every day except for Sunday. No one fished on Sunday. That was God's day, and in this predominately Catholic community, a day for church. But after church, most of the men in these parts could be found on the docks next to the lake, tending to their boats, fixing broken nets, drinking lots of beer, and communing with their own kind.

When I pulled my blue Honda Accord up to the Gaspard Fisheries boatyard early that afternoon, I found a line of beat-up Ford pick up trucks in the parking lot. I walked to the long pier, where over fifty shrimp trawlers and fishing boats were docked, then sauntered down the familiar planks until I came to launch number twenty-two, and a trawler named *Rosalie*.

"Uncle Jack," I called out to the empty deck of the old trawler.

All about the bleached wooden deck were scattered tools, an assortment of nets, and large coils of thick rope. Perched away at the far end of the deck, facing out to the expanse of the blue lake, was an old wooden deck chair. Over the top of the back of the chair, I could make out a faded blue cap, and sitting next to the chair was an open ice chest with two longnecks of beer protruding over the rim of the container.

"Jacques Mouton," I shouted one more time as I slung my purse securely over my shoulder. I made my way down the two four-by-four planks that served as a gangway until a sudden motion from the chair caught my attention.

"Who's there?" a raspy voice called out from the deck chair.

I hopped off the gangway and on to the deck of the boat. "Uncle Jack, its Nora."

Peering out from the side of the deck chair was a square, suntanned face with small, sky blue eyes. He had sunken cheekbones, a long pointy noise, and silver whiskers covering his chin and cheeks.

"Nora T?" He jumped from his chair. He was dressed in a greasy pair of jeans, a grungy white T-shirt, and no shoes. "What you doin' out here so early, girl?"

"It's after two, Uncle Jack. How long have you been asleep?"

"After two?" He pushed his blue cap back on his head, showing his sterling gray hair.

I motioned to the ice chest. "How many beers have you had?"

"Enough to lose track of the time." He walked over and hugged me.

He smelled of grease and sweat. His T-shirt clung to his back and I could detect the beer on his breath as his lips brushed my cheek.

"I've told you before, Uncle Jack, no more than two a day. It's not good for your blood pressure," I scolded as I pulled away from his arms.

He nodded his head and backed away from me. "I know, but it's just too hard for me, child. Old men can't change their ways."

"Old men had better change their ways or they'll be dead men." I placed my purse down on the boat deck, unzipped the top, and started going through it. "Go and sit in your chair," I ordered as I pulled out a blood pressure cuff and a stethoscope. "Let's just see how bad your pressure is today."

Uncle Jack went and sat dutifully in his deck chair, then held out his arm to me. "You don't have to come and take my pressure every Sunday, you know. I could go to that free clinic in town."

I rolled my eyes at him. "You would never go to the clinic. You would just tell me you were going." I placed the cuff around his arm.

"You look more like your mama every day," he said as his eyes explored my face. "You have her oval face, creamy skin, and her high cheekbones, but you got my blue eyes and blond hair."

"And my father's big mouth." I placed the stethoscope to my ears and began inflating the blood pressure cuff.

Uncle Jack sat patiently waiting for me to finish before he spoke again.

"Your father was a smart man, Nora T. You're smart, just like him."

I unwrapped the cuff from about his arm. "Yeah, well, four packs of cigarettes a day wasn't that smart." I sighed as I took in his blue eyes. "One forty-two over ninety-five; borderline, but still higher than I'd like, Uncle Jack."

"My pressure, she's fine." He reached over and patted my arm. "Stop worryin' 'bout me."

I rolled the blood pressure cuff up with my stethoscope. "If I don't worry, who will? Auntie Elise has been gone almost twelve years now, and Nathan has…." I wanted to kick myself for bringing up my dead cousin's name.

He turned and scoured the blue water of the lake behind him. "He's been gone six years. Six years since he drown in Katrina." He shook his head, reliving the nightmares of the past. "Seems like yesterday this was his boat. His problem, and now…." His eyes found mine. "How's your mama?" he asked.

I walked back to my purse and put my equipment away. "Driving me mad. She wants grandchildren. She says I owe her grandchildren."

My uncle rubbed the gray stubble on his face. "You do know that your mama is bracque…real crazy, she is. She done been that way ever since she was a youngin'. Always wantin' the world, and tellin' everybody how to get it for her. Don't pay her no mind."

"Well, today she really got to me." I paused for a moment and looked out over the blue water of Lake Pontchartrain. "Perhaps she's right. I'm thirty now and I should think about getting married," I mumbled.

"What about love, girl? Don't you want to be in love before you marry someone?"

I faced my uncle and shrugged. "Love would be nice."

He zeroed his blue eyes on me. "Nice? Child, love better be all you're after, 'cause the rest don't work without it. Don't be in a rush to marry, Nora T, if your heart ain't in it." Uncle Jack laughed, his warm cackle that always entertained me as a child. "You don't want to end up like your mama, do you?"

"No, I don't," I admitted with a smirk.

"So why you listenin' to her?" He paused and stared at me for a moment. "Anyways, I ain't known you to be serious about no beau."

"Most men bore me."

"So you one of those…those lesbots?" he queried.

"Lesbians," I corrected, shaking my head. "Mother asked me the same thing this morning. No, I'm not a lesbian."

"Now that's a damn shame!" a man's velvety voice said sarcastically behind us.

I turned to see the towering, muscular figure of a man, dressed in a casual pair of khaki slacks with a blue knit polo shirt, make his way onto the boat deck. He had wavy, black hair with a touch of gray around his temples, and deep brown eyes with long black eyelashes. His suntanned, square face had a protruding brow that only seemed to intensify the unsettling quality of his dark eyes, while his thin, red lips appeared to be frozen in a perpetual smirk.

"Nora," he said in his smooth voice as he nodded to me.

"Jean Marc. Didn't think you would be out among the working stiffs on a Sunday," I remarked in a curt tone as the potent aroma of his woody cologne assaulted my nostrils.

He gave me a thorough going-over with his disturbing eyes. "I always try to check on the crews on Sundays. Make sure everyone is ready for a full week's haul."

"Hi there, Jean Marc." Uncle Jack moved forward and took the man's thick hand. "Good to see you back in town. How was your business trip, son? And how's Ms. Marie doin'?"

"My trip was fine, Jack, and Momma's well." Jean Marc shook my uncle's hand. "She wanted me to thank you for the crawfish pies you sent over last week. She really appreciates how you and all the men have been looking out for her since my father died."

"That's what we do here in Manchac. We take care of our own." My uncle smiled up at the man. "How you doin', Jean Marc?" he asked with a lilt of fatherly concern in his voice.

Jean Marc placed his hands in his pockets and stared down at the deck. "Things have been all right, Jack. I'm just trying to keep the business going. I don't know how my father kept things afloat."

"Yeah," my uncle offered with a nod of his head. "With them local shrimp farms and that crawfish comin' in from China, things been hard on the lake." My uncle rubbed his head, displacing his cap to the side. "But things been hard on the lake before, son. Bound to get better."

"Well, I'm trying." Jean Marc raised his brooding, dark eyes to me. "How you been, Nora?"

I stepped to my uncle's side. "Fine, Jean Marc. Just came out to check Uncle Jack's blood pressure."

Uncle Jack placed his arm about my shoulders. "She comes out every Sunday. She's good to me, she is."

My irritation escalated as Jean Marc's eyes traveled down my body.

"I'm glad to hear it," he murmured. "You take care, Jack. I'll be checking in with you again on Thursday, once we get that new pump in for the fresh water holding tanks at the warehouse. I'll need you and LaSalle to help me put them in." He gave me a painful smile. "Nora," he added and dipped his head politely. Then Jean Marc quickly turned to go.

"God, I hate that man," I whispered as I watched him make his way down the gangway to the dock.

"Shhh." Uncle Jack waved his hand at me. "Jean Marc Gaspard is good people. Kept me out here shrimpin' longer than any other company would." He stopped and then tilted his head to the side as he continued to study me with his curious blue eyes. "Why you don't like that man?"

"Because he's an asshole, Uncle Jack!"

"Well, then you must know him better than me, 'cause I never seen no asshole in that boy." He bent over and picked up a wrench from the deck by his feet. "His family may be the best off in Manchac, but he's good to his people here. Never been no highbrow snob like your mama. When he went off to that college in Texas, he stayed away a long time, but he never came back all high and mighty." He paused and glanced back down the dock where the figure of Jean Marc Gaspard was growing smaller. "Now that his papa's gone, he got lots to do, him bein' Ms. Marie's only worthwhile son and all."

"Where is Henri these days?"

Uncle Jack shrugged. "Who knows? Better away from here, that's all I care. Never seen twins more different than those Gaspard boys. That Henri's been a peekon to his mama and papa since he was a youngin'."

I picked up my purse and swung it over my shoulder. "Jean Marc is the one who has always been a thorn in my side."

"Since when? Boy's never been nothin' but respectful to you. Been nice as pie to you all your life, even when you was a peeshwank. He used to sit and watch over you. I seems to remember you had a big crush on him. You even talked 'bout marryin' him one day."

"When was this?" I questioned, acting surprised that the disagreeable Jean Marc Gaspard and I were ever close.

"When your papa used to bring you out here. As soon as you stepped from your papa's car, you went runnin' to Jean Marc. Followed that boy all over the dock, you did." Uncle Jack pointed the wrench over at the dock next to the boat. "Jean Marc was always hangin' around helpin' to fix engines and such. Anytime you came to visit, he would volunteer to watch you so your papa and me could go fishin'. He even taught you how to dance. You don't remember that?"

I gave my uncle a bewildered side-glance. "Dance?"

"The Acadian Waltz. Your papa and me come back from fishin' early one day and found you two dancin' on the dock with no music. Funniest damn thing I ever see."

"I don't remember that," I mumbled.

"'Spect not. You was barely out of diapers then. That boy always has taken a fancy to you, Nora T. He liked you then, and if you ask me, he still likes you."

I walked over to the gangway made of two old boards. "He's an ass. He's always been short and rude with me."

My uncle cackled as I walked down the gangway. "That's the way his kind is," he called behind me. "They never know how to act 'round a girl. 'Specially a girl they fancy."

"Fancy?" I tried not to laugh as I peered down the dock. "The man looks at me with nothing but disgust."

"That ain't what I see."

I turned back to my uncle and frowned, wanting to change the subject. "No more than two beers a day, Uncle Jack." I waved my hand at him. "I'll see you next week."

CHAPTER 2

Over the course of the next few weeks, Mother began arranging meetings for me with a heavily screened line of suitors. An endless number of boring lunches with attorneys, engineers, bankers, and accountants began to clog my calendar. They were either divorced or never married, and they all looked at me with the eye of a butcher trying to discern which cut of meat from my hearty loins would taste the best. But a few of these casual lunchtime encounters led to dinner dates, where the real task of weeding the worthy from the worthless took place.

In my rapid-fire dating experience, perpetuated by my mother's frenzied excitement for grandchildren, I was dined from one end of the city to the other. Fed sumptuous grilled oysters by a rather portly tax accountant from Shreveport, to catfish fried in four-day-old oil and served on newspaper by a personal injury attorney on the lookout for wife number three.

I was courteous to each man, but I'm sure I lacked the bubbly charm they wished to see when meeting someone with long blond hair, blue eyes, and a well-endowed figure. Actually, most of my life had been filled with the subtle irony that my looks never matched my inquisitive, quiet, and academic nature. Mother used to say I was a librarian trapped in a stripper's body.

God knows how many mindless dates I had endured since my mother first impressed on me her need for the patter of little feet. But one evening, the prospect of finding Mr. Right for my mother suddenly took a turn for the better.

I was dining with a witless diamond dealer from New York that Lou had been forced to set me up with, when over the course of some poached salmon at a small bistro in the French Quarter, my date began to grab at his throat and turn a rather unusual shade of pink. Being a physical therapist, I went into full emergency mode, called for the waiter to dial 911, and helped my date stay calm until the rescue unit appeared.

An hour later, I was waiting in the emergency room at University Hospital when I was approached by a tall, slender, dark-haired man wearing a long white coat, and calling himself Dr. John Blessing.

"Your boyfriend had an allergic reaction to the shellfish stuffed into his salmon, Ms....." He looked me over with large gray eyes.

"Kehoe, Nora Kehoe," I stated as I stood from my chair to greet him. "And he's not my boyfriend. More like a blind date from hell."

That made the handsome Dr. Blessing laugh. "Yes, I, ah, have had a few of those myself." He glanced back down at the chart he was holding in his long hands. "Do you know his family or anyone we can call?"

"I'm afraid we never got that far, actually. I could call my stepfather in the morning. He set us up. Maybe Lou will know."

"Good idea." Dr. Blessing's gray eyes held mine for a second longer than necessary. "In the meantime, we will admit him overnight for observation; he can leave in the morning if everything is all right." He looked over my shoulder at the busy waiting room behind me. "Perhaps you'd better head on home." His eyes returned to mine and I noticed the way the bright fluorescent lights overhead highlighted the curve of his darkly shadowed jaw. "I'll get security to walk you to your car," he offered.

"Don't have one. I came with the ambulance," I admitted. I turned and surveyed the waiting area. "I'll just call a cab."

Dr. Blessing eyed his stainless steel watch. "It's almost two in the morning. You'll never get a cab here at this time of night."

I began rummaging through my purse for my cell phone. "I'd better call my stepfather then. Maybe Lou could come and pick me up."

"My shift ended twenty minutes ago and I was about to get out of here myself," Dr. Blessing spoke up. "Where do you live? Maybe you could let me drive you home?"

"I couldn't ask you to do—"

He smiled, silencing my protest. "Where do you live?" he asked again in a sultry voice.

"By the lake, off Milne Avenue," I answered, feeling a tweak of electricity travel up from my stomach.

"What a coincidence. I live out by the lake as well." Dr. Blessing's smile grew, showing his perfectly straight white teeth. "If you don't mind waiting a few minutes, I could drive you home." His smile quickly fell and he cleared his throat. "That is, if you don't think that would be too forward of me?"

"I think that would be just fine, Dr. Blessing," I assured him with a flirty grin.

His smile returned, deepening his five o'clock shadow. "In that case you will have to call me John."

* * *

Forty-five minutes later, John and I were headed outside of the city in his used but very clean dark blue BMW M3. I kept searching for topics of conversation, trying desperately to avoid those awkward silences that often creep into every nervous conversation.

"Where are you from?" I inquired.

"I'm from Dallas. My folks and my sister still live there. I go home from time to time, but not as much as I should. My residency has kept me busy over the past few years, but this is my last year at University Hospital."

"What are you going to do when you finish your residency?"

"I've had an offer from Southwestern University in Dallas to do a fellowship. Then there are the numerous emergency room staffing companies that I could work for, make my own schedule and so forth, but I feel I would like to stay in one hospital and not hop around. My mother wants me to come back to Dallas, but…." He shrugged.

"You don't sound too enthused about going back home," I surmised as I observed his strong profile.

"Let's just say my mother wants me home, but my father has never forgiven me for going into medicine."

"What father doesn't want a doctor for a son?" I asked in amazement.

"The kind that has a family business to pass on." He shifted down the car at a stoplight and turned his eyes to me. "My father has a geological survey company and works for a lot of the oil companies. My sister is a geologist and works with him, but that was never good enough for Dad. He wanted his son to take over the company, not his daughter."

"What does your sister think about all of that?"

"Nancy?" He sighed and rolled his head back. "Not only did she study geology to please my dad, she studied law to please my mother. Mom was an attorney before she married my father. So, my poor sister has taken on the brunt of both my parents' expectations. I, on the other hand, have always done the complete opposite of what they wanted."

"At least you're a doctor." I shook my head. "My mother's only hope for me is that I marry and have the right house in the right neighborhood with the right friends, and the perfect two point two kids."

"Yeah, my mother wanted that for my sister." He put the car into gear and started down the road ahead.

"How did your sister deal with it?"

"Well, she did get married, have the kids and the house, the whole pretty picture. Until Phil, her ex-husband, ran off with his secretary, leaving Nancy pregnant and poor. The whole divorce kind of cured my sister of my parents' delusions. She leads her own life now, not my mother's."

"It seems you lead your own life as well, John."

"To a point, but every now and then I hear my father's voice in my head, or worse my mother's voice, egging me on to be what they want. I'm not as free as my sister, but then again, I'm in New Orleans. I guess that's the real reason I don't want to go home. I can live my life here."

John Blessing expertly maneuvered his German machine through the slopes and around the numerous potholes that had plagued every city street since Katrina. He was still wearing his green scrubs with "Property of University Hospital" printed all over them, along with his grungy white coat. Identification tags hung from his lapel, while assorted pens, a stethoscope, and papers crowded his coat pockets. On the waist of his green scrub pants was clipped a black beeper.

"Your parents sound just like my mother. I guess that's why I became a physical therapist, because it's somewhere between a doctor and housewife."

"You're a physical therapist?" John's eyes brightened, as he looked me over with renewed interest.

"At Uptown Hospital. I manage the total joint replacement program."

"Really? I did a few rotations through there a year ago. A shame we never ran into each other." He turned down my street.

"Well, it's a big place. I'm one block up on the right," I said, pointing to my home up ahead. "The little yellow cottage," I added.

"When I was at Uptown Hospital I used to eat at this great little café around the corner…what was it called?"

"Lucifer's. I know it well."

He parked the car in front of my raised, single story home. "Why don't you and I go there this Saturday night? We can have dinner and perhaps head to the French Quarter after for some music."

"All right. That sounds like fun, John," I commented, trying to sound casual and not desperate.

"Good." He pulled out a pen and piece of paper from his coat pocket. "Write down your number for me, and I'll call you so we can work out a time."

I wrote down my cell number, and when I handed the paper back to him, our hands touched. The shock of his cool skin against mine made me shiver. Hoping to hide my blushing cheeks, I reached for the door handle.

"Saturday night then, Nora Kehoe," he stated behind me as I stepped onto the curb. "I hope you like jazz," he asserted.

I turned back to the car. "Of course I do. Jazz is required listening in these parts."

He gave me another killer smile, highlighting his smoky gray eyes. "I'll see you Saturday."

I shut the car door and headed up the walkway to my home while his dark blue BMW waited at the curb. When I was safely inside my front door, I heard the motor of the car rev, and watched the sleek machine pull slowly away from the curb. I flipped on my living room lights, still warm with an inner glow from our chance encounter, and wondered if this evening was going to turn into one of those life-altering moments. Suddenly, the future looked a little brighter than it had earlier in the day. I just prayed that the attractive John Blessing did not become yet another dating disappointment.

* * *

The following day at brunch with my parents, I made sure not to mention anything about my meeting Dr. Blessing. But later that afternoon, out in Manchac at my uncle's boat, my cautious attitude eased.

"I met someone last night, Uncle Jack. A doctor at University Hospital," I divulged after I finished checking his blood pressure.

"What was you doin' in that place, Nora T?" he asked as he gave me an odd look.

I rolled my eyes. "Some guy mother had Lou set me up with had an allergic reaction to shellfish when we were eating dinner. I had to go with him to the hospital."

"Don't trust no people that can't eat shellfish. Ain't normal." He walked over to the side of his boat.

"I would expect a shrimper to say that." I chuckled as I followed behind him. "The man I met is an emergency room resident. He was very nice to me, even drove me home from the hospital."

"He kiss you?" Uncle Jack questioned as he turned back to me.

"No," I answered, noting the frown on his face. "I thought you would be happy for me. I met someone interesting, and he's a doctor."

My uncle stepped inside the wheelhouse while I waited on the deck. I leaned against the weathered white boards that covered the wheelhouse.

"You want to marry this man?" His voice came from deep within the boat.

"Marry? Good Lord, Uncle Jack, we haven't even had our first date yet."

"You like him 'cause he's nice or 'cause he's a doctor?"

"Uncle Jack, I thought you would understand. I thought you would want me to date a nice guy who has a lot of career potential."

"You know, Nora T." He came out of the wheelhouse carrying a wrench in his hands. "You sound just like your mama when you talk 'bout this man bein' a doctor. More to a person than what he do."

From behind us someone cleared their throat. Uncle Jack and I turned around at the same time to see Jean Marc Gaspard standing in a pair of grease-stained blue jean overalls, old tennis shoes, and no shirt. I could not help but notice the thick muscles in his arms and beneath his bare chest.

"Nora," Jean Marc said in his usual condescending way. "Going to help your uncle and me fix the oil leak in the engine?"

I shook my head, trying to avoid his uncomfortable gaze. "No, Jean Marc. I just came out to—"

"Check his blood pressure," Jean Marc interjected. "Yes, I know. It's Sunday." He nodded to my uncle. "I can come back later if you want, Jack."

My uncle jumped forward and took Jean Marc's arm. "No, you come over here and help me. Nora can pass us the tools while we're down in the drink."

I gawked at my uncle.

"Wonderful!" Jean Marc exclaimed, clapping his rough hands together. He directed his eyes to me. "Shall we?" He motioned to the wheelhouse.

Uncle Jack placed his hands about my shoulders as he shoved me inside the darkened wheelhouse. "Come on, Nora T. Make yourself useful, girl."

* * *

Uncle Jack and Jean Marc had finished fixing the oil leak and were covered with more grime and dirt than I had thought humanly possible. The men climbed out of the lower part of the boat and made their way into the late afternoon sunshine up top. I followed dutifully behind, carrying the toolbox I had been assigned to take down below.

"Now, that should take care of the leaking oil," Jean Marc commented as he wiped his greasy hands on a rag. He turned to me, keeping his face devoid of any emotion. "Thank you for your help, Nora."

"Sure, no problem," I mumbled.

"Well, this calls for a beer," Uncle Jack proclaimed, going in search of his ice chest.

"No, Uncle Jack. You don't need any more beer," I chastised as he disappeared into the wheelhouse. I looked over at Jean Marc, my eyes pleading with him to agree with me.

"Ah, really, Jack, I don't need a beer," Jean Marc insisted.

Uncle Jack appeared from the shadows. "Yes, but I do." He popped the top off a bottle with his opener and took a long sip from his beer.

"I should be going," Jean Marc muttered.

I put the toolbox down on the deck. "I need to get back to the city."

"All right then, Nora T," Uncle Jack said. "I'll see you next week. You can tell me 'bout your date with that doctor."

I noticed a slight smirk creep across Jean Marc's thin, red lips.

Uncle Jack nodded to the younger man. "Jean Marc, I'm gonna finish up below. See Nora gets to her car all right."

"I don't need Jean Marc to walk me to my car," I blurted out.

"Nah," Uncle Jack protested. "It's late and Jean Marc can make sure you're safe." Uncle Jack did not even wait for my reply. He simply turned around and headed back into the wheelhouse.

I was going to voice my refusal when Jean Marc stepped in front of me.

"Come on, Nora, I'll walk you back to the parking lot." He quickly headed to the gangway.

I picked up my purse from the boat deck. "No, really, Jean Marc, I'm fine."

He narrowed his disconcerting eyes on me. "Your uncle asked me to see you to your car, and that is what I intend to do. So come on." He waved his hand for me to follow him and then he walked down the gangway.

I sighed and fell in step behind him. As I made my way across the gangway toward the dock, he held out his hand to me.

"I'm all right," I grumbled, refusing his assistance.

He pulled his hand away. "I was just trying to help."

"Well, I don't need your help." I started down the dock. "I've been coming here since I was a kid. I know this dock just as well as you," I added over my shoulder.

"I was there when you were running all over these docks as a kid. Remember?"

I did not say anything and kept on walking.

Suddenly, his hand was on my arm and he jerked me around with such force that it took my breath away.

"What's your problem? Every time we see each other, you have been nothing but rude to me. What happened to the fun little girl I knew?" he growled.

I shrugged off his hand and took a step away from him. "I grew up, Jean Marc."

"Only on the outside, Nora. I can't understand why every time we see each other you look at me with such loathing." He shook his head. "Your uncle is a good man, and he—"

"He's a good worker, you mean," I snapped.

He placed his hands on his hips and glowered at me. "Is that it? You think I don't give a damn? You think I like playing boss man around here, or is this tension between us attributed to something else entirely?"

His filthy body shimmered in the afternoon sunlight, accentuating the numerous muscles in his arms and chest. I quickly diverted my eyes to the blue water beside the dock.

"Why don't you just admit it? Your family has always hated mine," I declared, folding my arms across my chest.

"You still think after all these years that me, or any of my family, give a damn about your mother and what she did?"

"Your father never forgave her for marrying his brother," I replied, raising my voice.

"My father always spoke fondly about your mother, even after she left Uncle Etienne. No one ever blamed her for leaving the man. Hell, he was never any good. Everyone in Manchac knew that."

I glared at him. "But you always held it against her and me."

"What? How could I hold it against you when you never knew my uncle?" Jean Marc impatiently waved his hand at me. "He shot himself years before you were even born."

"He shot himself because my mother left him for my father. You and your whole family hate her for that."

"My uncle shot himself because he was dead drunk while trying to clean a loaded shotgun. Etienne Gaspard never wanted to kill himself."

"That's not what my mother heard at the funeral," I argued.

"That was thirty-five years ago, Nora. Who in the hell even remembers that far back?"

I held my head up and, deciding it better not to press the matter further, proceeded toward the parking lot.

"Nora, I'm not the one hung up on the past here," he shouted behind me. "You had better get rid of that big chip on your shoulder if you plan on spending any more time around my docks. And if you ask me, you're acting like a spoiled brat!"

I spun around to face him. "You arrogant piece of shit! Where in the hell do—"

"Piece of shit?" he bellowed, coming up to me. "What kind of language is that for a good girl like you? They teach you to speak like that in the city?"

"I'm not a little girl, Jean Marc. Stop treating me like one."

He moved in closer to me, his face inches from mine. I could smell the sweat and grease on him as the heat radiated from his skin. For a moment my stomach did a few nervous flips, but then I had to remind myself of my feelings for Jean Marc.

"I know you're not a little girl," he whispered to me. "It's been real damned obvious to me for quite a while that—" He abruptly stepped back from me. "Just watch your language. You shouldn't be cursing like that. Your momma wouldn't approve."

I snickered at him. "Then you don't know Mother; foulest mouth this side of the Mississippi, even if she does still curse in French."

Jean Marc raised his head and scanned the dock surrounding us. "Well, best you not be following her example. You're better than that, Nora. You've always been better than that."

I tried to think of some pithy reply, but my nerves were so rattled that nothing came to mind. Instead, I turned on my heels and quickly headed for my car. Once inside the safety of my Honda, I looked back to see Jean Marc still watching me from the edge of the parking lot. I gunned the engine and peeled out of the lot, wanting to put as much distance as possible between the infuriating Jean Marc Gaspard and me.

CHAPTER 3

The next day at work I forced myself to forget about my encounter with Jean Marc, and once again basked in the thrill of my coming date. I tried to think ahead to Saturday night and let the usual female matters of what to wear and how to do my hair and make up cloud my judgment. I even decided to consult with an expert about my approaching evening with the good doctor.

"John Blessing?" a wiry, silver-haired man commented as his penetrating blue eyes studied mine. "I don't remember him."

I took in my secretary's frown. "Come on, Steve. He was a resident here. Tall, kind of thin, but good-looking. He has brown hair and deep gray eyes. Surely you would remember him?"

He leaned across my desk with a naughty glint in his eyes. "Nice body?"

"I don't know. I haven't seen much of it." I picked up a memo on my desk.

"You didn't look hard enough." Steve stood from his chair, pressed out the slight crease in his dark pants, and came around to my side. He sat on the edge of my small chrome and faux wood hospital issue desk and folded his arms.

Steve Seville had a killer smile, sharp, aquiline features attributed to a Nordic ancestry, and a slender but muscular body that he trained rigorously at a local gym.

"So?" he asked after several seconds of silence. "When is the big date?"

I tossed the memo back on my desk. “Saturday. He wants to take me to Lucifer’s.”

“That’s a good first date place. Casual.” Steve nodded approvingly and then stared at my dark green scrubs. “I think the twins should come out for this one,” he stated, pointing to my bosom.

“Actually, I thought I would go casual but conservative. I was thinking maybe a pantsuit with my hair up?” I glanced up at him, grimacing with self-doubt.

“No way.” He stood from my desk and eyed me up and down. “Tight dress to highlight your curves, hair down, and soft shades of brown for make up. Makes you look mysterious when you wear brown eye shadow, and it highlights the blue in your eyes.”

“Anything else?”

“Yes, sleep with him.” He walked toward my office door. “All doctors want sex on the first date,” he proclaimed.

“No, all *men* want sex on the first date.”

Steve faced me, grinning. “Not the ones I’ve been out with lately. If this one doesn’t work out for you, there’s always next year. I know dead people who have more sex than you.”

“I shouldn’t have said anything to you.” I picked up a chart sitting on the side of my desk.

“Too late.” His face became serious again. “Back to business. You have a nine o’clock with Peterson about the infection rates on the hip implants this month, and I’m supposed to remind you about the quality management meeting tonight at six.”

“Thanks.” I sighed heavily as I began to go through the chart in my hand.

He reached for handle on my office door. “I’ll see what I can dig up on your Dr. Blessing. Never hurts to check them out first.”

“All my mother needs to hear is that he’s a doctor and she’ll be booking the reception hall, no matter what type of felony he may have committed in the past.”

“Oh, God…mothers.” Steve rolled his eyes dramatically. “Wait until this guy meets yours.”

*   *   *

The following Saturday, John arrived promptly at seven dressed in a casual pair of black slacks and a freshly ironed white Oxford shirt. His hair was still wet and he smelled of crisp cologne. His stainless steel watch gleamed against his right wrist.

"I like your outfit," he declared as he took in my clingy, black, low-cut dress. "Elegant and simple."

I shut my heavy front door with a thud. "And tight in all the right spots," I remarked as his gray eyes lingered over my bosom.

"You said it, I didn't. But I'm a man who has learned how to appreciate the finer points of anatomy." He held out his arm to me.

"Spoken like a true physician." I took his arm.

"Man first, physician second. But the physician part of me is definitely off tonight. Look." He flourished his hand over his outfit. "No beeper."

We started down the path to his car. "Should I feel honored?"

He shrugged. "I just didn't want to give the wrong impression on our first date."

"What wrong impression?"

We stopped in front of his dark blue BMW, and he opened the passenger car door for me. "That what I do is who I am. Many people only see the title 'doctor' when they look at me. But you saw me for who I am. I have to admit when I first noticed you in the ER waiting area, I thought you would be just like every other woman I had ever met. But you didn't flirt with me or try to be someone you're not when I drove you home the other night. You're different from all the rest. That's why I'm here."

I smiled into his handsome face. "Thank you, John."

He eyed me quizzically. "For what?"

"For noticing that I'm different."

His eyes traveled down the length of my body. "Good thing for both of us you weren't wearing that dress the other night. Otherwise, I might never have noticed."

He leaned in closer, and a flutter of excitement gripped my stomach.

"Nora," he whispered in my ear. "Perhaps you should get in the car so we can actually go on our date." He stepped back from me and raised his head.

I tried to discern what he was thinking at that moment, but his gray eyes lacked any hint of desire. His face was oddly detached.

I quickly climbed into the waiting car, feeling a little let down by his reserved manner. Perhaps he was nervous. Not every man was as blatant with his emotions as the insufferable Jean Marc Gaspard. Maybe John Blessing was one of those men you had to get to know before he revealed his inner workings to you. How refreshing to meet a man who did not begin every conversation with a scowl, and whose eyes were not filled with a dark distrust. Funny, I remember thinking at the time, how Jean Marc's aggravating idiosyncrasies had been seared into my memory.

* * *

We made our way in his fine German automobile through the heart of the Crescent City, along the old streets and into the Garden District. While we headed to the restaurant, John talked about his love of New Orleans homes and their unique architecture.

"James Gallier, Sr. built several homes in the uptown area in addition to the former city hall off Poydras Avenue," he explained. "He was renowned for his use of delicately carved cypress and the inlay of marble and tile in his long entrance halls."

"You're quite an expert on the architecture around here," I said, admiring his slender hands on the steering wheel.

"Always loved New Orleans architecture, with its mix of French and Spanish influences melding together in a Caribbean-like climate. It's one of the reasons I came here to study medicine and do my residency. The first place I went after moving here was Jackson Square. I remember being enthralled with the architecture around the square. It's always been my favorite spot in New Orleans." He paused and shifted the car down in the slowing traffic. "Everything in Dallas is new and filled with stainless steel and glass. Here everything is as it has always been for a hundred years or more."

"So are the people," I insisted. "New Orleanians have a strange kind of Southern apathy. Progress is a dirty word, and instead of moving forward, sometimes I swear we go backwards."

"But it's like any other large American city," John objected. "The problems here are no different than any other place in the U.S."

"People here are different. They're locked in to the land with a deep sense of tradition and obligation to the ways of things past. It's that sense of holding on to the past that drowned the city after Katrina."

"But the past is comforting to many people," he countered.

"Comfort in the past is a luxury that holds people back from embracing the future. Schools without air-conditioning, houses without electricity, people without basic elementary education, and levees that failed when we needed them most. These are all things the love of the past has given us." I paused and took in some of the run down homes we passed on our way down Prytania Street. "'Embrace the past, but save room for the future,' my father used to always say."

John pulled the car up to a red light. "He was an advocate for progress?"

"He wanted to see the city move ahead. He encouraged me to become interested in politics and current affairs when I was little. Dad believed it was important to be well informed. When I was a kid, he used to sit at the dinner table and quiz me on topics from the newspaper, on television—oh, everything and anything to stimulate my mind."

"What about your mother? Did she join in on those conversations?"

My eyes went wide. "Mother? She used to think Dad and I were nuts to talk about such things at the dinner table. Claimed we gave her indigestion."

"I'm surprised you didn't become a lawyer," he admitted as the light changed to green.

"I wanted to follow in my father's footsteps when I was younger and work side by side with him one day. But when I was fourteen, Dad got cancer and I put those ideas on the back burner. I had to spend a great deal of time taking care of him. My mother wasn't any good at being a nurse. She freaked out at the whole sick husband thing." I shook my head, trying to force those bad memories from my mind. "Anyway, when Dad was near the end he told me I should become a nurse. He said I cared, and he wanted me to do something with my life that would help people. But I didn't want to be a nurse. I didn't want to take care of the sick and dying, especially after my dad. Then on a field trip in high school, I found out about physical therapy and decided to study that in college."

"You could still go to law school. It's not too late."

I shook my head and gave him a weak smile. "When my father died I lost my desire to become a lawyer, but I still like to keep up with current affairs. Makes me feel like he's with me in a way."

"You two were close?"

I sighed as I thought of my father. "We were the same. Mother was always foreign to us. She still is to me."

"I'm sorry. Must have been hard to lose your father at such a young age."

"It was, but after my father died, my Uncle Jack, my mother's brother, was there for me. He has always helped me get through the tough times."

"What does your Uncle Jack do?"

"He's a shrimper in Manchac, and the complete opposite of my mother. He's down-to-earth, practical, rational, and is more impressed by a man's handshake than the size of his wallet."

John chuckled. "You're more like your uncle than your mother."

"Thank God." I rolled my eyes. "You've never met anybody like my mother."

He shifted down and the car slowed. "I've met your mother many times before. I know the type too well. Doctors are on their husband-hunting list. You would be amazed at how many women out there are like your mother. I think I've dated most of them."

"How can you be so sure I'm not one of those women on the hunt for a doctor-husband?" I joked as he pulled into a parking spot about a block from the restaurant.

He turned off the engine and then smiled at me. "Because you're more impressed by a man's handshake than the size of his wallet. I'm also a very good judge of character."

"Ever been wrong about someone?"

John opened his car door. "Never. I can size people up pretty fast." He exited the car and came around to my door. "I like to figure out early on how someone will fit in my life," he told me after opening my car door.

I stood from the car. "Shouldn't you get to know someone before you make such a decision?"

John placed his arm about my shoulders. "I don't like to waste my time with people who will never matter. I'm sure you're the same way." We started toward the restaurant entrance.

I didn't bother to enlighten John as to my true feelings. Normally, I would have expressed my opinion without reservation, but suddenly my mother's voice popped into my head, warning me about my ticking biological clock and my limited prospects for a desirable husband. It was the first time in my life I could remember holding back my thoughts. That night marked a turning point for me. I realized that my wants and my desires had finally been usurped by my need to please another.

* * *

After we had dined on shrimp and pasta, and strolled along the broken sidewalks of the French Quarter, John pulled his car up in front of my Lakeview cottage. When he turned off the engine, he reached for my hand.

"I had a great time tonight," he said with a bright smile.

The electricity rose up my arm as his hand squeezed mine.

"Tell me, Nora Kehoe, why hasn't some guy swept you off your feet?"

I shrugged. "Probably the same reason you dropped out of the dating scene. There aren't a lot of interesting people out there to date. At least, I don't find them interesting."

"There must have been someone special."

I thought back to the roller coaster of dating that I had endured for the last fourteen years. There had been great first dates that turned into horrible second dates. First dates that had me grabbing at my cell phone wanting to call a cab. Third and fourth dates with men who had turned from Dr. Jekyll into Mr. Hyde, and one steady boyfriend in high school named Thomas. He had been sweet, and always insisted on kissing me good night only on the cheek. Following graduation we parted ways. A few years later, I heard Thomas was gay.

"No, the past couple of years I've devoted to furthering my career and little else." I nodded to him. "What about you?" I asked, itching with curiosity.

"A few girlfriends here and there. The last relationship I had was in medical school before I began my residency. Her name was Monique and she applied to a residency program in Florida. I never pursued the relationship after graduation." He reached for the handle on his car door. "It wasn't the right time to commit to anything long-term."

I remember thinking how peculiar that comment sounded to me. There never was a right time for most of life's curveballs, but where would the game of life be without them?

When John walked me to my front door, he was holding my hand in his and moving very slowly, as if trying to squeeze in a few more seconds together.

"I'm off Thursday night. How about we have dinner again?" he inquired as we climbed the three steps to my door.

"I'd like that." I reached into my purse and pulled out my keys. He was standing right next to me, and I motioned toward the front door. "Do you want to come in?"

A shadow of apprehension rose in his eyes, and I found the change in his features disturbing. I began to question what I had done wrong, and then the look quickly disappeared.

"I'd better not, not tonight anyway." He leaned over and kissed me very gently on the lips.

But before I could respond to his kiss, he pulled away. "I'll call you later to talk about Thursday," he whispered as he took a lock of my blond hair in his fingers. "Go to bed, Nora Kehoe. I'll see you again Thursday." He turned and headed down my walkway to his car.

I pushed my heavy front door open, and no sooner had I stepped into my living room, when I heard the sound of his car starting.

"A gentleman," I whispered as I closed my door. "I've never been out with one of those before."

I leaned back against the thick oak door and smiled, intrigued at the prospect of seeing the kind Dr. Blessing again.

* * *

"So you like this boy, for real?" Uncle Jack asked as we sat on the deck of his boat, enjoying the cool spring breezes from Lake Pontchartrain the following afternoon.

I nodded my head. "Yes, I do, Uncle Jack."

"Too bad." Uncle Jack took a sip from his beer.

"Why do you say that?" I stood from the deck.

"'Cause when you realize that this boy ain't right for you, you'll break his heart."

I hovered over him. "What makes you think he's not right for me? You've never even met him."

"He's a doctor, right?"

I shrugged. "Yes."

"Come from Texas, you say. From money?"

"I guess."

"Took you to a nice place in his nice car and was a real gentleman to you last night?"

I glared at him. "What's your point, Uncle Jack?"

"No spark. When sparks fly, girl, there ain't no nice dates and no gentlemanly ways. There's only passion."

"He's polite," I assured him.

Uncle Jack scowled. "He's afraid." He put his beer down on the boat deck and stood up from his chair. "A gentleman is only a man afraid of doin' what he really wants to do. I've seen it time and time again. You just wait and see. I'm right." He winked at me.

"But you don't even know him."

He frowned at me. "Yep, but I 'spect I'll meet him soon enough."

"You'll change your mind when you meet him. I know you will."

"Will I? We'll see 'bout that." He turned away and headed to the wheelhouse.

CHAPTER 4

Monday morning, Steve Seville was waiting at my office door with a playful grin on his face.

"How did it go?" he inquired, standing behind me as I struggled to open my office door.

"Fine," I told him as I pushed my door open.

Steve leaned against the doorframe. "Fine? Honey, I want to hear more than fine."

I turned on the lights and headed to my desk. After placing my brown bag lunch and purse on the desk, I turned back to him. "We had a good time."

"Good time?" Steve snorted. "Good time as in he was sweet and kind, or a good time as in we screwed each other's brains out?"

I took my seat behind my desk and frowned "You sound like my uncle. For your information, there were no intimate relations between Dr. Blessing and myself. We had dinner, went to the Quarter, and then he brought me home. My clothes never left my body at any time during the date."

Steve hurried to my desk. "Oh, Lord! At least tell me the twins made an appearance."

I nodded. "They got some air. It was a rather low cut dress."

"Well, at least you followed my advice in that department. As for the rest...." He rolled his eyes.

"He was a nice guy, Steve. A real gentleman."

Steve lowered his gaze to me as his sharp blue eyes intently analyzed my face. “Nora, there are no gentleman in the world. There are only two kinds of men: the kind who want to sleep with you and the kind you’ve already slept with. So either he wants to sleep with you or he’s gay.”

“Now you definitely sound like my uncle.”

“Your uncle sounds like my kind of man.” He paused and folded his arms across his chest. “Are you going to see him again?”

“Thursday. We’re having dinner.”

“When will you tell Claire?”

I sat back in my chair and sighed.

Steve shook his head. “That’s what I thought.” He stepped back from my desk. “I don’t blame you. If she were my mother, I would have become a serial killer.”

* * *

Three weeks later I broke down and told my mother about John.

“A doctor!” Claire screamed into the speaker of my cell phone. “You’re seeing a doctor!”

“Mother, please. It’s just been a few dates,” I said, trying to calm her as I fumbled putting on my mascara in the bathroom mirror.

“How many dates have there been?”

“Tonight will make four dates. John is taking me to an Indian place in the Quarter for dinner. He says he loves Indian food.” I paused and made a face, trying not to smear the mascara as I applied it to my lashes.

“Is that unofficial or official?” she persisted.

“You’re kidding?” I put the mascara wand down on my vanity.

“No, I’m not kidding, Nora,” she clucked. “Official dates are the dinner kind made in advance. Unofficial are the impromptu lunches and last minute get-togethers. So, how many official and unofficial?”

"Where do you get this stuff?" I asked staring dumbfounded at my cell phone.

"Every woman knows this. My God, Nora, where have you been all these years? Don't you have girlfriends you talk to about boys?"

"No, Mother, I have colleagues, and, we talk about men, not boys. Right after we discuss taxes, health insurance, IRA'S, and interest rates."

"You've got to get some better influences in your life, child. No wonder you've never snagged a man."

"He's a man, Mother, not a fish in a trout stream."

"He's a man, dear. All men have to be rounded up, broken in, and branded in order to be of any use to a woman."

"How many times have you been down to the corral, Mother?"

"Never mind that." She brushed aside my rib with all the grace of a tow truck. "We are not talking about me. This is about you."

"When isn't it about me?" I muttered and proceeded to re-apply my mascara. "Look, Mother, officially or unofficially, we have only had a couple of dates. We've gone to dinner a couple of times, a movie, and had lunch once. Pretty generic dating stuff."

"You haven't slept with him then?" Her voice was harsh and flat, the way it would always get when she was frustrated with me.

I almost dropped the phone. "Are you kidding? Mother, you do realize that there are several versions of sexually transmitted diseases circulating out there that can make vital body parts shrivel up and die."

"Obviously that means no." She sighed and I could hear her playing with the assortment of gold bracelets she always wore around her right wrist. "Well, I can't tell you what to do."

"Since when?" I balked.

"But if I were you, I would hook this man as soon as possible." She paused as the tinkle of ice filtered in from the background. "You know, there are plenty of other girls who would die to have a doctor for a husband. Think of all the prestige and free health care you could get."

"Mother!" I waited a beat as I tried to readjust my tone. "I don't want to even think about what you're suggesting. Maybe I should play this casual and not read too much into the situation. Besides, I don't know much about the man. He could be a pervert, or a workaholic, or even mentally unbalanced."

"Darling," my mother purred as I heard the sound of her five o'clock bourbon pouring into a glass. "The initials 'MD' behind any man's name forgives a multitude of sins. So don't go off with this man and bore him to death with your opinions and your too highly educated brain. I told your father not to try and make you so smart. I said it would ruin you for marriage. Now look at you…thirty years old and not even a decent marriage under your belt." She paused and I could hear the clink of her glass as she shot back some bourbon. "Try to wear something revealing Nora, and act like a woman, for Christ's sake. Don't try to act too intelligent. Offer to cook for him; flatter him a lot, laugh at his jokes, and listen to his opinions, don't express yours. That's what a man wants…a woman, and not some news anchor from CNN."

* * *

Later that evening, as John and I walked hand in hand along the black wrought iron fence around Jackson Square in the French Quarter, my mother's words came back to haunt me, and I found myself actually wondering if the lunatic that bore me did not have a point when it came to the desires of men.

"You're awfully quiet tonight," John observed as he put his arm about my shoulders.

At six-foot-one, John dwarfed my five-foot-four inch frame, and I often had to find ways to adjust to his size. I curled a bit closer into his side to get comfortable next to him.

"I was just thinking about something," I mumbled against his chest.

"I thought you seemed a little preoccupied tonight. Not your usual talkative self."

The remark made my stomach curl into a knot. I pulled myself free of his arm. "John, do you think I sound…." I hesitated, trying to find the words. "Well, do you think I talk too much, like an anchor on CNN?"

John laughed, a deep, musical sort of laugh that made people around us stop and smile.

"Where is that coming from?" He placed his hands on my shoulders. "This isn't you. You're usually so sure of yourself. That's what I like about you. When you speak, Nora, you say something of value. This uncertainty is not like you."

My shoulders sagged under the weight of my mother's expectations. I looked down at the ground, taking in the way the cobblestones lay perfectly side by side with each other. There were no gaps and no breaks between them. Why can't people be more like cobblestones? I gazed back up into John's face and marveled at his deep gray eyes.

"Sorry. My mother called me before you came over tonight, and she kinda got to me."

"Oh, I see. Did you finally tell her about me?"

"I mentioned you." I turned away from him, hoping to hide my embarrassment.

"Let me guess." He came up next to me and placed his arm about my shoulders.

"'He's a doctor, a great catch, and you need to work harder to snag him,' or some such thing."

I laughed, feeling slightly relieved by his comment. "How did you know?"

"I've heard it all before. My mother is a lot like yours. I remember when I was in undergraduate school, Nancy brought home a medical student she had been dating to meet my parents." He rolled his eyes playfully. "My mother acted as if the pope had come to call. Nancy broke up with the guy soon after that. To this day my mother still brings up the doctor my sister let get away."

"Your mother and mine sound like they have a lot in common."

"No, just a different generation. For our mothers, what a person does for a living defines the kind of person they are. You and I look at people differently. I know for the most part society is still hung up on labels—doctor, lawyer, Indian chief, and so forth. But the truly enlightened among us realize that what makes a person is not their profession, but what they believe in; or, more to the point, who they believe in."

"Are you talking about God?"

"God to some, or religion, or a belief in a person or ideal. That belief is what defines them, because that is what makes them who they are." John stopped walking and turned to me. "I'm a physician, but I believe in the Catholic Church, and that all the world is not one big medical research problem to be solved. There is a time and place for all events. I also believe that jazz music, and a good bottle of scotch, are the second and third best things in life." He paused and rested his forehead against mine. "So, Nora Kehoe, what do you believe in?"

My mind went blank. I had always had an opinion about world affairs, causes, and other people's problems, but could not for the life of me think of a single, overwhelming person or cause that dominated all others. The epiphany made me wonder where I had been all those years. I had spent so much of my life chasing other people's dreams and passions that maybe I had forgotten to foster my own.

"I can't break it down as easily as you," I finally confessed and took a step forward.

John enveloped me in his long arms. His face was inches from mine and I could feel the heat of his body through his casual shirt and slacks.

"Try," he whispered to me.

Suddenly, the nearness of him made me uncomfortable. "John, please." I spied the people milling about the square. "People are staring at us," I pointed out as I struggled in his arms.

He held me even closer. "I like it when you put up a fight."

Before I realized what was happening, he kissed me—not just kissed me, but pressed his lips against mine with a passion I had never felt from him before. Sure, I'd had butterflies in the pit of my stomach when we had kissed prior to this moment, but this time, for the first time, he kissed me and it was as if he really wanted me.

He stepped back from me, the desire shining in his gray eyes. "Let's get you home."

Perplexed by the intensity of his kiss, all I could do was nod my head in agreement. He took my hand and led me away from Jackson Square, heading toward the parking lot where his dark blue BMW was waiting.

* * *

Once we had returned to my yellow cottage near Lake Pontchartrain, John followed me up the walkway to my front door. In the past, he had respectfully kissed me good night and not tried to venture into my home. But tonight as I placed the key in the lock, I could feel his teeth gently nibbling my earlobe.

"Hurry up and get that damned door open," he whispered to me as I struggled with the key. "I want to show you what I believe to be the number one best thing in life."

"I'm trying," I complained. "But you keep distracting me."

He raised his arm from about my shoulders and held his hands away from my body, then he flashed me a devious little grin. The thick oak door finally gave way and John pushed me inside.

I barely had time to reach for the light before his cool, slender hands were all over me, caressing the curves of my breasts and kneading his palms into my rear end.

"Dr. Blessing, I thought you were such a gentleman," I commented after I came up for air from one of his kisses.

John took the keys from my hand and threw them on the table by my front door. Then he reached for my blazer and expertly peeled the jacket from my body.

"Oh, I can be," he said as he began to unbutton my blouse. "I have been a real gentleman up until tonight." He kissed me, and then started unbuttoning his shirt. "But I thought it was time I try a new approach." He pulled his shirt open to expose his chest. "What do you think?"

I let my hand wander over his smooth chest and slowly pushed the shirt over his shoulders, watching as the fabric fell effortlessly to my hardwood floor.

He picked me up like I was a rag doll and threw me rather unceremoniously over his bony shoulder. Then he slapped my bottom with his hand. He laughed as he carried me across my living room. "I presume your bedroom is this way," he declared as he walked down the short hallway that led to my bedroom. After he kicked open my bedroom door, he plopped me down on my king-sized, four-poster bed.

He stood back from the bed. "Take off your clothes."

Happy that he finally seemed interested in getting intimate, I grinned and sat up. He intently watched as I removed my blouse, bra and slacks. After tossing my underwear to the floor, John approached the bed.

He pushed me back on my beige comforter as he began kissing my neck. His tongue teased my right nipple and my body arched with anticipation. His hands caressed my breasts and hips, and when his fingers slid in between my legs, I moaned in his ear. Suddenly, he stopped touching me.

"What is it?" I asked, looking up into his face.

"Condoms," he replied as he sat up and pulled out his wallet. "Better safe then sorry."

"Yes, you're right," I agreed, trying to get back in the mood.

He put two condoms on the circular nightstand beside my bed and then left his wallet next to them. He quickly shed his trousers and boxers and flung them to the floor. John wrapped me in his arms and hungrily kissed my mouth. His lips went along my cheek to my delicate earlobe.

"Put your hands on me," he whispered in my ear.

Flustered, I reached up and put my hands on his chest.

"No, not there." He took my right hand and guided it to his erection. "Now, stroke me," he directed.

I soon learned that the entire sexual experience to John was something akin to following instructions for operating a DVD player. At specific intervals I was told to "touch me here" or "kiss me there" or "move against me like this." By the time we had come to the end of our very brief encounter, I was so emotionally frazzled that I had forgotten to fake an orgasm.

"I really like being with you, Nora," he murmured to me after. "We make a great team."

Unsure of what to say, I simply mumbled, "I really like you, too, John."

He snuggled next to me. "I also like scrambled eggs for breakfast." Then he chuckled.

I playfully slapped his arm. "Good. You can make extra for me."

John kissed my cheek. "You're going to be a handful, aren't you Nora?"

I didn't offer a reply. I figured that was one of those tidbits of information he would eventually discover about me. At least, I hoped he would get to know the real Nora Kehoe. I had been keeping much of my true nature from John, and I began to question if he would even like the outspoken woman I had sequestered away.

I nestled in his arms, and my apprehension quickly dissolved. We were just beginning, I reasoned, and there would be time enough for getting to know each other. I listened to the steady sound of his heartbeat and was reassured that everything was as it should be between us.

But when I closed my eyes, my mind was seized with a whirlwind of activity. Images of my mother's tantrum about grandchildren, John's directions during sex, and my uncle's warning about passion all flashed before me. Then, I saw Jean Marc Gaspard looming over me with his thick arms folded across his bare chest. He was staring at me with his black eyes gleaming, and a smug grin on his handsome face. My eyes flew open and I became gripped with dismay. Why on earth was I dreaming of him?

CHAPTER 5

The smell of coffee from the kitchen stirred me from a very restful sleep. The clock next to my bed read five-fifteen in the morning. I yawned lazily, and as an idea hit me, I leapt from the bed. I ran to my closet and pulled out a short robe I had been saving for just such an occasion; the kind where you want to look like you just woke up and fell out of a Victoria's Secret advertisement. I put on the pink satin robe, checked myself in the mirror, gave my long, blond hair a quick run through with my fingers, and then ran to the bathroom and shot back some mouthwash to complete the illusion. When I stepped into my small green and white kitchen I felt confident, sexy, and sure I would be able to lure John back into bed for another try.

"You're up," he said when he saw me enter the brightly lit kitchen.

I had to squint for a moment, having forgotten to stick to the shadows so as not to reveal too much of my morning after self. After my eyes had adjusted, I was relieved to see John Blessing standing by my cooktop next to the built-in oven, tending to scrambled eggs and wearing only his trousers. His eyes had dark circles beneath them, and his constant five o'clock shadow had turned into a thick stubble.

He came up to me, pulled me into his arms, and kissed me on the lips. It was a long, deep kiss that was mixed with the comforting sense of familiarity, as well as a hint of sexiness.

"You look good in that." He playfully tugged at the belt on my robe.

I stood back from him and nodded to the cooktop. "Early breakfast?"

"My beeper went off." He kissed my forehead and returned to his eggs. "One of the residents under me had some questions about a patient. I couldn't get back to sleep after that."

I came up behind him and placed my arms about his waist while he stirred the eggs in the pan. "Everything all right?"

"Sure." He turned off the flame on the gas cooktop and picked up the frying pan. "Just routine stuff. First year residents are always nervous about making decisions. They feel they have to get back up opinions for everything."

"Were you like that?"

He shook his head. "I always knew what my limits were when I was a first year. But I tried to solve the problem before I asked for help; didn't want to appear weak. These first years are pitiful." He divided the scrambled eggs between two plates waiting on the counter. "I was hoping to bring you this in bed, but now that you're up, you can make the toast."

I headed to the refrigerator to get the bread. "Are you going back to the hospital this morning?"

"Afraid so." He carried the plates to my small pine breakfast table next to the kitchen window that overlooked my back garden. He pulled out a chair and sat down. "Life of a resident," he affirmed.

I placed the bread in the toaster and stepped over to the table. As I came up next to him, he placed his arms about my waist and glanced up at me from his chair. It was then I got a good look at his body. I noticed how pale and slender his arms and shoulders appeared. The grueling years of his residency obviously left little time for exercise or outdoor activities.

"If this is going to be a bother, we will have to sleep at my place. I get called in at odd hours a lot."

I fingered his shiny stainless steel watch. "No bother."

"Good. I'll bring some things over tonight. It'll make it easier for me." He reached up and ran his hand along his thick stubble. "My razor for one, a toothbrush, a big box of condoms." He paused and grinned. "That is, if you don't mind?"

"I don't mind. But I have one question."

John turned back to his eggs and picked up his fork, intent on eating and listening to me at the same time.

"What changed last night?" I asked.

"What do you mean?"

"When I said I thought you were a gentleman, I meant it. It just seemed like you suddenly got turned-on or something."

John laughed and put his fork down on his plate. He reached out and grasped my hands.

"Nora, we have gone out on how many dates, five or six? It was time."

"Time?"

"Yes, time to go to bed; time to go to the next level of this relationship. That is, unless you think I was wrong. Was last night a mistake?"

I shook my head. "No, not a mistake."

He let go of my hands and went back to his eggs.

I heard the bread pop-up from the toaster. "I was just a little swept off my feet, I guess."

"I aim to please," John stated, and then shoved a large forkful of eggs into his mouth.

I refrained from telling John how I really felt about the previous night. The whole experience had left me more puzzled than pleased. I went to the toaster and reached for the warm bread. As I began buttering the toast, I wondered why men always patted themselves on the back after sex, as if they had just climbed Mt. Everest, thinking that they had satisfied a woman when they had actually done nothing of the kind. Maybe if I had voiced my displeasure, John would have made more of an effort to appease me. But like most men, I figured critiquing his technique would only lead to his hasty departure through my front door. I thought it odd how they could be deemed the stronger sex, when ours was the one who had to put up with all of their imperfections.

"Nora," John called. "Bring me some more coffee when you bring the toast."

I looked at him huddled over his plate of food and smiled. "Sure, John."

In an instant I had gone from sexy morning after girl to waitress, and that was the first moment I became acquainted with the little nagging feeling deep within the pit of my stomach; a small, burning sensation known to appear when the heart and the head begin to disagree.

* * *

After John left, I tried to go back to sleep, but my mind was spinning with questions about our night together. Just when I was getting a little drowsy, my cell phone rang. I sat up in bed and glanced over at the clock.

"Who would be calling at six in the morning?" I muttered as I reached for the cell phone on my nightstand.

"Hello?" I said, secretly hoping John was on the other end of the line.

"Nora?" The smooth voice sounded familiar, but I could not place it. "It's Jean Marc Gaspard. I need you to come to Hammond Hospital right away. Your uncle's had an accident."

My heart trembled with fear. "What, what is it?"

"He's all right. Just a sprained ankle," Jean Marc went on quickly, sensing my distress. "He fell at his house and called me." He paused again and I could hear him sigh. "He was really drunk, and they're asking me a lot of questions I can't answer. Can you come?"

"I'm on my way," I answered, throwing off my covers.

"I'll tell them," Jean Marc affirmed.

"And, ah, Jean Marc." I paused and my throat tightened. "Thank you for calling me."

* * *

I was running through the emergency room entrance to Hammond Hospital when I spotted Jean Marc. He appeared as if he had just climbed out of bed, complete with a very wrinkled white T-shirt and rumpled pair of old jeans.

"I called as soon as the doctors told me what was going on." His features looked stern and cold as usual. "Jack didn't want me to call you, but I knew you'd want to be here."

I scanned the empty emergency room waiting area. "Where is he?"

Jean Marc gently placed his rough, callused hand on my elbow and motioned past the waiting area to a wide red door with "Exam Rooms" printed across it. "The doctors need to speak to you about something they found," he mentioned as we approached the front desk. "They had to do blood work when he came in, Nora. They found out his liver is in bad shape."

I closed my eyes and pushed down the scream that was climbing its way up my throat.

Jean Marc put his arm around my shoulders. "They said he needs more tests. I told them you're in the medical field and the only family that gives a damn about him, so they want to talk to you." He pulled me alongside of him as we walked through the red door to the exam rooms. "It's all right, Nora," he whispered to me. "I'm right here. I'm not going anywhere."

Jean Marc's presence gave me courage. I found it remarkable that a man I had previously detested insisted on being there for me. But then I reminded myself that Jean Marc was my uncle's friend and employer. I chalked up his dedication to nothing more than polite concern, but the way his arm felt about my shoulders was eliciting an entirely different response from me. I quickly shrugged off the funny tingle in my stomach as indigestion. Over-cooked scrambled eggs, nervous tension about my uncle, and lingering doubts about my night with John had overloaded my system. What else could it be? I figured the unusual sensation would soon be gone and I would have nothing to worry about. I forced the unsettling tickle out of my mind and focused on my uncle's situation.

*   *   *

The sun was just coming up over the horizon by the time Jean Marc and I were escorting Uncle Jack from the emergency room entrance. Uncle Jack had been given a pair of crutches, and a splint covered his right ankle. Jean Marc walked closely beside him, making sure he did not crash to the ground as he struggled to keep the crutches underneath him.

"Goddamned doctors," Uncle Jack cursed as he hobbled to my car. "Never trust the bastards, Nora. Always tryin' to find problems where none exist. Killed your Aunt Elise that way. They tested her to death."

"Uncle Jack, Aunt Elise died of a stroke because she didn't take care of her high blood pressure." I sighed as I fumbled to get the keys from my purse. "This is something different. You heard the doctor. You have to have further tests to find out how bad your liver is, and you need to cut back on the drinking."

"Non! Jamias! I didn't want to come here 'cept that this bon rein dragged me here." He nodded to Jean Marc.

"I didn't know how bad you had hurt yourself, Jack," Jean Marc admitted in his reserved way. "I had to bring you here, for liability reasons."

"Bullshit!" Uncle Jack barked.

"Enough!" I shouted. "Uncle Jack, get in the car." I pointed to the door of my Honda.

My uncle glared at me, but he said nothing while Jean Marc opened the door for him. Uncle Jack settled into the front seat while Jean Marc placed his crutches in the back seat.

"Thank you for everything," I said to Jean Marc.

"No problem," he mumbled as he shut the back passenger side door.

I motioned to my uncle. "I appreciate what you did for him today. It was kind of you to bring him here and stay with him. You really didn't have to, but you did, and I'm grateful."

He lowered his eyes. "Like I said, there was a question of liability. He's my employee and I felt responsible for him."

I shook my head, feeling more than a little frustrated with the man. "You know, it wouldn't kill you to be nice to me for once, Jean Marc."

He raised his eyes to me. "Nice to you? I've always been nice to you. I try and go out of my way to be nice to you." He waved his hand at me. "You're the one who is always...." He stopped and looked around the parking lot. "Forget it, Nora. Take your uncle home. I'll see if I can find someone to stay with him tonight."

"I'll stay with him," I told him, walking around to the other side of my car. "You needn't bother."

"You know, Nora, despite what you may think, I do care about people around here, whether they work for me or not. I don't hold thirty-five-year old grudges, and I most certainly would like it if we could at least be civil to each other."

My mouth fell open slightly as I gawked at him across the top of my car. "Civil? How do you expect me to be civil with you when every time I see you I feel like you're about to chew me up and spit me out?"

He ran his hand through his wavy, black hair. "That has never been my intention. We were so close once when we were young. Why can't we be that way now?"

"That was a long time ago, Jean Marc. We have both lived very different lives since them."

"Do you think we could at least try to be friends?" he softly asked.

I instantly felt very foolish. Here I was arguing like a child with a man who had come to the aid of my uncle. I cast my eyes shamefully to the ground.

"Well, obviously not," I heard him say.

When I raised my head, he had his back to me and was beginning to walk away.

"Jean Marc," I called out. I saw him stop and arch his back for a moment before he turned to me. "I'm sorry. You're right. We seem to have always been at odds with each other over the past few years. For my uncle's sake, I promise to try and be friendlier to you in the future, all right?"

For the first time, he smiled at me. Not a simple easy going grin, but a great smile that lit up his face and seemed to warm him from within. My stomach did an uneasy flip as I absorbed that smile. What in the hell was wrong with me? The man only brought out the worst in me, but at that moment something stirred within me. It was an uncomfortable sort of feeling that I was not quite sure how to interpret.

"I'm glad to hear it. Jack will be pleased." Jean Marc's dark eyes lingered on my face. "I'll see you again, Nora."

When I climbed into the car, Uncle Jack nodded to Jean Marc's figure, heading toward the emergency room entrance.

"What did you say to him?"

"Nothing," I replied as I started the engine.

"Well, whatever it was, it sure must have been somethin'," Uncle Jack proposed as he fidgeted with his splint. "Haven't seen that boy smile like that since…I can't remember when."

* * *

The next day, a dozen yellow roses arrived at my office in a large green vase.

Steve smirked as he carried the roses into my office and ceremoniously placed them on my desk. "Slept with him, eh? How was he?"

I put the chart I had been reading to the side and inspected the roses. "I don't kiss and tell, Steve," I pronounced, and plucked the small white envelope from the bouquet. I was going to open it, but decided to wait until I was alone.

"Must not have been that great, otherwise you'd be blushing." Steve waved at the roses. "Anyway, it's a classic post first-time-in-bed-move to send flowers." He ran his fingers over the yellow buds. "Means he wants more sex. If he didn't send flowers then the sex wasn't so great, and you would never see him again."

I sat back in my desk chair and stared at him. "Am I missing something here? Some unpublished phantom handbook that floats around on the particular elements of dating? You and my mother keep quoting these rules to me."

"Ah, you must have told Claire about him. Now it will get interesting. Did she ask you to bring him over for dinner yet?"

I grimaced with apprehension. "Not yet."

Steve laughed, a loud sounding cackle that filled my small office. "She will!"

"I don't know if I'm up for that." I paused as I inhaled the sweet aroma of the roses. "Knowing Mother, she'll probably scare him away."

"Hell, Claire will probably abduct him." He took in my concerned frown. "Don't look so worried, Nora. If he's serious, he'll want to meet her."

"How do you know that?"

He shrugged. "All men approach dating the same way, and meeting the future in-laws is always a serious step. Except it's a much bigger deal to women."

"How would you know what women are like?"

He waved his hand dramatically in the air. "I went with girls in high school. Where I came from in Mississippi, no one even knew what a homosexual was, let alone how to act like one. So, I started out with girls, but when I was ready I switched to men."

"When did you decide you were ready? Do all men have some unwritten schedule when it comes to dating? When to date someone, when to sleep with them, when to get serious?"

Steve gave a heartfelt laugh. "That's silly, Nora." He started toward my office door. "The only people I know who do stuff like that either need medication or are already on it," he added over his shoulder.

After Steve shut my door, I took the white envelope out of my hand and opened it.

"Sorry I was such an ass. I apologize, and hope we can be friends." The card was signed Jean Marc Gaspard.

I had to read the note twice to make sure I was not hallucinating.

"Great, just great." I slapped the card down on my desk. This was completely unexpected. Then, another thought crossed my mind. Why didn't John send flowers?

I picked up the phone and pressed the intercom button to Steve's desk.

"Miss me already?" he said into the intercom.

"Steve, see if you can find the number for a Gaspard Fisheries in Manchac," I stated, still looking at the flowers on my desk.

"Why, are we having a crawfish boil or somethin'?"

"No."

"Then why do you need the number?" he persisted.

"Because the owner of Gaspard Fisheries, Jean Marc Gaspard, is the one who sent me the flowers."

There was silence on the other end of the line, and then my office door flew open.

"Who in the hell is Jean Marc Gaspard? Have you been keeping another man from me, Nora?" Steve called from my doorway.

I gave an exasperated sigh. "He's an old family friend, not a man in my life."

Steve stared me down with his intimidating blue eyes. "And I'm straight." He took a step inside my office. "So who is he?"

I sat back in my chair. "A friend…no, not a friend, more like an adversary. He and I never got along well, except when I was little. He used to watch over me when I was younger." I waved a dismissive hand at him. "But that was a long time ago."

"Obviously his feelings haven't changed." Steve nodded to the flowers. "Is he cute?"

"Cute?" I shook my head. "I don't know. He's dark and moody. He always seems to be in a foul temper, and talks to me like I'm eight years old. Oh, and the way he looks at me, it's as if I have the plague. And he's always got—"

"Nora." Steve rolled his eyes at me. "You're in trouble."

I furrowed my brow at my secretary. "What makes you say that?"

He grinned at me. "The doctor never got you this hot and bothered."

"I'm not hot and bothered. I'm aggravated," I corrected.

Steve snickered. "Darlin', for you it's the same thing." Then he quietly pulled the office door closed behind him.

* * *

It took three different transfers on the phone with Gaspard Fisheries to finally get through to Jean Marc's offices. I was about to give up after holding on the line for several minutes, when I suddenly heard a smooth, deep voice come over the speaker of my cell phone.

"Gaspard here," he said in his usual brisk, businesslike tone.

"Jean Marc, it's Nora Kehoe."

There was a moment of silence. "You got them," he whispered.

"Yes, thank you, but it was not—"

"Yes, it was," he cut in. "I shouldn't have jumped all over you like that. Your uncle was hurt and you were scared for him. I was out of line and I wanted to apologize for the way I acted."

I fidgeted in my chair, unsure of how to respond. "Well, I've said some things in the past that I shouldn't have, but no matter what we say or do, Jean Marc, we will probably always feel at odds with each other."

"I don't feel that way about you." He paused, and I could hear a phone ringing in the background.

"You're busy," I surmised, brushing off his words. "I just wanted to thank you for the flowers, and I promise I'll try to do better with us in the future."

He sighed heavily into the phone. The ringing stopped in the background and I heard a woman's voice calling his name.

"Nora, I didn't send you the flowers to make you feel guilty." There was another awkward moment of silence. "I was going to invite your uncle to stay a few days over at the house with my mother. Momma's got plenty of room in that old mansion, and when I told her what happened, she insisted on looking after Jack. She even went out and bought one of those electronic blood pressure cuffs for him."

"I don't know what to say, but thank you, Jean Marc. That makes me feel so much better. I know Ms. Marie and Uncle Jack go way back."

"Yes, they do." I heard him shuffle some papers about. "Did you know my mother turned your uncle down for a date to the senior prom? Went with my father instead."

"I've never heard that story," I confessed, somewhat taken aback, because my uncle always loved to tell stories about growing up in Manchac.

"Have Jack tell you about it some time," he stated, just as more ringing began in the background.

"Yes, well, thanks again, Jean Marc. I won't keep you. I know you're busy."

"All right, Nora." His voice seemed to return to its usual detached tone. "I'll get word to you when I get your uncle set up at the house. Good-bye." Then he hung up.

I stared at my cell phone as I mulled over our conversation. But just as I was about to put my cell phone in my purse, my intercom beeped in.

"John Blessing is on line one," Steve announced into the speaker. "And he sounds divine."

CHAPTER 6

Three weeks later, John decided that the time had come to meet my parents.

"I think we are due an evening with Claire and your stepfather. Better to make the introductions at this point in our relationship," he had said early one morning while I was cooking his breakfast.

"Are you sure about that?" I had questioned.

"They need to meet me, Nora. It's time."

I noticed how everything about our relationship seemed to be set according to some imaginary schedule John had predetermined. But I attributed his behavior to the rigorous demands of his medical training, and figured all residents probably approached dating in the same way.

A few days before our dinner with my parents, John determined it was necessary to discuss the proper term for our arrangement.

"I think the time has come for you and me to consider ourselves an item," he proposed while we were getting ready for bed.

A gentle spring rain pattered on my roof as I eased my nightshirt over my head.

"We should agree to tell everyone we know that this is an exclusive relationship," John insisted.

I pulled the beige comforter back on my four-poster bed. "John, you have been spending every night you're off from the hospital here with me. I think it's pretty obvious we're not seeing other people."

He tossed his scrub suit top on a chair next to the bed. "But we haven't discussed it. I want you to know that exclusive means you and me, Nora. No dating other people," he added with a stern frown.

I climbed onto my bed. "You mean like going steady?"

"If you like." He removed his scrub pants and boxers.

I sat back and took in his naked body. "All right, John. If that's what you want."

He nestled next to me. "I'm glad we sorted that out," he whispered against my neck. "Now why don't we seal the deal," he suggested, and his teeth grazed my shoulder. "Take off that nightshirt and let's have some fun."

I slipped the nightshirt over my head and John's hands eagerly went to work exploring my body. As he whispered instructions to me like a motion picture director supervising a love scene, I began to wonder if sex with John was always going to be like this. It wasn't that I disliked having sex with him; it was more like I no longer felt spontaneous.

Determined to try something different, I tried to shift John's body to the side. "Why don't you let me get on top? It could be fun to change things up a bit."

"Just do it this way," John impatiently muttered as he gently guided my body back underneath him.

I didn't have a vast amount of experience in the bedroom, but my few previous lovers had taught me that some degree of variety in bed helped to keep the relationship from getting stale. But John seemed to enjoy the same old routine.

"Don't you want to try something new?" I asked as his hands began to spread my legs apart.

"No," he said breathlessly. "Now, shift your hips up to me like I showed you."

I decided not to pursue the subject further. I just wondered how long it would be before I began to want more.

* * *

On the evening when we were to meet my parents for dinner, John resolved the time had come to affirm our true feelings for each other.

"I think we should iron out the exact emotional level of our relationship," he stated as we headed along the interstate in his always perfectly clean car.

I turned from the window and peered over at him. "What are you talking about?"

He kept his eyes on the road. "Your parents will want to know my intentions, and I think—"

"Correction," I interrupted. "Only my mother will want to know your intentions. Lou is the normal one."

"Well, I think we need to discuss how we feel about each other. Your parents will want to know if we are serious."

I gave him a questioning look. "We've agreed not to see other people. I thought that meant we are serious."

He cleared his throat as he took the exit off the interstate to St. Charles Avenue. "Yes, but we have never really talked about how we feel about each other, have we, Nora? Most women want to know where a man stands, emotionally."

"Do they?" I shrugged my shoulders, never having felt the need to know where John stood on our relationship. I already knew.

That gnawing little burn in my stomach began to churn ever so slightly as we descended the exit ramp. I chalked up the feeling to motion sickness, not wanting to analyze the sensation any further.

After an odd silence filled the car, he said, "I love you." He paused for an uncomfortable second or two as he pulled the car up to a red light. Then he turned to me. "Now, tell me how you feel," he insisted.

"I, ah…." I stuttered as the burning sensation in my stomach intensified to an uncomfortable irritation. "I love you, too, John," I finally told him.

John leaned over and tenderly kissed my lips. Then he put the car into gear just as the light changed to green.

"I'm glad we discussed that. It makes our relationship stronger," he affirmed and directed his attention back to the road ahead.

I said nothing as he drove down St. Charles Avenue. I just kept running our conversation over in my mind. I had never told a man I loved him before, but somehow I thought the experience was supposed to be a bit more emotional. Or at least that was the way it always appeared to be in the movies. But life was not a movie. No matter how much we desperately wanted the fantasy, reality would always triumph.

By the time we pulled into my parents' driveway, I had come to the conclusion that John definitely had some unromantic ways about him. But I shrugged off my pessimistic attitude and decided, what was romance between two medical professionals? Romance was for the hapless housewife starved of affection, and her nose buried inside some steamy novel. I could not afford such trivialities in my life. A relationship was a business, an intimate business between two contractual partners. Love, romance, and passion only clouded the mind and blinded one to the harsh reality of life. We are born, we mate, and then we die. Everything was biologically predicated on the need to continue the species, just as Darwin had concluded all those years ago.

I looked over at John as he turned off the engine and opened his car door. His physical appearance was appealing, he was successful, and he was dependable. What else could a girl ask for?

As we approached the front door of my parents' uptown double-gallery home, complete with white Doric columns, long balconies, and wide french doors, I could not help but question if some of my mother's ravings over the past few years had not rubbed off on me. Here was a fine specimen of a man that I had roped and corralled. But could I find contentment in a life of branded bliss with him? I gazed from John's profile to the leaded glass front door of my old home.

Let's just see what mother thinks of this one, I thought as the door opened before me. *The old librarian has finally come through.*

"Darling," Mother cooed as she stood in the doorway.

She was in one of her finer designer dresses, a shimmering silver piece that was cut very low at her bust and fit a little too snuggly about her hips. The dress clashed with the extraordinary amount of diamonds she had around her neck, her ears, and about both wrists. She had even teased her usually conservatively coifed red hair into a round bun above her head. She reminded me of a Christmas ornament, the kind one leaves in the box and does not put on the tree. Standing behind her in the foyer, Lou was wearing one of his ill-fitting dark suits, thick-rimmed black glasses, and holding a glass of bourbon in his hand.

"Mother, Lou." I turned to John. "This is John Blessing."

John stepped into the rosewood-inlaid foyer and kissed my mother on the cheek. He then reached over and took a firm grasp of Lou's outstretched hand.

"Welcome, John," Mother purred as she took his arm. She walked him into the living room beyond the foyer, leaving Lou and me to take up the rear.

"You'd better be prepared," Lou whispered to me. "She's gone hog wild. Even wanted me to hire a butler for the occasion."

I frowned at Lou as we entered the living room. "I knew she would be impossible tonight. Ever since she found out John was a doctor, she's been pestering me to bring him over."

Lou nodded to John holding my mother's arm ahead of us as Mother showed him to the bar at the far end of the living room. "You like this one, No?" Lou asked, calling me by the nickname he had given me ever since the first day Mother had brought him home to meet me. "I mean, his being a doctor is great and all, but do you really like the guy?"

I stopped and stared into Lou's bloodshot, hazel eyes. "You know something I don't, Lou?"

"Nah, I just was wondering how you felt about him." He motioned over to my mother, who was smiling and preparing a drink for John at the bar. "We know how your mother feels. She'd marry him if she could."

I elbowed my stepfather playfully. “She loves you, Lou. You know that.”

He looked at me, his eyes tinged with uncertainty. “I wonder about that sometimes, No.”

“You’re the only person who understands her, Lou. I’m her daughter and I don’t even understand her. But you do.”

Lou took a swig from his glass. “Yeah, I guess I do.”

Mother had gone all out for John, as I discovered when we entered the dining room to sit down for dinner. Her best Royal Worcester china and Baccarat crystal were displayed on top of the fancy Irish linen tablecloth she kept under lock and key. The expensive candles in the antique silver candelabra, which prior to tonight had been a blasphemy to light, were burning away, dripping their expensive, rose-scented wax down the polished silver. The table even had the best of the silver dining utensils and serving pieces laid out in an intricate array probably not seen on this side of the Atlantic Ocean in over a hundred years.

“My God, Mother!” I exclaimed, almost laughing at the garish presentation. “Is the Queen of England coming to dinner?”

My mother tittered nervously. “Really, Nora, you act as if you were raised in a barn. You know very well I always use the best china for special occasions.”

“The last special occasion I remember was when you brought Lou home for dinner fifteen years ago.”

“I think it looks wonderful, Claire.” John gave my mother one of his winning smiles, the kind that made his deep gray eyes twinkle.

“Oh, thank you so much, John,” my mother chirped as she came around to his side and showed him to his spot at the table next to her. “I do try my best,” she humbly added.

“Would you look at that, they’re already cozy,” Lou whispered as he nudged me to my spot across the table from John.

“Everyone sit and I’ll get the first course,” Mother commanded.

I leaned over to Lou. “We’re having courses?”

He placed his glass of bourbon down on the fine linen tablecloth. "I told you, she's gone hog wild tonight."

"So, Lou," John commented. "Nora tells me you're a jewelry dealer."

Lou pulled his chair up to the table. "Ah, yes. I deal in antique and custom jewelry. I have stores here, in Houston, and New York."

John placed his linen napkin in his lap. "Really? I didn't realize you were a franchise."

"I started the business in New York years ago; opened the store down here after I met Nora's mother."

John reached for his water goblet. "Where did you and Claire meet?"

"At her husband's funeral, actually." Lou picked up his bourbon and took a sip. His wane complexion almost matched the fancy white tablecloth. "Kehoe and I had done some business together in Houston. I'd never met Claire until I came to New Orleans for the funeral. After that, well…." Lou put his drink back down on the table and smiled. "I could never get myself to go back to New York," he confessed.

"Here we go," Mother proclaimed as she marched into the dining room carrying a white china tureen. "Cream of curry soup to start." She placed the tureen on the table in front of to John. "Nora told me you love Indian food, John."

John smiled at me. "Yes, I do love it."

"Good," Lou remarked. "Claire's cooked enough for ten people. You two get all the leftovers to take home. Damn curry gives me the runs."

After that, dinner became a series of exotic Indian dishes lovingly prepared by my mother and paraded out for John's approval. By the time we got to dessert, Lou was on his third bourbon and had been through at least seven glasses of water, trying to quench the fire in his mouth. All of us had downed several glasses of water with the meal. Mother's motto with seasoning was "more is always better," something not particularly recommended when using curry.

* * *

After dinner we gathered in the cozy living room for coffee and Courvoisier. The room was decorated in soft tones of green with floral print upholstered couches and dark walnut furniture. On the walls were expensively framed photographs of my mother with her influential society friends. Mother served coffee and chicory from her antique silver coffee urn set up on the table in the center of the room, while Lou poured the Courvoisier at the bar.

"Well, your job sure sounds exciting. I've watched those television programs about emergency rooms and it seems so fast-paced." Mother, always the consummate hostess, kept the conversation going by commenting on John's litany at dinner about his adventures in the emergency room.

"Yes, but you must be used to hearing about medical stories with Nora and her job." John took the cup of coffee my mother offered him. "She has quite an important position at Uptown Hospital." He sat down next to me on one of the two bright green and yellow floral couches.

Mother had a seat on the other floral couch across from me. "Nora is just a physical therapist, after all, John. You doctors are the real decision makers."

I rolled my eyes at her. "Thanks, Mother."

"Nora is well-respected by the staff and doctors she works with," Lou insisted as he approached the couch where John and I were sitting. He placed two brandy snifters, partially filled with Courvoisier, on the coffee table before us.

"How would you know how respected she is?" Mother asked, glaring at Lou.

"Because half the people she works with are my clients, Claire." Lou turned to me and winked. "Nora has sent me a ton of business from Uptown Hospital. Most of the doctors there are my clients."

Mother looked down at the coffee cup in her hands. "Oh, I wasn't aware of that."

After we were all settled on our perspective couches, the clang of the doorbell made my mother jump.

"Now who could that be?" she fussed.

"It's probably one of your friends dropping by, Claire. I'll take care of it," Lou told her and went to answer the door.

A few moments later when he returned to the living room, he had an unexpected guest with him.

"Nora T!" Uncle Jack held out his arms to me as he limped toward me, still wearing the splint on his right ankle.

"Uncle Jack." I placed my coffee down on the table in front of me and went to hug him. "What are you doing here?" I inquired as I stepped back from his embrace.

"Oh, for God's sake, Jacques. Can't you call like any normal person?" Mother barked from her couch. "I hope you can forgive the intrusion, John," she added, smiling sweetly.

"Nora told me 'bout dinner, so I thought I would stop by and meet the new beau." Uncle Jack raised his long nose in the air. "Jesus, it stinks in here. What in the hell you been cookin', Cece?"

My mother hated many things in life, but above all she hated being called by her childhood nickname of Cece. My uncle, however, reveled in reminding my mother of her humble upbringing at every opportunity.

"Reminds me of when we used to fry catfish on the back porch in Manchac," Uncle Jack went on as he placed his arm about my waist.

My mother began gnashing her teeth like a mad squirrel.

Uncle Jack examined my mother's outfit. "Lord, have mercy, Cece. What in the hell you done to your hair? You look like a hooker on Decatur Street."

"Not fully recovered yet from your drunken tumble, I see?" Mother's brown eyes appeared ready to shoot flames at Uncle Jack. "You still can't hold your liquor, can you Jacques Mouton?"

"Cece, I'm glad to see that your outsides may look a hell of a lot older, but on the inside you're still the same old bitch you've always been."

"Uncle Jack," I quickly interceded. "There's someone I would like you to meet." I motioned to John sitting on his couch, holding his white china coffee cup in his hands. "This is John Blessing."

"Well, hello." Uncle Jack left my side and limped over to shake hands with John.

John put his coffee down and stood to greet my uncle. They were the same height and had the same square jaw. But my uncle looked stronger and more agile than John. Years of hard living on bayous of Louisiana, I surmised.

"My brother is a little rough around the edges, John." Mother asserted, trying to sound as condescending as possible. "You will have to excuse him."

Uncle Jack carefully inspected John with his crafty blue eyes. "So, you're the doctor." He turned to me. "This is the fella you told me 'bout?"

"Yes, Uncle Jack." I walked back to the couch and stood by John's side.

"I'm glad to hear she told you about me." John paused and looked down at my uncle's right leg. "How's the ankle?"

"Better, thanks, 'cept for all them damn tests you doctors keep doin' on me. They keep lookin' for somethin', when nothin' is wrong."

I scowled at my uncle. "You know that's not true, Uncle Jack. The doctor told you what you needed to do to get better."

"I've cut back on my drinkin' like he wanted, so why I need more tests?" Uncle Jack sat down on the couch next to John. "Marie Gaspard even thinks I don't need all of them tests. Ms. Marie, she's been real good to me."

"I can't believe you accepted her invitation to stay at their place, Jacques. Those people are no good scum," Mother chided. "The Gaspard's will never be accepted in polite society. There have been stories floating around about them for years. Smugglers, that's what they are."

"Ain't no polite society, Cece," Uncle Jack argued. "It's Manchac."

"What do you mean, smugglers?" John asked as he picked up his coffee from the table in front of him.

"Gaspard's come from an old family of smugglers," Uncle Jack began. "Their great, great, great grandfather smuggled supplies to the Confederates durin' the Civil War. Then their great grandfather made money runnin' rationed food and rare imports through the swamps durin' the First World War. Grandfather Jean Louis ran whisky through the swamps for the New Orleans Mafia. When Jean Louis decided to go legit, he used the money he made to buy his trawlers and started Gaspard Fisheries. But he didn't do such a good job runnin' the place. Damn near bankrupted it when Cece's first husband, Etienne, and his brother, Emile, took over the business. So, Jean Louis went back to what he knew best, smugglin'." My uncle turned to John. "The swamps of Louisiana are like a maze. For years the government's been tryin' to stop the drugs and stuff that comes through our swamps and gets into the States, but the Coast Guard don't know how to navigate all them bayous and small canals. They get lost and give up. Only people that can make it in the swamps are the ones raised in them."

John raised his dark eyebrows in surprise. "I've never heard that before."

Mother snickered. "You know as well as I do, Jacques, that Gaspard family is still in the smuggling business. I heard stories for years from Etienne. Then there is Jean Marc and that business in Texas."

My uncle shook his finger at his sister. "Don't you be goin' and sayin' bad things 'bout that boy, Cece. Jean Marc's been good to me."

I anxiously stared at my mother. "What about Jean Marc?"

Mother sighed as she demurely placed her hands in her lap. "When Jean Marc was in Texas, after he finished at that fancy college, I heard he got involved with a notorious smuggler. That boy's no good, just like his Uncle Etienne."

"Jesus, Mother! I can't believe you would buy into such gossip."

"It's not gossip, Nora. It's just another reason why Jacques shouldn't be taking any handouts from the Gaspards," she defended.

"What's wrong with Uncle Jack staying at Ms. Marie's, Mother? Why can't one old friend help out another?"

Mother's cheeks began to turn a pale shade of red. "Since when are we ever friends with any of the Gaspards?"

Uncle Jack made himself comfortable on my mother's floral print couch. "Just 'cause you ran 'round on Etienne when you was married to him, Cece, don't mean the rest of us can't be friendly with that family."

"Hush up. We've got company, you old fool." Mother turned to John and smiled. "No need to go airing all our dirty laundry and boring poor Dr. Blessing to death."

"Why not? You afraid I'll tell some secrets 'bout you, Cece?" Uncle Jack persisted.

"My uncle and my mother love to spar every time the family gets together," I explained as I looked from John to Uncle Jack.

"My brother is from the side of the family that one tries to forget about, actually," Mother remarked as she rolled her perfectly made up eyes.

"What side of the family you talkin' 'bout, CeCe?" Uncle Jack struggled to his feet and walked over to the bar. "You from the same side of the family as me, girl." He grabbed a glass and started to search through the bottles behind the bar. "'Cept me ain't the one talkin' snooty. You don't need to be actin' so high and mighty all the time."

"Let me help you with that, Jack," Lou offered as he got up from his couch.

"Uncle Jack, I thought you said you cut back on the drinking."

His robust cackle filled the living room. "Cut back don't mean quit, child."

Lou went behind the bar, grabbed one of the bottles, and began to fill Uncle Jack's glass with whiskey.

Mother nervously played with her diamond necklace as her eyes went from Uncle Jack to John. "I'm sorry about this, John. My brother has a bad habit of just dropping by without warning."

John smiled reassuringly at my mother. "No, this is wonderful. I'm getting to meet the whole family."

"Tell me, boy." Uncle Jack, now armed with his whiskey, limped over to the couch where John was sitting and took the spot next to him. “You and my niece, this serious or you just sportin’ her?”

“Uncle Jack!” I gave him a stern reprimand with my eyes. “Don’t start threatening my date, all right?”

“I’m not threatnin’ him. I just wanna know his intentions.” Uncle Jack turned from me to John. “You got any intentions, son?”

“Jesus, Jacques, shut up!” Mother got up from her couch and walked back to the bar. She placed her empty brandy snifter on the bar and motioned for Lou to refill it.

“Actually, I have very honorable intentions,” John declared as he stood from his spot on the couch next to my uncle and stepped to my side. He took my hand and then faced the others. “Nora and I are in love, and I want to marry her,” he announced.

At this point, my mother broke out into huge fits of screaming, my Uncle Jack frowned, while Lou just stood behind the bar, seemingly unfazed, and poured my mother another Courvoisier. I, on the other hand, almost hit the floor after John’s little disclosure.

“Nora, my baby!” My mother came toward me, hands outstretched, and then she embraced John. “Lou, did you hear that? Our little girl is getting married.” She turned to my stepfather, who was still standing behind the bar.

“I heard,” Lou calmly said, his eyes steadily glaring at me.

“Nora T, you want this?” my Uncle Jack demanded, staring up at me from the couch.

All eyes in the room turned to me.

“Ah, I….” I looked over at John smiling at me. “We never talked about marriage, Uncle Jack, but we do love each other, and I think we would make a good team.”

“Team, ha! Are you happy with this, Nora T? Bein’ happy, that’s what makes it last fifty years.”

Mother spun around on her high heels and yelled at my uncle. “Frem la bouche. Tu es couyon, Jacques. Je vas te passé une collette.”

My Uncle Jack chuckled and rose from the couch. “Now, she wants to slap me.” He winked at me. “She only speaks a français when she boudé.”

"What?" John softly asked me.

"She only speaks French when she gets angry," I replied, translating for my uncle.

Lou stepped from behind the bar. "I guess this calls for a toast."

Mother clasped her hands together gleefully. "Definitely. Go get the champagne, Lou. Let's have a celebration."

John's hand squeezed mine as he whispered, "I thought it was about time I made my intentions known. Sorry it was so public." He kissed my cheek. "I hope you don't mind."

I examined John's happy face. His gray eyes seemed soft and caring. His profile looked like a marble statue, forever supportive and dependable. The nearness of him, the warmth of his touch, felt comforting to me. But deep within the recesses of my body, the acid churned and that nagging pang of doubt began to eat away at me.

When does it feel right? I mused, and then I looked over at my mother's beaming countenance. It was the happiest I had seen her in quite some time. Even tears of joy seemed to be smearing her perfectly applied mascara. Maybe it was just me. Perhaps I had been on my own for so long that the idea of joining forces with another needed time to settle in. I figured we would probably have a long engagement to allow me to get used to the idea of marriage. At least I hoped it would be a long engagement. With John, things tended to move quickly, according to his master plan.

* * *

As we drove home later that evening, I questioned John's announcement of our impending nuptials.

"You could have said something to me ahead of time," I told him as we headed away from the city.

He maneuvered his BMW M3 through some slower moving cars on the interstate. When he glanced over to me, the smile he had used on my mother all evening had been replaced by a perturbed scowl.

"What did you expect me to say to your family?" He paused as he sped around a puttering Volvo. "Your uncle was asking what my intentions were while your parents were standing there. What could I say? Yes, I'm having sex with your daughter and no, I'm only hanging around until I get bored with her." He turned back to me. "I don't think your uncle would have been too pleased. I was afraid the man was going to pummel me if I didn't say the right thing."

I began to feel a little flushed. "You want to marry me?"

"Of course I want to marry you, Nora. I thought we could announce our engagement officially in June, and then plan a wedding for the late summer. My residency will be finished by then." He winked at me. "Hopefully, I'll have a job lined up by the time we get married."

"This summer?" I noted the close proximity of the red taillights of the cars in front of us. "But June is only two months away."

His winning smile returned. "Yes, that's good, isn't it? I don't believe in long engagements. We'll also need to start looking for a new place to live. As a matter of fact, the other day—I was going to tell you about it—I saw the best house for us. In the same neighborhood as your parents, but bigger."

"What's wrong with my place?" I argued as he took the turn off the interstate, heading toward Lake Pontchartrain.

"Your house is too small for both of us. We're practically tripping over each other in your bedroom. My home is even smaller, so I thought we could get a new one with extra room for kids."

"Kids?" I hesitated, holding back the expletives I desperately wanted to shout out.

"I figured we could have two. Their sex doesn't matter to me, but I want to wait at least a year or two after the wedding before we begin trying for a family."

"Christ, John, have you already selected their names?"

He gave me a funny look. "What are you talking about? I thought that would be something we decide together. But I have to admit, I always wanted a John Edward Jr. around."

"This is all a little sudden." I gulped back the panic rising up my throat. "What if we make a mistake? What if it doesn't work out between us?"

John patted my thigh. "Of course it will work out. We're perfect for each other. We are a good team, you said so yourself. How could we not succeed? Besides, we are older, not some teenagers going on a whim. I've thought this out carefully and planned our future together. It's our time."

"I see," I muttered as some newly constructed lakefront homes, built since Hurricane Katrina, passed by my window. "What about your parents?" I turned back to him.

His face flickered with anger as we traveled beneath the streetlamps. "Never mind about them. All they will need is an invitation to the wedding. Your parents are the important ones. After all, you will be the bride, and that's who a wedding is for, isn't it? For the bride?"

But sitting there, in John's immaculate car, I did not feel very much like a bride. I started having visions of long, white trains and a dozen velvet-sheathed bridesmaids. Leading the wedding party through the whole sordid affair was my mother, dripping with diamonds, covered with white lace, and serving curry to the five hundred guests she would cram into some grand old hall for the reception.

As we made our way back to my small cottage by the lake, I began to entertain the idea of a late summer wedding in New Orleans, complete with torrid heat, high humidity, hurricanes, and pre-season Saints football. While weighing the benefits of a Las Vegas wedding, the burning in my stomach took hold, making me reach reflexively for the car door.

"You all right?" John felt my cheek with the back of his cool hand. "You look a little flushed."

"I think the curry has gotten to me," I said, placing my hand on my stomach.

"I'm sure it did." John nodded as he eased the car into a parking spot right in front of my house. "Your mother may be many things Nora, but a cook is not one of them."

CHAPTER 7

A few days later I was sitting at my desk going through patient charts when Steve came into my office carrying some papers in his hands.

He leaned over my desk and examined my face. "You don't look so good."

I took the papers from him. "I think I have a stomach bug," I grumbled and tossed the papers to the side of my desk.

"Everything all right in the bedroom?" He raised his silver eyebrows to me. "You haven't said much about Dr. Blessing lately, and I haven't seen any more roses from the other guy. What's going on?"

I sat back in my chair and gazed down at my hands, fidgeting nervously on my desk. It was moments like this that I wished I had acquired a slew of girlfriends on whom I could deposit all of my problems. For the better part of three years I had confided my troubles to no one, feeling the burden of confession too much for most people. But as I sat there and felt Steve's eyes on me, I figured he was all I had.

"John is talking marriage," I blurted out. "He met my parents last weekend and he announced that he intended to marry me."

"Congratulations?" Steve furrowed his high brow. "You don't seem like the happy bride, kiddo." He had a seat in a chair in front of my desk.

"You noticed. I don't feel like one. I think it's all too fast."

"Then slow it down. It is your life after all."

I stared at him. “Is it?”

He sat back in his chair as he studied me for a few seconds. “Do you love John Blessing?” he finally asked.

I shrugged. “I told him I loved him.”

Steve slammed his hand down on the desk. “Nora, you’ve got a problem. You’re not in love with the doctor. I can see it written all over your face. And if you ask me—”

“Which I haven’t,” I cut in.

“I think the fish guy is still swimming around in your head.”

My jaw dropped. “Jean Marc?” I laughed more out of shock than humor. “The guy is a pompous ass who thinks he’s better than me. He is condescending, a male chauvinist, conceited, arrogant and—”

“Those are more adjectives than you have ever used to describe the dear doctor, Nora.” Then Steve slowly smiled. “If I were you I wouldn’t hang my fishing pole up quite yet.”

I waved off his smug grin. “Steve, you’re being ridiculous.”

His inquisitive blue eyes locked on mine. “Nora, I may not know a whole hell of a lot about women, but I do know when someone is trying to fit a round peg in a square hole. You need to ask yourself if this is what you want.”

I took in a deep breath and let it out slowly. “John and I are a lot alike. It’s a good match between us.”

Steve stood from his chair. “Honey, it’s not about what you have in common, it’s about love. That’s the only tie I know of that can keep two people together for a lifetime. Make sure it’s love, Nora. Don’t settle for anything less.” He walked to my office door.

“How do I know when it’s love?”

Steve grinned as he turned to me. “You won’t have to ask. You’ll know.” He shut the office door behind him, leaving me to wrestle with my growing apprehensions.

* * *

The following Sunday, I joined my parents for our usual brunch. It was while we were seated at the mandatory mahogany table that my mother delighted in informing me that she had already come up with a list of possible reception locations.

"Nora, you and John are going to have to set a date sooner than later," Mother told me after I enlightened her about John's plans for our engagement. "It takes months to organize a wedding. Some of the places on my list have to have at least six months' notice, especially Gallier Hall. They're impossible. However, Jenny Auquin, from the Ladies Auxiliary, knows the manager of the hall and she said we could get you squeezed in this summer, but they would have to know right away." She smiled, seeming very pleased with herself.

"Mother, stop." I raised my hand and looked to Lou for support. But he just sat hunched over in his mahogany chair, staring down at his plate of ham and eggs. "John and I have just started talking about marriage. We have no date, no plans, nothing."

"But, darling," Mother whined. "It's Gallier Hall."

"I really don't care." I pushed my plate of food away. "I will not be rushed into this."

"Quite right," Lou finally spoke up as he forked a large piece of ham into his mouth.

"Don't encourage her, Lou," Mother reprimanded. "If we don't make the arrangements for her, God knows what kind of wedding she'll end up with. Some nightmare complete with kegs of beer, a barbeque buffet, and an accordion player banging out polka tunes."

I stood from my chair. "What if I wanted to elope?"

"Elope!" Mother fumed. Her face turned a deep crimson, almost matching her hair. "You wouldn't dare elope and humiliate me out of all the best social circles in town." She stood from her chair, her brown eyes fixed on me. "No self-respecting Catholic girl in this town elopes. It's not done, Nora, and you will not do it to me."

Lou looked up from his plate. "Why not? We eloped."

"That was different; we were older and it wasn't our first marriage." Mother threw her linen napkin on the table. "This wedding has to be done the right way, or I will never be able to hold up my head in this town again." She pointed her finger at me and shook it, making the collection of gold bracelets on her wrist jingle. "You will not cheat me out of this, Nora. I will have this wedding or I will never forgive you." She turned from the table and stormed out of the dining room, her high heels clicking on the old oak floor as she went.

Lou raised his dark eyebrows high over the rim of his black glasses and let out a sigh. "You know how she is, No. She'll be impossible unless she gets her way." He leaned in closer to me. "It's just one day. Your mother always wanted a big social wedding, and despite being married three times, she never got one. Let her have this one day. After all, you only have one mother and she only has you to live vicariously through. Just think about it." He returned his attention to his pile of scrambled eggs.

I took my chair and reached for my plate. I watched Lou fill his fork with some overly cooked eggs and my heart broke for the man. Not only would my life be hell if my mother did not get her way, but his would not be much better.

"All right, Lou, I'll think about it." I picked up my fork and started to play with the grits on my plate. "But I will have to talk with John about all of this," I asserted.

Lou glanced up at me and smiled, his pale skin contrasted the redness in his eyes. "That would be good, No. That would be real good." He reached across the table and patted my hand. "You going out to see Jack today?"

"Yeah, he's working on his boat again and has moved back into his house. I figured I'd go up and check on him since he's not at the Gaspard's anymore." I put my fork down and pushed my chair away from the table.

"Your uncle said they were real good to him."

"They were. Uncle Jack told me Ms. Marie took his blood pressure every day, and Jean Marc checked on him every night."

"Well, that's good for Jack." Lou looked down at his plate, deciding what to devour next. "I'm glad he has friends up there to help, especially with you and Claire being in the city."

"I better get going." I rose from my chair, wanting to leave Lou to his brunch.

"See you, Lou," I added as I waved good-bye.

Lou just grunted, having just taken a bite of his ham.

* * *

An hour later, I found Uncle Jack in Merle's Bar, located next to the Gaspard Fisheries boatyard. I knew I would find him at the closest bar when I arrived on board the *Rosalie* and found a new captain had been assigned to the trawler.

Merle's was popular with all the local fishermen, especially after a long day in the hot Louisiana sun. My uncle was seated at the far end of the long wooden bar, next to a soundless television that flashed sports scores over pictures of U.S. soldiers in Afghanistan. On the dusky gray walls were assorted pictures of boats, along with stuffed and mounted fish caught by the owner. The large room reeked of stale beer, fried food, and bleach used to clean the cement floor. The place was not crowded, and only a few of the many tables in the dining area were filled. Merle's was also a restaurant that served fresh boiled and fried seafood brought in by the fishermen who frequented the bar.

"Uncle Jack?" I softly said to his back as he sat on the bar stool before me.

My uncle never faced me. He just picked up his shot glass filled with dark liquid and brought it to his lips. He emptied the small glass with one gulp.

"Don't do this," I begged as I took a seat on the torn red leather stool next to him.

"They took my boat." He slammed the glass down on the bar. "They took my *Rosalie*. She was my boat. She was my son's boat. Been on that boat better than twenty years." He turned to me and I could see the dark circles underneath his bloodshot eyes. "How in the hell am I to make a livin' now, Nora T?"

"You could go to New Orleans. Move in with Momma and Lou."

"Move in with your mama?" He crossed himself as if he had seen an evil spirit. "Livin' with that woman would be the death of me. She's been the death of two husbands already, and Lou don't look so good these days."

"Stop it, Uncle Jack. I talked to the new captain of the *Rosalie*, Teddy Breaux, and he told me that the Gaspard's insurance company won't cover you anymore because of this." I pointed to the shot glass on the bar. "The insurance company thinks you're a liability."

"Insurance company, ha!" He spit on to the floor. "When I started in this business over forty years ago, we don't have no insurance on these boats." He held up his callused hands to me. "These the only insurance a man had. If you had hands, you could work."

"Times are different, Uncle Jack. Jean Marc has to do things by the book." I was about to give him a lecture on his drinking when I heard footsteps come up behind my stool.

Uncle Jack was the first to wheel around. Before I even knew what was going on, my uncle swung his big fist to hit the person standing behind me. I turned in time to see Jean Marc Gaspard duck expertly out of danger. When he missed connecting with Jean Marc's jaw, my uncle lost his balance and fell from his stool.

"Merde!" Uncle Jack hollered as he hit the cement floor.

Jean Marc was the first to his side. I jumped from my stool, and knelt down beside him.

"Get away from me," Uncle Jack growled at Jean Marc.

Jean Marc took a step back as I helped my uncle to his feet. He appeared unharmed as my eyes did a quick assessment of his body.

"What you doin' here, boy? Passé!" Uncle Jack howled as his blue eyes spewed venom at Jean Marc.

"Uncle Jack, shut up."

"Look, I came to see how he was," Jean Marc explained.

"You just like that possedé brother of yours, stabbin' men in the back," Jack shouted as he made a move toward Jean Marc.

I jumped in between the two men. It was then I noticed a few of the patrons intently watching our every move. I nodded at Jean Marc. "Let's get him home."

But Uncle Jack would have none of Jean Marc touching him. Instead, he grabbed his faded blue cap from the bar and then proceeded to the entrance. I followed him as Jean Marc fell in step behind me.

Once outside in the full light of day, Uncle Jack did not appear as steady on his feet as he had inside the bar. I went to him and placed my arm about his waist.

"Come on, Uncle Jack," I urged as I tried to guide him to the parking lot.

He pulled away from my arm. "Non, I'm not goin' home. Too early to go home. I got things to do. I should rewire some crab traps and run a new tow line, but...." He pointed at Jean Marc. "He took that away from me."

"You did it to yourself, Jack," Jean Marc insisted. "Once that hospital filed a report with our health insurance company, you were screwed. The doctor at the hospital ran a blood alcohol level on him." He came up to my side. "When he ran the blood tests to check his liver. The doctor made a diagnosis of chronic alcoholism on the insurance report. Once it was filed, my insurance company called me and told me I had no choice but to pull him from the boat, otherwise they would not cover him for liability." Jean Marc turned back to Jack and threw up his hands. "There was nothing I could do. I even tried to get you coverage working dry dock, at least around the boats, since you couldn't be out hauling. But the insurance company nixed that, as well." Jean Marc placed his hands in the front pockets of his black slacks. "I can't hide the drinking anymore, Jack."

I gave Jean Marc a reassuring smile. "I'm sure you did all you could."

"Don't you take his side," Uncle Jack barked at me, and then without warning he fell back against the shell-covered lot, passed out cold.

"Uncle Jack!" I cried out as I ran to him.

Jean Marc picked up my uncle like a sack of crawfish and slung him over his broad shoulder. "I'll put him in the back of my truck."

I followed him to a red Ford pick up truck, newer than the others in the lot, but still old compared to the standards of city folk.

Jean Marc tenderly laid my uncle out in his truck bed and covered him with an old blanket he had folded up in the back of his cab.

"Follow me in your car," Jean Marc instructed. "We'll get him home and put him to bed."

As we drove out of the parking lot, I watched his bright red taillights in front of my car and thought about all that Jean Marc had said. Silently berating myself for not stepping in sooner and curtailing my uncle's drinking, at that moment I swore I would take a more active roll in my uncle's life, even if it meant spending time away from John and my responsibilities in the city. When I began to consider the hours away from my home and fiancé, I realized I didn't feel anxious or upset. I was relieved. And that feeling, more than my uncle's guarded health, disturbed me.

* * *

My uncle lived in a two-bedroom cypress cottage next to a small bayou. His front yard was filled with several imposing bald cypress trees and a vast collection of painted ceramic animals. My Aunt Elise had decorated each of the ducks, squirrels, rabbits, frogs, and turtles that lay scattered about the lawn. Her artistry had not stopped there; Aunt Elise had also painted every color of the rainbow on the exterior of her home. The little raised Cajun cottage resembled something out of a child's drawing. But even after so many years since her death, the paint still looked fresh and vibrant thanks to my uncle's loving care.

When the red pickup truck stopped in front of the old porch, I jumped from my car and ran ahead to open the front door for Jean Marc. Being from the city, I was surprised to find the door unlocked, but I figured that was probably the way people were on the bayou. Trust was a commodity still evident in small communities across rural Louisiana. It was only the city folk, like me, who were jaded and disheartened by the cruel acts of others.

"Thank you," I said after Jean Marc had carried my uncle to his bedroom and laid him out on his old oak bed.

"You're welcome. I was worried about him," he told me as he walked out of the bedroom with its pink wallpaper and paintings of Jesus covering the walls.

I followed him down a dark-paneled hall to the kitchen.

Jean Marc pulled out a chair next to the pine breakfast table that filled the tiny yellow kitchen. He sat down with a thud, looking as if all his energy had been siphoned away. "One of my men told me he was at Merle's," he admitted.

I took the seat across from him. "When did you find out about the insurance?"

"Wednesday afternoon, after I got back in town from a business trip."

I placed my hands on the table before me. "You told him then?"

He rubbed his face in his large hands. "I told him after he came in from trawling that day. But he didn't believe me. Not until he saw Teddy Breaux taking his boat out the next morning." Jean Marc paused and I could see his dark brown eyes were distorted by anguish. "I've known your uncle all my life. He taught me how to rebuild a boat engine, gut a catfish, even how to ask a girl out on a date. Telling him he could not shrimp anymore was one of the hardest things I've ever done."

"I didn't realize you and my uncle were so close."

Jean Marc smiled, a warm and uplifting smile that muted the sadness in his eyes. "Jack was always a second father to me. My dad was too busy with the business, and when he wasn't doing that, he was bailing Henri out of some mess."

"I'm sorry. I'm his niece. I should have been more involved, and then maybe I could have helped him."

Jean Marc reached across the table for my hand. "Don't blame yourself. You didn't know. You aren't responsible for your uncle, Nora."

"Then why are you?" I questioned, feeling a sudden twinge of something strange as his strong hand held mine.

"Your uncle has been good to me." He let go of my hand. "He's been there for me and listened to me." He lowered his eyes to the worn surface of the old pine table. "I owe him a debt."

I shook my head. "You owe him the debt of friendship. I owe him the debt of family."

"'It's better to owe a debt of love than blood,' my grandfather used to always say. I never realized what he meant until now." He paused and the chill returned to his dark eyes. "I can look after Jack here. You won't have time to keep coming back and forth."

I stared at him, a little taken aback by his comment. "I can't ask you to do that."

"Nora, you have a great deal going on in your life. You have your wedding to plan and all the changes your new life will bring."

"Did Uncle Jack tell you I was getting married?"

"He mentioned you were going to marry a doctor." He paused and once again his eyes changed and a glint of warmth appeared in their darkness. "But he doesn't believe you're in love with this guy."

I sat back in my chair, feeling slightly dumbfounded. "He said that?"

Jean Marc rose from his chair. "Make sure you love the man you're going to marry, Nora. Otherwise, marriage can be a real bitch."

I looked up into his face. "You were married once, weren't you?"

He nodded. "Lasted less than a year. She was the daughter of a business associate I knew in Dallas. It was wrong from the start."

"Wrong?" I asked, realizing how little I actually knew about the man.

He snapped his fingers. "There was no spark, no passion between Cynthia and me. Love needs passion to ignite. Without it you just have hormones." He directed his attention to the small clock on the far wall. "You'd better get back to the city. It's getting late. I'll come back in a few hours and check on him. He's much more reasonable when he's sober." Jean Marc placed a reassuring hand on my shoulder. "Don't worry, I'll find something for him to do at the crawfish farms or, if need be, at the house." He gave me an encouraging smile.

I stood from my chair. "Thank you, Jean Marc. You've been a good friend to my uncle and I'm very grateful." And then, without thinking, I stood on my toes and gently kissed his lips.

The electricity that passed between us was unlike anything I had ever experienced. I could feel my body throb with the touch of his lips against mine. But before I could pull away, he threw his muscular arms about me and deepened his kiss. I could smell his woody cologne mixed with the scent of the bayou out back. I could hear the wild chirping of the birds in the trees along with the pounding of my heart. All my senses came to life, and the effect made me slightly dizzy. John's kisses had never been like this.

I pulled away first, overwhelmed by the frenzy of sensations raging within me.

He took a step back from me. "I'm sorry," he murmured, but the way the light reflected in his eyes, I sensed he really wasn't.

I smiled, trying to appear unflustered. "Don't worry about it." I turned to go and grabbed on to the back of the chair beside me to keep my knees from giving way.

"Nora?" Jean Marc whispered.

I straightened up and faced him. My stomach clenched as I took in his smug grin and the way he was dissecting my features as if he were a detective interrogating a murder suspect.

After several agonizing seconds, he finally said, "Are you sure you want to marry that doctor?"

I hastily lowered my gaze to the old linoleum floor. "You don't know John. We are a good team and—"

But before I could finish, he stormed out of the kitchen. A few minutes later, I heard the gun of an engine and the screech of tires on my uncle's shell-covered drive.

I kicked the little pine table next to me. "Damn it!"

I fought to regain control over my emotions. I was engaged to another man, so how could I possibly have feelings for a man I had always despised? I assured myself that I was simply exhibiting some nerves over my impending marriage; at least, I hoped that's all it was. To consider any other reason was, quite simply, dangerous.

CHAPTER 8

I returned home to find John preparing dinner in my kitchen. Standing next to my green cabinets, he was holding a mixing bowl, and stirring what appeared to be biscuit dough. He still had heavy dark circles under his eyes and was dressed in only his scrub pants. The pale skin on his thin chest and lean shoulders looked gray under the fluorescent lights of the kitchen.

I eased up next to him and tenderly kissed his rough cheek. "Tough night?"

"Knife and gun club after ten every weekend at University. I had three gang fights. Four guys with knife wounds, six with gunshots. Lost about half. But that wasn't the worst of it."

I patted his chest. "Damn drugs. Sorry it was so bad."

"I'm used to it." He put his bowl of dough down on the white-tiled counter. "But I will never get used to the really weird stuff. Had a woman last night, about twenty, who was involved in some bizarre cult thing. She was even wearing a long white robe when she came in." He picked up his blue coffee mug. "Her musculature supporting both eyeballs had been cut away. Never seen anything like it. Looked like a surgeon's work. Left both eyeballs just hanging by the retina; no blood and no blunt trauma to the head. Luckily, the woman was out of it...some drug they gave her at whatever twisted ritual they performed." He let a long sigh escape his lips. "She's on a ventilator now. Probably won't survive the night. The things people do to each other, and then we have to clean it up." He took a sip from his mug.

"Do they have any idea who did it?"

He shook his head. "I had the police up my ass half the night asking a lot of questions. They took her blood to their lab for toxicology screening to try and find out what she was on. Nothing I've ever seen. Bad night all around." He paused and looked over at me. "How was brunch with your parents?" he asked, and then took another sip from his coffee mug.

My stomach suddenly curled into knots at the mention of brunch. I debated for a moment if I should mention the incident with my uncle and Jean Marc.

"Brunch was fine," I told him.

John peered down into his coffee. "Uh huh. Don't try and lie to me, Nora Kehoe. Something happened today. What is it?"

My heart rose to my throat.

He grinned at me. "I can just imagine what Claire had to say today after our dinner last weekend."

"Oh." I sighed as a wave of relief spread throughout my body. "Yes, she was impossible." I leaned my hip against the counter and folded my arms across my chest.

"Did she have any lists?"

I squirmed and tried to avoid John's probing eyes. "Lists?"

"Oh, let me guess. Was it reception or church lists? Or did she have the guest list already started?" He rolled his head back and gave a warm, genuine chuckle that eased the knots in my belly.

I forced my mind back to earlier that morning and the brunch with my parents. After my kiss with Jean Marc, the conversation with my mother did not seem so intimidating anymore.

"Reception list," I stated as I unfolded my arms.

"Where?"

"I think she said something about Gallier Hall."

John nodded his head approvingly. "Difficult place to get, I hear. Have to make reservations a year in advance."

"Mother has friends. She can get it without the wait." I made my way to the sink.

"Really? Everybody who's anybody has their reception there. It's such a wonderful historic building. Can you imagine if we had our reception there?" I heard him say behind me. Then there was silence.

My hands gripped the edge of the sink as I waited for John to announce his next plan.

"Tell your mother we'll take it!"

"We would have to set a date," I clarified without turning to look at him.

I heard his bare feet slap against my kitchen floor as he went to the far wall where I kept my calendar. Instantly, he was at my side, holding the calendar in his hands.

I watched, feeling suddenly detached, as he flipped through the months until he came to August.

"The beginning of August?"

I stared into his face and he smiled at me. His gray eyes sparkled despite their fatigue. He flipped the calendar again.

"September? How about the seventeenth."

I lowered my gaze to the stainless sink. "John, we're not even officially engaged. You haven't asked me, and we haven't worked out where we want to—"

He put the calendar down on the counter and grabbed my hands. "Nora, marry me." He placed my hands against his bare chest. "Just say yes and it will all work out. There's nothing to be afraid of. We love each other."

He felt so sure against my hands, and for a moment I believed that John Blessing could remove all the burdens from my shoulders. He loved me and he was good to me; what else could there be?

"Yes, John. I will marry you," I whispered.

He put his hands about my face and very tenderly kissed me.

"September seventeenth," he declared and stepped back from me.

I examined his eyes and felt his strength flow into me. "September seventeenth."

He gave me one of his winning smiles. "Go call your mother and I'll take a shower." He glanced down at his watch. "There should be some jewelry stores still open. Let's go and get you a ring." He kissed me once more on the lips and turned away, heading for the bedroom.

Wanting to stifle my growing feeling of unease, I searched my kitchen for a distraction. I retrieved John's blue coffee mug and bowl of biscuit dough from the white-tiled counter. When I placed the items in the sink, the memory of Jean Marc's kiss drifted across my mind. I shook my head, forcing the vision from my thoughts. Without hesitation, I reached for the phone on the kitchen counter and dialed my mother's cell phone number. It was time to get back to reality.

* * *

Lou would not hear of John and I shopping at any other jewelry store than his. The following day, after I left work, John met me at Lou's store located on Canal Street.

John was still wearing his green hospital scrubs when he came running up to meet me at the front entrance to Schuller's Jewelry Store. He kissed my cheek hurriedly and opened the door for me.

"I've only got about an hour and then I have to get back for the evening shift, Nora."

"We can do this another day, John, when you have more time."

He shook his head and ushered me into the store. "No, I know exactly what we're looking for. Shouldn't take us too long to find it."

I shrugged my shoulders and walked inside, not exactly sure what John thought we were looking for.

When I stepped into the front of the store, I spotted Lou talking with another man. The gentleman's back was to me as he and Lou stood before a long display case. I noticed his dark, wavy hair, and the way his broad shoulders flexed beneath his snug, black polo shirt. Something about him reminded me of someone I could not place. When Lou nodded to me, the dark-haired man turned to face us, and the sight of him made me gasp with surprise.

"Nora, John, why don't you come over here and say hello?" Lou proposed, waving at us.

As John pulled me further into the store, the stranger's black eyes took in my figure. I recognized the square face and protruding brow, but the long white scar down his right cheek was something I had not seen before. Around his thick neck was a gold rope chain, and at the end of the chain was a strange medallion, a square with a circle inside of it, and then a triangle inside of the circle.

I looked up from the medallion and the man seemed to sneer as I came closer, almost as if he were a demon coveting a righteous sinner.

Lou nodded to the gentleman beside him. "Nora, you remember Henri Gaspard, don't you?"

Except for the scar, Henri was identical in every way to his twin brother, Jean Marc. But Henri's eyes were different. They seemed darker than his brother's, as if they truly were made from something sinister.

"My God!" Henri exclaimed. "Little Nora Kehoe." His voice did not have the same velvety smoothness as Jean Marc's; it was harder and edgier, as if tinted with a touch of desperation. "I haven't seen you since…must be ten years at least."

I held out my hand to him. He took it, and I noticed the array of fine gold rings and the expensive gold watch about his wrist.

"How are you, Henri?"

"Doing real well, Nora." He turned and patted Lou on the back. "Been making my own way here in the city for some time now."

"I was sorry to hear about your father. Jean Marc told me about his passing a few years back."

Henri laughed, more like a bellow. "Yeah, my brother the great, Jean Marc. Daddy always preferred him to me." He waved a hand covered in gold rings before me. "But I don't care. Let him have that smelly old fish business." Henri's eyes wandered to John. "Is this the fiancé Lou's been telling me about?"

John stepped forward and held out his hand to Henri. "John Blessing."

Henri took his hand. "Glad to meet you, John, Hope you're gonna take good care of our Nora here. I've known her since she was in diapers running around Daddy's pier with my brother chasing after her."

"Really?" John turned and raised his eyebrows to me. "She never told me about that."

"It was a long time ago," I admitted.

"Oh, yeah," Henri went on. "Nora was like the little sister me and Jean Marc never had. My brother just adored her." He smiled, or should I say leered at me, then Henri turned to Lou. "Well, I've gotta head out, but I'll be back next week to pick up my order."

"All right, Henri," Lou said as he shook the man's hand.

Henri gave me one last glance and then set his eyes on John. "Good luck you two."

"Thank you," John replied.

I waited until Henri had left the store before I confronted Lou.

"You know him?" I asked, astonished that Lou had business dealings with the black sheep of the Gaspard family.

"Yeah, for a couple of years now. He brings in silly designs for gold and diamond pieces he wants. Sometimes he brings in his girlfriends and buys them tokens." Lou nodded to the door Henri had just exited through. "He's a pretty good customer, pays cash every time."

"Does Mother know you do business with her former nephew?"

Lou shook his baldhead and rolled his pale hazel eyes. "No, and you can't tell her. I'll never hear the end of it."

"Her former nephew?" John questioned.

"Mother was married to Etienne Gaspard before she met my father. Etienne was Henri's uncle. When she left Etienne for my father, Etienne Gaspard shot himself."

"Your mother is just full of surprises," John quipped as he looked from me to Lou.

"It's not what you think, John," Lou insisted. "Etienne Gaspard was a drunk, a liar, and a hustler. He shot himself by accident while cleaning a loaded gun."

"But Mother prefers telling the story so it sounds like Etienne died of love for her. She had me believing it for years until Jean Marc set me straight."

John arched one dark eyebrow at me. "Jean Marc? Isn't that the guy your mother mentioned the other night at dinner?"

"Yes, he's Henri's twin brother," I explained. "He runs the family business, Gaspard Fisheries."

"I've heard that Jean Marc is the better half of the Gaspard boys, despite what Claire says of him. I've never met him." Lou patted my shoulder. "But Nora knows him real well."

"Not that well," I quickly corrected with a nervous titter. "He's a friend of my uncle's and his boss, so I've seen him around Uncle Jack's boat quite a bit," I added, hoping to avoid any further explanation of my relationship with Jean Marc.

John shrugged and eyed his stainless steel watch. "Look, I don't mean to rush you, but, I've only got an hour and then I have to get back to the emergency room."

Lou held up his hands to assuage John's worry. "No problem. Come on in the back and we will find something wonderful for Nora." Lou started toward a metal door to the side of the display counter.

John took a few paces to catch up with my stepfather, leaving me behind. "Lou, I was thinking of a pear-shaped, three-carat diamond to start, set in platinum."

"Sounds good," Lou agreed as he moved up to the door and punched in a security code on the keypad next to it.

"Then I thought perhaps some baguettes," John continued as he stood behind Lou, waving his hands about as he shared his design.

I slowly approached the two men just as a loud buzzer sounded and the heavy metal door snapped open. As I walked through the security door to the back of the store and listened to John describe his idea of the perfect engagement ring, that nagging pain started up again in my stomach. Only this time it was stronger than it had ever been before.

CHAPTER 9

Two weeks later, I was sitting behind my desk at work, going through some figures for the monthly reports, when Steve waltzed into my office, fifteen minutes late as usual. I never minded and over the past few weeks, I had come to savor those extra few minutes alone before my day began.

"Oh, my God!" Steve gasped as he stood dramatically holding the doorframe of my office. "When did you get that?" He pointed to the platinum three-carat, pear-shaped diamond that was on the third finger of my left hand.

I looked down at the diamond. "Oh, that," I stated, nonchalantly.

"'Oh, that,'" Steve mimicked. He bounded to my desk in two steps and grabbed my left hand, pulling it to his face. "We could have plugged the breach in the Seventeenth Street Canal with that thing."

I sighed. "Yeah, it's a little big."

He looked up from the ring. "Most women I know would be jumping up and down with joy, showing this to every employee and patient in the hospital, and not have the expression on their faces that you have right now."

I yanked back my hand. "What expression?"

"The one that makes you look like you're going to your gynecologist appointment."

"You're being silly." I directed my attention to the figures before me.

"No, I get it, Nora." Steve stepped back from my desk. "You're not in love with this guy. Any woman in love with a man who gave her a rock like that would be ethereal, vibrant, glowing. You're as pale as a ghost."

"Steve, stop it. I have a lot on my plate right now. In addition to planning this wedding, I'm working full time here, getting ready for budget review next week, and I have to start house hunting with John. On top of all of that, I've been worried about my uncle."

"I thought you called him on Monday?"

"I did and he says he's all right, but I haven't been to see him in over two weeks and I feel guilty, like I should be taking care of him."

Just then my office phone rang. Steve, being his impossible self, grabbed for the phone.

"Orthopedics, Nora Kehoe's office," he announced into the receiver. He listened for a few moments then he hit the hold button. "A guy with a very sexy voice said to tell you it's Jean Marc." He leered at me. "Two-timing on the doctor already with the fisherman, you hussy!"

"Drop dead."

He smirked. "Only if you give me that ring, and the man who goes with it." Steve whirled around and headed for my office door.

"Hello, Jean Marc," I said after Steve firmly closed the door behind him.

"Hello, Nora." His delectable voice came over the line, making my insides warm over. "I was calling to give you some good news."

I glimpsed the large diamond on my hand. "I could use some good news."

"I got your uncle working at the house." I could hear the happiness in his voice. "Mother was the one who suggested it. She's been bugging me to send out a handyman for a while, and told me to hire Jack for the job." He paused and I could hear another phone ringing in the background. "I think it will be good for both of them. Give Jack something to do and Mother someone to look after."

"Jean Marc, that sounds wonderful." I sighed with relief. "Thank you, thank you so much."

"Don't thank me. My mother is the one who insisted on the arrangement." He paused and I could hear the shuffle of papers. "I'm just glad that everyone is happy. Jack came over to the house this morning and my mother had a long list for him. She'll pay him out of her house funds, and we don't need to worry about the insurance company anymore."

"Jean Marc, I don't know what to say." I could feel my heart beating a little faster as I listened to his deep voice over the phone.

"I'm just glad I could help out."

"You have been so good to him, and to me. I really appreciate it."

"Yeah, well…" He became very quiet and I could hear other voices in the background.

"I ran into Henri a few weeks ago at my stepfather's jewelry store. Apparently, he is a pretty good customer there. He says he's doing well," I told him.

"I wouldn't know." The cool, hard voice was back. "Henri and I haven't spoken since I came back from Texas over twelve years ago."

An uncomfortable silence hovered between us. "I'm sorry; I shouldn't have mentioned it," I finally admitted.

"No, it's my fault. I don't like to talk about my brother."

I removed the ring from my finger, suddenly feeling encumbered by it. "I understand. I don't like talking about my mother."

That made him laugh; a heartfelt laugh that sent a pleasurable tingle through my body. "Yes, Claire is a piece of work." His laughter abated and again the silence loomed. "Well, I'd better let you get back to your job. I know you must be busy, and then you have your wedding to plan."

I placed the ring on my desk. "Yes, I have that."

"Why don't you come by the house this Sunday? You can check on Jack, and I know Mother would love to see you. She hasn't seen you in years."

"I would like that, Jean Marc."

"I want to see you again, Nora." The voices in the background began getting louder. "I, ah, have to go. Bye, Nora." He abruptly hung up.

I sat there holding on to the receiver as his words replayed in my head. I wasn't sure how long I was lost in my thoughts before a sudden loud rap on my door startled me. I looked up to see the door to my office open.

"Sorry to disturb you, Ms. Kehoe," Steve began trying to sound uncharacteristically professional. "But there is a gentleman here to see you."

"I don't know any gentleman, Steve."

I stood from my desk as John stepped out from behind Steve.

"Hello, Nora." John moved toward my desk.

I quickly picked up my ring and placed it back on my finger.

Steve was standing behind John, holding his hand to his chest and mouthing the words, "I'm in love."

"Thank you, Steve," I commented, trying not to laugh.

John, fortunately, did not turn around to see Steve sending several rather obscene gestures my way.

"This is a surprise," I said, taking in John's wrinkled scrubs and tennis shoes. His hair seemed a little windblown and he had his usual five o'clock shadow, despite it being only eight in the morning.

He sank into the chair across from my desk. "Keating, the faculty head of the emergency room for LSU, sent me home for the day."

I sat down in my chair. "Why did he send you home?"

"Too many fish in the pond. He had more residents than he knew what to do with. Several first years started rotating through the ER today, so he told me to take the day off."

I noted the dark circles under his eyes. "Why don't you go home and get some sleep?"

He shook his head. "Nah, I got three hours last night in the lounge. It was slow in the ER for a change."

"How can you keep going on so little sleep?"

"You get used to it during your residency. Most of us feel great after two or three hours. It's just the way of it in medicine; no one sleeps, no one eats, no one has a life."

I perused the arrangement of charts and budget proposals on my desk. "I would love to take the day off with you and play hooky, but I'm up to my elbows." I motioned across the desk with my hand.

"I didn't come by to ask you to play hooky. I'm on my way to your mother's house. She needs someone to help her with some decisions about the wedding."

"Since when does Mother need help deciding anything?"

He grinned at me. "She left a message at the house this morning, but she must have called after you left for work."

I fidgeted in my chair. "No, I just didn't pick up the phone. She's been calling my cell phone for days. I've been avoiding her."

His gray eyes peered into mine. "She seems to think you're not interested in planning our wedding."

"John, my job here has been rather hectic lately. I really haven't had time to think about our wedding."

"I figured it was something like that." He leaned forward in his chair, looking very serious. "Why don't you get another job?" I opened my mouth to object, but he stopped me. "You don't need the money anymore. I make plenty for both of us, and you will need your free time to plan the wedding, set up our new home, and get settled."

I rose from my chair. "I like my job," I angrily asserted.

"Yes, but you don't need it anymore. I think it's time you slow down a bit; get another job working less hours, or at least something that is less stressful."

I went around to the front of the desk. "It took me over two years to get this position, John. I worked my ass off in the physical therapy department before the surgeons trusted me enough to take over the total joint program. I can't just walk away."

"Nora, everyone can be replaced, even you. Your orthopedic guys can find someone else to oversee their hip and knee replacements. It can't be that hard to do."

A wave of outrage mixed with stomach acid churned inside of me. "John, I like to work. It gives me purpose and a sense of accomplishment."

He stood from his chair and came to my side. "Nora, you will feel differently when our children come along. Then you will want to stay home and take care of them. All women do. They will be your sense of purpose and your accomplishment."

"I'm not just a breeding machine, John! I can think. I can create, and I certainly intend on working, even after we have children."

He put his hands on my shoulders. "All right." His voice became soft and soothing. "Calm down, Nora. All I'm saying is perhaps you should consider changing jobs, or at least asking if you can cut your hours here."

"If and when I choose to change jobs or cut my hours, I'll make that decision, is that clear?"

"But at least start looking into some other options. I don't want my wife looking tired all the time." He kissed my cheek.

"I don't look tired all of the time," I refuted.

"Nora, you haven't really looked at yourself in the mirror lately. You look tired and drained, like you have a lot on your mind. I want a beautiful bride, not a shell of a woman." He stood back from me. "I promise you will be much happier when you aren't working so hard." He waved to me and then turned for my office door. "I'll tell Claire you've been too busy to call," he added over his shoulder as he left my office.

Steve immediately entered my office, looking backwards toward John as he made his way down the corridor.

"Oh, the inhumanity," Steve cried out and pretended to faint on my office floor.

I looked over at him sprawled out in front of my desk. "Get up, you ass."

"Don't say ass." He jumped to his feet and fastidiously began dusting off his pants. "Makes me think of that fine little number that just left here."

I returned to my desk. "It's not as fine as you think. It comes with a lot of bullshit attached to it." I plopped into in my chair and sighed.

He curled his thin lips into a sardonic smile. "Trouble in paradise, eh? What did he say?"

"He wants me to get another job. Says I work too hard at this one."

Steve folded his arms over his chest. "He wants wifey home, barefoot, and pregnant with the brood."

I glanced down again at the paperwork on my desk. "Something like that, yes."

"What did you say?"

I continued to stare at my paperwork. "I'm still thinking."

Steve walked toward my open office door. "Well, kiddo, it's your life. The key to living it is not to listen to anyone who tells you how to live it."

"Including a husband?"

"He ain't your husband yet." Steve chuckled, and then he quickly shut the door behind him.

CHAPTER 10

The following Sunday John was to join me for brunch with Mother and Lou. Mother had insisted that John start being a part of the weekly ritual since he was soon to become a member of the family. When he arrived at my parents' uptown home fresh from a full night of work, he looked completely worn out.

"You sure you're up for this?" I questioned when I opened the leaded glass front door.

"I'm fine. I got an hour or two of sleep before I came over." He put his arm about my waist as we stepped through the doorway.

I put my purse down on the table by the door. "You look like you're going to fall flat on your face. Maybe we should keep the brunch brief today. No going over wedding plans or anything."

John shook his head. "Your mother has got several things she needs to discuss with us today. I assured her I would be here to work it all out."

I turned to the ornate rosewood-inlaid foyer that led to the living room. "All right. Let's hurry up and get this over with."

But my mother was determined to enjoy every moment of planning the wedding, as I found out when we sat down to eat at the compulsory mahogany dining table a short while later.

"Now I was thinking something along the lines of a deep red brushed velvet for the bridesmaids, and gray morning suits for all of the groomsmen," Mother began as she spread out two different swatch samples on the table.

I gawked at my mother, and pushed away my untouched plate of eggs and grits. "Velvet in September? The bridesmaids will pass out with heatstroke." I reached for my glass of orange juice.

"But velvet looks so good in the pictures," Mother whined as she held a swatch of velvet up to my face.

"Nora's right, Claire," Lou jumped in. "I told you it's too hot for velvet down here."

Mother pouted for a few moments. "All right, fine. We can go with the lighter satin, but I still think the color is perfect." She pulled out a piece of dark red satin from her pile of swatches.

"How many bridesmaids are we having?" John asked as he looked over his plate of scrambled eggs.

"Nine," Mother answered.

"Nine!" I almost choked on my orange juice. "I don't even know nine people, let alone have nine friends to ask to be bridesmaids." I banged my glass down on the table.

"They won't all be your friends." She searched the table for one of her many lists. "John has family, too," she asserted.

John nodded as he loaded his fork with scrambled eggs. "Yes, I've got my sister, Nancy, to think of. Then there are my two cousins, Emily and Patrice, and I was thinking of having Nancy's two little girls as bridesmaids as well. They're eleven and twelve, and I know they would love to be part of the wedding."

"Then we have your friends to consider, dear." Mother gave me a worried look. "Well, at least the ones you knew in high school. If they won't do it, I can ask some of the daughters of my friends to be your bridesmaids. You've got to have somebody stand by you at your wedding."

"Uncle Jack will be standing by me, Mother. I won't need bridesmaids."

"Jacques? My brother?" Mother appeared horrified. She placed her hand to her chest and wrinkled up her brow. After the amount of Botox that brow had been exposed to, I was surprised she still had use of it.

"Uncle Jack is going to give me away," I declared, folding my arms defiantly in front of me.

My mother shook her head. "My brother cannot be shown in public, child. I can't have my friends exposed to the ravings of that drunk."

"Mother, all of your friends are drunks. Uncle Jack will fit right in."

"My friends are all good, upstanding people." Mother turned to Lou, her nostrils flaring. "Did you hear what she said about our friends, Lou?"

Lou glanced up from his ham and eggs. "Nora is right. Your friends are drunks, Claire."

"Lou!" Mother shrieked.

He waved his fork in the air. "Well, it's true. Every time those people come over for dinner they drain my bar. I agree with Nora, Jack will fit right in."

"You always liked my brother," she grumbled.

Lou stabbed at a piece of ham on his plate as he smiled rebelliously at my mother. "Yeah, I do like Jack. So what?"

"Perhaps," John broke in. "Five bridesmaids is plenty."

Mother turned to John. "Of course it isn't. No self-respecting Catholic wedding would have less than nine bridesmaids." Mother scanned the list of possible bridesmaids in front of her. "I guess we can iron this out later." She reached across the table for another piece of paper. "But this can't wait." She handed the paper to me.

I tried to decipher my mother's unintelligible scribble. "What's this?"

"Father Delacroix gave me a list of dates for you and John to go over to St. Rita's and begin your Pre-Cana sessions."

I stared at my mother in disbelief. "Pre-Cana? You're joking."

John put his fork down. "Nora, we have to go to Pre-Cana in order to have a mass during the ceremony. You want to be married in the eyes of God, don't you?"

"God doesn't have to sit through his own Pre-Cana classes." My stomach rolled with disgust. "Look, Mother, I don't have time to go to Pre-Cana sessions, and I don't see why John and I should have to—"

"But John wants to go," Mother interrupted. "He's a very devout man and he told me last week that he wants your marriage to be sanctified by the church. I told him I would call Father Delacroix to set up the Pre-Cana."

I scowled at John, suppressing a sudden urge to choke the living hell out of him. "But how can you make time for these sessions?" I asked him, sweetly. "You're at the emergency room six days and nights a week."

He patted my hand. "I can make arrangements. Don't worry."

"There, that's settled." Mother leaned slightly to her left and elbowed her husband. "Isn't it exciting, Lou?"

Lou, who had been watching the entire conversation with his arms folded over his chest, grinned at me. "It's not too late, No. I know a real good rabbi if you want to convert."

"Lou!" Mother screeched.

After the subject of Pre-Cana, I began to tune out of the rest of the wedding conversation. Mother and John seemed to be planning everything, even down to food selection at the reception.

"Nora and I would love a mixture of tastes—Indian, Chinese, Mexican—that way people would have some variety. And we must have champagne," John added with a flourish of his hand. "We want the very best champagne and lots of it."

I stared at John and wondered exactly when in our relationship he had decided to start speaking for me. I had known the man almost two months, but in all that time I had never felt more insignificant to him than that morning, sitting with my mother and Lou.

"Now, Nora," Mother badgered as she made notes on one of the growing scraps of paper on the table. "We will have to go over to Chopin's next week and pick out the flowers. First the service flowers, your bouquet, bridesmaids' bouquets, reception arrangements, and of course corsages for John's parents and Lou and me."

"Roses," John announced as he pushed his empty plate aside. "Make it yellow roses. Put them in everything."

My body reflexively twitched at the mention of yellow roses.

I turned to John. "Since when do you like yellow roses?"

He smiled at me, making the lines beneath his gray eyes appear even deeper.

"Always. They're my favorite."

"Nora's, too," Mother squealed, clapping her hands together excitedly. "Now we have to look through these invitation samples. I want to get our selection to the printer on Monday."

I sat back in my chair. "Mother, John is wiped. He's been up all night and I'm pretty beat. Can't we do this another time?"

"I'm all right, Nora," John insisted as he held my hand.

I analyzed his bloodshot eyes and frowned. "Well, I can't stay," I stated and let go of his hand.

"Can't stay?" Mother frowned at me. "Nora, we have a lot to go over."

"John can finish up here. I promised Uncle Jack I would go to Manchac this afternoon and check his pressure."

Mother waved an impatient hand at me. "Tell the man to go to a doctor like everybody else. And stop calling him Jack. His name is Jacques. I hate it when you call him Jack. It's so blue-collar." Her face began turning red, a sure sign she was getting angry. "Nora, you can't just leave. We have a wedding to plan. You have obligations."

I quickly stood from my chair. "I can't disappoint Uncle Jack." I smirked at her. "You know how he looks forward to my visits, and I haven't seen him in a while."

John stood up next to me. "I'll come with you."

I placed my hand on his arm. "No, I'll go. You stay here and help my mother. She's right, we have a lot to plan."

"I wish you would stop making promises to that old drunk." Mother's face was growing a darker shade of red. "He's just like Father. Drank himself into an early grave, Francois Mouton did. My poor mother had to suffer such humiliation. I swore I would never be like her." She pointed a finger at me. "It does you no good to spend so much time with your uncle."

I ignored her warnings and kissed John's cheek. "I'll see you back at the house." Then, without another word to my mother, I fled from the dining room.

"Nora, don't be silly," Mother called behind me. "That old fool will be high as a kite all afternoon. You're wasting your time."

"Yes, Mother," I shouted as I grabbed my purse by the front door. "But it's my time to waste." I stepped through the leaded glass front door and slammed it behind me. Instantly, I felt better. Reprieved of my oppressive wedding duties, I happily ran down the steps, eagerly wanting to get into my car and speed away.

CHAPTER 11

During the entire drive to Manchac, I kept such a tight grip on the steering wheel that by the time I pulled in front of the Gaspard's home, I could barely pry my fingers off the leather. I sat in my car, outside of the white plantation style house, and took in a few deep breaths. That didn't help. I still wanted to rip my mother's red hair out by the roots.

I was reaching for my purse when a tap on my car window distracted me. I turned and saw Jean Marc Gaspard standing next to my car door, wearing a pair of jeans and a crisp white T-shirt. He was smiling at me, or more like grinning from ear to ear.

I opened the door and could not help but notice the thick muscles in his suntanned arms.

"Glad to see you made it," he remarked, offering me his hand.

I took his hand and a little twinge of excitement coursed through me when my flesh touched his.

"Mother has been asking me every hour on the hour when you were coming," he added as he helped me out of the car. His hand stayed on mine for a few seconds after I was standing from the car, and then he let go.

"I got hung up at my mother's." I sighed and I tugged at my purse strap. "She was in her glory with the wedding planning."

Jean Marc briefly chuckled. "Thank God I avoided that mess when I got married. Cynthia, my ex, wanted a quick, simple ceremony in Dallas, no family or friends. Mother has never forgiven me for that."

"You're lucky. My mother is insisting on the whole big ceremony fiasco," I said as we started slowly down the narrow shell-covered path toward the house.

"Yeah, my mother would have wanted the whole blown out affair, too. She claims I cheated her out of her one chance for a nice wedding."

I shook my head. "I don't know if all the hoopla is really worth it."

"It's worth it when you're in love, Nora."

I took in his profile. "Were you in love with your ex-wife?"

He stopped and turned to me. "I thought I was, I really did. But after we were married, I discovered she was missing something. Something I could never quite put my finger on until I came back to Manchac."

"What was she missing?"

He simply smiled and nodded to the house. "Come on. My mother is waiting."

As we neared the end of the path, the full majesty of Gaspard House came into view. It appeared a little more worn and faded than I remembered, but the home still had its long sunlit balconies supported by the four round, white columns that ran along the front of the three-story dwelling. The roof was covered with terra cotta tiles, hard to find nowadays, but worth their weight when the setting sun made the tiles glow red against the evening sky. The exterior was covered in plaster and painted white. The tall french windows still had the original old, imperfect wavy glass in place. The front door had been freshly painted a deep shade of red, reminiscent of the swatches my mother had produced earlier that day. Surrounding the property were grand oak trees brushed with long strands of Spanish moss, and limbs so heavy with age that they reached down to the ground. There were pink crape myrtle trees and red azalea bushes growing wild in the front gardens. Off to the side, away from the oaks, but close enough to the entrance of the house to spread its sweet aroma indoors every May, was a large magnolia tree, mandatory in any respectable Southern garden.

I gazed up in awe at the impressive structure. "It hasn't changed."

Jean Marc laughed as he took my elbow and ushered me onward. "Oh, it's changed, all right. A year ago I had to put new plumbing in all of the bathrooms. I just replaced the central air-conditioning system last spring, had the kitchen overhauled last winter, and," he took a breath, "refinished all the old pine floors just last month. Costs me a small fortune to keep the place up, but she's still in pretty good shape, considering she just made a hundred and thirty-three."

"That old?"

He looked up at the house. "The original home burned down in the eighteen seventies. This was the more luxurious replacement my ancestor built with profits from his smuggling escapades during the Civil War."

"Your family has had such a colorful past."

"Yes, we Gaspards claim descent from a pirate who traveled in the company of Jean Lafitte named Jacques Gaspard. He settled in this area and spent his days smuggling goods through these swamps. But today's Gaspard family is not quite as colorful as our predecessors. Oh, we have the occasional delinquent, like my brother, but at heart we're just simple fishermen."

"Not according to my mother. She still believes the Gaspard family is filled with men such as your ancestor the pirate." I paused and turned to him. "She even mentioned something about your time in Dallas. Mother believes some nasty rumor flying around that you were involved with a notorious smuggler."

He stared at me as his dark eyes shimmered in the sunlight. "Maybe it's not a rumor."

"Is it true what they say about you?"

He shrugged his broad shoulders. "My former father-in-law, Lawrence Castille, was a very wealthy importer of rare and hard to acquire items. Some say he was a smuggler, and I did witness more than a few illegal transactions between him and other international businessmen. When he took me under his wing and I married his daughter, more than a few people began to believe I was a smuggler as well."

"But you weren't, right?"

Jean Marc rubbed his hand across his chin. "I did things for my father-in-law that I'm not proud of, Nora."

As I took in Jean Marc's troubled features, I could not fathom how a man I had known all of my life could be someone so different from what I had imagined.

"What kinds of things?" I finally asked.

"Perhaps I've said too much already." He sighed and took in the surrounding greenery. "I can understand if you think less of me because of—"

I placed my hand on his forearm, silencing him. "I don't care about what you did, Jean Marc. How could I ever question you or your past? You have always been there for my uncle, and as far as I'm concerned that erases any of your former sins."

He put his hand over mine. "One day you might care," he whispered.

A tingling sensation passed through my body as his hand rested against mine. I quickly removed my hand from his arm and nervously took a step back.

Jean Marc waved toward the house. "We should go."

We were almost at the front porch when two monstrous brown, blue, and white speckled hound dogs, with long tails and tall bodies, approached me.

"Oh, the welcoming committee," Jean Marc declared. "Napoleon and Nelson, Dad's old Catahoula dogs."

I held my hand out to the closest of the hounds, a dark brown creature with black and white spots on his rump. Instantly, my hand was covered with a layer of slobber. The second of the dogs, a blue and tan mix, came forward and reached for my hand, wanting the same attention as the first.

"Careful, if you get too friendly with them, they might just try and sit in your lap," Jean Marc cautioned as he rubbed one of the dogs on the head.

When we stepped onto the sprawling front porch, complete with a wide assortment of rockers, a familiar woman's voice called from inside the open front door.

"Is she here?"

The voice was soon followed by the figure of a petite woman, delicate almost in her bearing. She had deep brown hair, smooth, silky white skin, and the warmest brown eyes I had ever known.

"Nora T!" The woman held out her slender arms to me. Her oval face was bright with love and her pale cheeks were flushed with warmth.

"Ms. Marie!" I ran to her waiting arms.

Ms. Marie held me back and carefully inspected every inch of me. "Why, look at you. You're all grown up, mon p'tit'." She pulled me to her once more and squeezed me tight.

When I could finally come up for air, I saw Jean Marc standing off to the side, beaming as he watched me with his mother.

"Oh, I have thought about you every day, Nora T." Ms. Marie put her slender arm about my shoulders. "I've been tellin' Jean Marc to invite you out to the house for ages."

"Nora works, Momma. She has a big job at a hospital in the city. She can't always get away," Jean Marc informed her as he walked up beside us.

"Well, that's no excuse," Ms. Marie scolded and pointed her finger at me. "You're family, child. You always must come and see me."

Just then, Uncle Jack appeared from around the side of the house, wearing a pair of worn blue jean overalls and his old, faded blue cap. He had gained some weight and there was a bounce in his step.

"Nora T!" He came forward and hugged me.

I stood back from him and explored his face. His blue eyes were brighter and there was a hint of color in his cheeks. "You look great, Uncle Jack."

"All Ms. Marie's good cookin', I 'spect." He patted his belly. "I didn't think you'd be comin' today. Figured you'd be too busy plannin' your big weddin'."

"Jacques told me you're marryin' a doctor," Ms Marie admitted with a smile. "That be a fancy catch, girl."

I shrugged as Ms. Marie's eyes carefully observed me. "His name is John Blessing, and he's not a fancy catch. Just a nice guy."

Ms. Marie clapped her hands together. "If he makes you happy, child, that be all that matters." Then she turned her head curiously to the side and studied me for a moment longer. "You love that boy, Nora T?"

"Of course I love him, Ms. Marie." I smiled for her. "He's a great guy," I added, trying to sound convincing.

"That's what you say, Nora T," Uncle Jack remarked. "But that ain't what we see."

Ms. Marie patted my arm. "When you're in love, child, you glow. You walk on air. You have no doubts. You're happy, a 'once upon a time' kinda happiness, like in a fairy tale."

I took in an unsteady breath, feeling as if the world was closing in on me. "Times have changed, Ms. Marie. Couples have a lot more obstacles to overcome, more pressures to live with. Happiness is not the primary concern. Expectations are different for couples nowadays."

Jean Marc's eyes focused on me. "Are they?" He shook his head and then hurried inside the house.

"Never mind him. He's just feelin' the sting from his own failed marriage," Ms. Marie assured me as she waved her hand after her son. "He's never been the same since that Texas girl broke his heart."

"Broke his heart?" I asked.

"She ran off with a colleague of Jean Marc's. Them married only nine months, and she was already lookin' for greener pastures." Ms. Marie winked at me. "That girl wasn't right for my Jean Marc. She would have been better for my other son, Henri."

"Why do you say that, Ms. Marie?"

"'Cause she didn't care for no one but herself. Selfish just like Henri, she was. But Jean Marc, he's my good son. He's gonna make some good girl a fine husband one day."

Uncle Jack pushed back his cap and rubbed his forehead. "Yep, he's gonna be a fine man once he learns to speak his mind," he commented, and then stepped through the front door.

* * *

Ms. Marie, Jean Marc, Uncle Jack, and I were seated around the thick oak breakfast table in the enormous kitchen. The kitchen was the size of most living rooms, with a huge red-bricked hearth at one end of the room with its original swinging iron arms still intact. The white-tiled counters I remembered from my youth had been updated with deep umber granite countertops. The small hand carved cypress cabinets that had hung on the light sand-colored walls had been replaced by pine ones painted beige. A gourmet cooktop and twin convection ovens now sat in the place where the old gas stove had been. Even the Sub-Zero refrigerator was new and built into the wall next to the ovens.

"Everything looks so different," I commented, taking in the renovated kitchen.

"Everythin' 'cept the floors," Ms. Marie illuminated as she tapped the old red-bricked floor with her shoe. "I kept that. Didn't want to take it out. This here's a good ole floor."

I reached for the glass of fresh lemonade Ms. Marie had prepared in my honor. "The rest of the house is still the same as I remember."

"I didn't have the strength to do the whole house," Ms. Marie declared. "It was bad enough havin' the workman in and out of my kitchen for three months."

Uncle Jack took a sip from his lemonade. "The place, she sure needed it, but still more needs to be done." He put his glass down on the table and stood from his chair. "I best be getting' get back to work." He removed his old blue cap from the front pocket of his overalls and placed it on his head. "You come and see me again, Nora T." He leaned over and kissed my head. "Don't bring that man of yours when you come back."

I thought Uncle Jack was joking, but when I looked up into his steely blue eyes, I realized he was serious.

"How can you say that, Uncle Jack? John is a great guy."

Uncle Jack moved away from the table toward the open back door next to the hearth. "Non, he no good for you, no sir." He turned and walked out into the afternoon sunshine.

I anxiously noted the grin spreading across Jean Marc's thin lips. "My uncle has not taken the time to get to know my fiancé," I explained, and then took a sip from my lemonade.

"No, child." Ms. Marie rose from her chair and picked up Uncle Jack's glass from the table. "Your uncle, he's a good judge of how people really are." She carried the glass to the sink. "Jacques knew he wasn't the right man for me, just like he knows that doctor ain't the right man for you."

Jean Marc frowned at his mother. "Momma, that's Nora's business. Stop filling her head with such nonsense."

"Nonsense? No such thing." She stared at her son for a moment and then smiled. "Jean Marc, remember when you was a p'tit' boug and you used to dance with Nora T outside in the sunlight?" She nodded to me. "You taught her how to waltz, the Acadian Waltz."

His dark eyes nervously darted about the room. "I don't remember that, Momma."

"Sure you do." She waved at the open kitchen floor in front of her. "Go on over there and show Nora T the way you used to dance with her."

"Momma, we're not little children anymore," Jean Marc griped.

"Then dance for me, once more. Make this vielle happy. Show me how you two used to dance."

"You're not an old woman, Momma." Jean Marc stood from the table and begrudgingly took my hand. "Come on. She will pester us until we do this."

He pulled me to the center of the kitchen, and when he faced me, my legs became weak. I swallowed hard as his hand went around my waist and moved my body closer to his.

"Follow me, Nora. Just do what I do," he whispered.

He moved back and then to the side, and the seductive grace of his movements unnerved me. I stared down at his feet, hoping to alleviate my growing discomfort.

"Look into my eyes. Don't follow my feet," he said softly to me.

When my eyes found his, a burst of heat sliced through me. His body pressed into mine as we swayed back and forth to some unknown melody. I became lost in the sensation of being held in his strong arms. The aroma of his woody cologne swirled around me as the warmth from his body quieted my unease. For a moment it was just the two of us, joined together with no knowledge or care for the world beyond that kitchen door.

Ms. Marie's frenzied clapping broke the spell between us. "That's it," she happily cried.

Jean Marc stopped dancing and stared into my eyes. An unfamiliar passion began coursing through my veins. I suddenly ached for him, and as the hot flush of longing rose from my gut, I pulled away.

I directed my attention to the clock on the stainless microwave, sitting on the kitchen counter across from me. "I should be heading back to the city," I mumbled.

Ms. Marie frowned at me. "So soon, child? It's still early yet."

"Nora has things to do, Momma. She has a fiancé, a wedding to plan, and a very busy career," Jean Marc asserted.

"Oh, I don't know how you girls today find the energy." Ms. Marie waved her hand at me. "In my day raisin' children and keepin' house was more than enough."

I reached for my purse on the kitchen table. "My fiancé shares your sentiments, Ms. Marie. He wants me to quit my job and stay home after the wedding."

"I hope you told him to go to hell," Jean Marc barked.

I slung my purse strap over my shoulder. "No, I'm considering finding another job. Perhaps something not quite as hectic as my job at the hospital."

"But I thought you loved your job. Why are you going to let him dictate your life?" he demanded.

"He's not dictating my life. I'm not even sure if I'm going to get another job," I defended, raising my voice to him.

Jean Marc's scowl returned. "You shouldn't let him push you around, Nora. If he loves you, he won't care where or how much you work. He should only want you to be happy, not—"

"Arrete toi," Ms. Marie harshly called to her son. "It's not your place to tell her what to do, Jean Marc."

There was a moment of nervous silence between the three of us, and then Ms. Marie smiled. "He was always so protective of you when you were a peeshwank. You must forgive him, Nora T. Old habits die hard in my boy."

The kitchen walls began to close in around me. "I must get going," I insisted as I stepped over to Ms. Marie and kissed her cheek. "Thank you for a lovely afternoon."

She placed her loving arms about me and held me close. "You come back anytime you like." She released me and nodded to her son. "Jean Marc can walk you to your car."

Jean Marc turned from the table and disappeared into the house.

He was waiting on the front porch when I stepped out the front door. His eyes impatiently scanned my body, and then Jean Marc started down the steps. He walked ahead to the little shell-covered path that led to the long driveway. I had to break into a slight jog to catch up with him.

"What's your problem?" I asked as I came alongside him.

"Nothing," he muttered as he kept his eyes on the path ahead.

"All right, fine. Don't tell me. Sulk all you want."

He jerked to a sudden stop. "You think I'm sulking?"

"You seem very…." I shrugged my shoulders. "I don't know, disturbed."

His eyes were distracted for a moment by the glister of my diamond engagement ring in the afternoon sun. "Disturbed?" He gave a disgruntled snort and started back down the path.

I raced to catch up with his long stride.

"So what is it? Is it the business, or your mother, or my uncle? What?"

"There are some things that need not concern you, Nora. You lead your life and I'll lead mine."

I grabbed his arm and pulled him around to face me. "Jean Marc, talk to me. Let me help."

"Help?" His face was contorted with frustration. His eyes were like black fire. "All right, you want to help? Fine." He pulled me to him, and then his lips came down hard on mine.

The heat from his kiss spread quickly throughout my body, making me forget who I was and where I was. All I could feel, all I knew was the sensation of his mouth pressed against mine. Then as quickly as it started, it stopped. He let me go and pushed me away.

"I shouldn't have done that." He ran his hands through his dark, wavy hair. "Damn it."

"You want to explain what just happened?" I questioned, trying to control my shaky voice.

The fire in his eyes was gone, replaced with the pale light of regret. "I'm sorry. I, ah, lost my head." His chilly demeanor instantly returned. "It won't happen again."

I searched his features, desperate for some clue as to what he was thinking. "Jean Marc, is there something you want to talk about?"

"Talk?" He shook his head and stepped back from me. "I think I've said about everything I need to say. Good-bye, Nora." He turned and quickly headed toward his family home.

CHAPTER 12

Two weeks later I was sitting in my small office at Uptown Hospital going over my reduced schedule with Steve. Eager to shave some money from her budget, my supervisor had happily granted my request to cut back my hours at the hospital. I also put in for some overdo vacation time in order to plan my wedding.

"Are you doing this for him, or are you doing this for your mother?" Steve pestered as he sat across from my desk. "Because I just don't see you doing this for yourself." He paused and his worried blue eyes probed my features. "I thought you liked this job, Nora."

I shrugged. "I can't keep up these hours and plan a wedding. I'm doing this for my future with John. I like my job, but to tell you the truth, I want more."

"Like what? Kids, the white picket fence, and the golden retriever?"

I shuffled around a few of the papers on my desk. "No, I want to grow, to be more, to learn more. I want to change myself."

"Change yourself? I've never heard you talk like this. When did all this start?"

I opened a red manila folder in front of me. "I don't know. Over the past couple of weeks I've been doing some real soul-searching, and I have discovered I really don't like myself very much."

"Soul-searching? I thought it was called dieting. You look like you've lost ten pounds since you first walked in here with that rock on your finger." He waved to my left hand. "I know quite a few brides diet, go dress shopping, reception hunting, and even fine china reconnoitering, but I have never heard of a bride soul-searching before the wedding." He folded his arms over his chest. "Honey, soul-searching is what you do before the divorce."

"It's difficult to explain, Steve. You're not a woman. You wouldn't understand." I hurriedly started putting some of the papers into the red folder.

"Wouldn't understand?" He snickered and stood from his chair. "Darlin', I understand a lot more than you think. For instance, does any of this soul-searching have to do with the guy who sent you the roses?"

I slapped the folder closed and shot him a dirty look.

Steve smiled, a great big smile, showing all of his perfect white teeth. "I see, so the fish guy is part of the problem."

"There's no problem. And no to what you're thinking." I pointed at his smile. "Jean Marc is just an old friend." I picked up the red folder and opened my desk drawer.

He leaned in closer to me. "Has he kissed you?"

I almost dropped the folder in my hand.

"Aha!" Steve clapped his hands together, laughing like a hyena. "He did kiss you." He stopped laughing and placed his hands on his hips. "Oh, you little slut."

"It was nothing," I insisted as I put the folder away in my desk drawer.

"Bull. Look at you. You're blushing."

I covered my face with my hands and could feel the heat on my cheeks.

"Must have been one hell of a kiss…or was there something more?"

"No! None of it matters now." I slammed the drawer of my desk closed. "I won't be going back to Manchac, and I won't be seeing Jean Marc again!"

"What about your uncle? I thought you wanted to keep a closer eye on him?"

I reached for a patient chart from the pile on the side of my desk. "Uncle Jack is fine. He has a job working at the Gaspard's house, and he won't need me checking up on him anymore."

"Avoiding the problem doesn't make it go away, Nora."

I looked up at him. "Please, Steve, this is hard enough for me without you throwing Jean Marc in my face all the time."

Steve threw his hands up in resignation. "All right, I'll behave for now, but you do realize all you have done by cutting back your hours is cram more into the days you are here. The orthopedic doctors will still expect their reports on time, just like the operating room and the hospital administration will expect their reports on time. Seems to me this fiancé of yours is being more of a hindrance than a help."

I glimpsed the tall pile of patient charts next to me and sighed. "I know, but for now this is what I have to do to keep him and my mother off my back."

Steve strutted to my office door. "Whenever you need to get away from your man and your mother, let me know. I think you need a good old-fashioned girls' night out to get rid of all that pent-up frustration." He glanced back at me as he put his hand on the doorknob. "When you're ready to get wild and crazy let me know." He winked at me. "I know all the best spots in town."

* * *

The following morning I rose early to prepare for a day of presentations to several organizations around the city. Part of my job was being an ambassador for the hospital and going into the community to teach people about knee and hip replacement. But I had to do some last minute scrambling with my wardrobe to find something presentable to wear.

"How's this?" I asked John who was standing in the kitchen, drinking coffee.

He took in my double-breasted gray pantsuit and nodded. "Very professional. But you could do to gain a few pounds, Nora." He eyed me up and down for a moment. "You're getting awfully thin."

I pulled at the loose-fitting waistband of my pants. "Yeah, well, brides are supposed to lose weight for their wedding, aren't they?"

He leaned against my kitchen counter. "Not three months before the wedding; and besides, there was never anything wrong with your weight."

"Fine," I responded, waving away his concern. "I'll eat ice cream for lunch. Anything else?"

He sipped his coffee and slowly looked me over again. "Don't forget we are to meet your mother at Gallier Hall at five o'clock to go over the reception menu." He went to my refrigerator and pulled a yellow slip of paper from the door. "Then you and your mother are to go to your first dress fitting at seven," he added, handing me the yellow piece of paper. "This is the address of the dress shop. Claire wanted me to give it to you."

I stared at the paper in my hand. "I haven't even picked out a dress yet. How can I be fitted for something I haven't even chosen?"

"Your mother has a selection of dresses she picked out over two weeks ago waiting for you at that dress shop. You just choose the one you like and they will start fitting it on you."

I grimaced at John, dreading the yards of silk, lace, and white chiffon that would be awaiting me. "What if I don't like any of them? You have no idea how bad my mother's taste can be."

He put his coffee mug down on the counter. "Look, Nora, no one is going to make you wear something you don't want to, or make you have the kind of wedding you don't want to have. I won't let them. This is our wedding. I only want you to be happy."

I recalled Jean Marc saying something similar the last time we had seen each other. My mind swarmed with visions of our dance together on Ms. Marie's old bricked floor, the way he had kissed me and then walked away.

"Let's get you some breakfast." John's voice catapulted me back from my memories. "Then you go do your presentations." He snapped his finger in the air and walked into the living room. When he reemerged, he was carrying a handful of papers. "Drop these off at St. Rita's Church on your way. They're for Father Delacroix, for our Pre-Cana." He handed the papers to me.

I gleaned through the small stack of papers. "I thought we were going to fill these forms out together. When did you do this?"

"Last night at work. Father Delacroix needs them by today so he can schedule our sessions." He pointed at a small piece of paper stapled to the form on top. "I left him a note asking him to schedule our sessions on Thursdays after five, when I can get off from the ER without any hassle."

I felt the weight of the papers in my hands and sighed. "All right, John." I walked out of the kitchen.

John followed me into the living room. "What about breakfast?"

I reached for my purse by the front door and stuffed the papers inside of it. "I've suddenly lost my appetite," I muttered and rushed out the door.

* * *

After spending forty-five minutes watching my mother and John decide on grilled red snapper and oysters Bienville for the reception at Gallier Hall, I drove to the exclusive bridal shop on St. Charles Avenue for my first dress fitting. Displayed in the store window was a flowing white gown with a fifteen-foot train draped around a mannequin. I wondered if I would ever come anywhere near to looking half as good as that lifeless doll.

"What's wrong with you, Nora?" Mother nagged as we walked into the dress shop. "You never said a word at Gallier Hall, and poor John had to make all the menu decisions."

"I don't think he minded one bit."

She went to a counter by the door and rang a small bell. "Of course he minded, Nora. He was just too nice to say anything to you in front of me. Lord, don't you care about what is served at your wedding? People will form their impressions of the caliber of your wedding based on the food you serve."

I smirked at her. "That's why I've got you, Mother. To make sure we make the best possible impression for all your friends."

"What in the hell is that supposed to mean?" she snapped.

A pale, short woman with dark hair pulled back in a bun appeared from behind a wide, red curtain in the wall. She stepped behind the counter and smiled meekly at my mother.

"May I help you?" she asked in a timid voice.

"We have a seven o'clock fitting with Ms. Lillian. The bride's name is Kehoe," Mother told her.

The pale woman simply nodded and then retreated behind the curtain.

I scanned a few of the white lace dresses displayed at the entrance. "What is this place anyway, Mother?"

Mother proudly smiled. "Lillian Nash. She is one of the best wedding dress designers in the South. Her gowns have appeared on the cover of several prominent magazines. She's very exclusive, but I had some friends put in a good word for us."

I sighed and rolled my eyes. "I should have known."

A petite woman with Asian features appeared from behind the curtain. She had long, black hair, and a small porcelain face with dark blue, almond-shaped eyes. She looked from me to my mother and then she smiled.

"Mrs. Schuller?" She walked around the counter, holding her tiny hand out to my mother. "How nice to see you again." After shaking hands with my mother, the woman's eyes turned to me. "You must be our bride, Nora. I'm Lillian Nash, but you must call me Lily." She placed her hands on my shoulders and gently turned me to the side, inspecting every inch of me with her deep blue eyes. "Very pretty," she commented. She nodded to my mother. "Let's go in the back and see what Nora thinks of your selections, Mrs. Schuller."

I followed my mother and Lily behind the counter and through the red curtain. We stepped into a narrow hallway that led to a fitting room. The walls were covered with mirrors, and in between the mirrors were large hooks. In the center of the room was a raised, circular platform. Off to the right was a dressing room, and waiting by the far wall were racks of white wedding dresses covered in clear plastic bags. Lily glided over to the racks and began pulling out dresses. She carefully placed them on the hooks spread along the walls of the room.

As I watched the dresses being displayed, an oppressive sense of catastrophe descended over me. It was worse than I feared. There were rhinestones, an overabundance of white beads, large bows, an excessive use of lace, and even big, puffy sleeves on every dress. I tried my best to hide my disappointment, but Lily, being an expert at this sort of thing, must have sensed my reaction.

"I just love this one," Mother cooed over a balloon-shaped taffeta nightmare with shimmering silver beads sewn into the bodice.

"Perhaps Nora would like something a little simpler," Lily reflected as she moved back toward the rack.

"No, I think any one of these would be perfect," Mother assured her as she took in the dresses spread about the room.

Lily moved through the racks until she found what she had been looking for. She removed the gown from its protective cover and came back to me.

"This one, I think," she suggested, gazing from the dress to me. "It reminds me of you." She held it before me, fanning out the fabric so I could get the full effect.

It was a sleeveless empire dress, designed to hang from wide straps at the shoulders, and gathered at a raised waistline. It had no bows, beads or rhinestones, just yards of pale white silk chiffon arranged in a petal style that gently flowed down the front skirt.

I carefully examined the gown, and as I touched the soft fabric, my dread abated.

"Oh no, that won't do, it's too plain," Mother objected. "Nora needs some sparkle to make her stand out in the church. No one will see her in that thing."

"A wedding dress is meant to complement the bride, Mrs. Schuller, not outshine her," Lily extolled as she turned from my mother to me. "Why don't you go and try it on?" She carefully handed the garment to me.

"All right, Lily." My mother sighed and shrugged her shoulders. "Come on, Nora." She waved me toward the dressing room. "Let's go see what you think of this one."

As I placed the long silk creation on the hook inside the dressing room, Mother came in and closed the door behind her.

"Why on earth do you want to try on that one?" She waved her hand toward the fitting room. "I picked out some beautiful gowns for you."

"I like this one, Mother." I began unbuttoning my pantsuit jacket while kicking off my shoes at the same time.

"Why don't you try on one of mine after this, and you'll see how much nicer you will look with a little extra sparkle."

I pulled off my blouse. "I don't want to sparkle, Mother."

When I stood before my mother in my bra and panties, her eyes traveled down the length of my body. "Good God, Nora, what has happened to you? You're so thin!" She raised her eyes to mine. "What are you doing to yourself? I know you want to look good for your wedding, but you're emaciated."

"I've been busy and skipped a few meals. Never mind that. Help me with this," I declared, unzipping the dress.

After I stepped into the gown, Mother zipped up the back as I stood in front of the full-length mirror.

I objectively analyzed my reflection. The dress would definitely have to be taken in several inches in the waist, but the way the fabric cascaded down the front skirt reminded me of a waterfall. It was simple, classic, and elegant.

"I want this one," I stated as I turned a little to each side to watch the motion of the gown as I moved.

"Oh God, it's so plain." Mother contemplated my image in the mirror. "Maybe we could glamour it up a bit with a few choice pieces from Lou's store."

"What, a tiara and a diamond drop necklace?"

"Don't be silly, Nora. Diamond drop necklaces are so last year."

"Mother!" My voice reverberated off the walls of the dressing room. "I am not wearing a tiara."

"Just think about it, Nora. Mixed with a lovely long veil, a tiara can make such a statement."

"It's a wedding, Mother, not a political rally." I turned once more to the mirror. It was then I noticed the small white tag hanging from the right shoulder strap of the dress. I reached for the tag.

"Fifteen thousand dollars!" I gasped as I read the price tag again. "This is fifteen thousand dollars," I repeated as I gaped at my mother through the mirror.

She searched my face as if I were five and had just discovered my first mud puddle. "Of course it's fifteen thousand dollars. It's an exclusive shop. Everything is expensive."

I gazed down at the gown with abject horror. "I could feed an army of homeless people for a month with this thing."

"Lucky for us there won't be any homeless people at the wedding," Mother scoffed. Then she waved her hand nonchalantly over the dress. "What did you expect? It's an original."

"An original what? Because unless it's got *The Last Supper* painted across it, I don't see how it's worth that much."

She sighed and undid the zipper on my back. "That's what people spend, Nora."

"This is ridiculous," I muttered, pulling the dress off my shoulders.

Mother shrugged at me. "That's nothing. The gowns I picked out for you start at twenty thousand."

I began pulling the dress back on my shoulders. "Then this is the one I want."

"Nora, what do you care what it costs? Lou is paying for everything. He wants you to have a nice wedding, and he told me money is no object."

I stepped around and showed my unzipped back to her. "I'm not going to bankrupt Lou over a dress. Now zip me up and let's get this one fitted."

Mother zipped me up and stared at me through the mirror with her lips pinched tightly together, the way they did when she was upset. "I want you to try on the other ones first, before you make up your mind."

When I turned to face her, I felt some slender thread inside of me snap. "Mother, this is my wedding, and I will have what I want. I want this dress, and I do not want to sparkle, or glitter, or shine brighter than the Virgin Mary at the altar. We are buying this one, or else I'm walking down the aisle naked!"

Mother recoiled slightly with surprise. "All right, all right, Nora. You don't have to get so emotional about it."

As I walked out of the dressing room to begin my fitting with Lily, a surge of exhilaration rushed through me. For the first time in weeks I had voiced my opinion, and it felt wonderful. Relief washed over me as I realized the outspoken girl I used to be before John came into my life had not shriveled up and died. I was there, despite all of the chaos swirling around me. In that moment I knew that I had to take control again. I had to start speaking up for myself, before anyone else did it for me. I wanted my life back, and from now on I was not going to let anyone tell me how to live it.

CHAPTER 13

John and I stood before St. Rita's Church on St. Charles Avenue, ready for our first night of Pre-Cana. He held my hand as we gazed up at the solemn spire on the high steeple.

"In just a little over three months, Nora, we will be here, exchanging our vows," John voiced, sounding almost giddy.

A ripple of panic pervaded my body as I imagined our wedding day. I closed my eyes and pushed the sensation back down into the depths of my being. Now was not the time to entertain such emotions. Perhaps the wedding would be postponed due to a hurricane or an asteroid hitting the earth. Images of natural disasters delaying my wedding had a calming effect on me. I knew this was not normal bride behavior brought on by the demands of planning a big wedding. What I was feeling was something completely different.

When we stepped inside the arched entrance of the church, a short man dressed in black trousers and a black shirt with a white collar greeted us. He had dark hair touched with gray, and a round, chubby face. His cheeks were as red as his lips, and when his large brown eyes spotted me, he gave a welcoming smile.

"Nora Theresa Kehoe," the priest called out as he came toward me and offered a hug. "It's been a long time," he added as he pulled away.

"Father Delacroix." I motioned to John. "This is my fiancé, John Blessing."

John took the priest's hand. "Thank you for arranging to see us this evening, Father. My schedule at the hospital has been rather hectic lately."

Father Delacroix waved away John's concern with his plump hand. "Don't think anything of it, son. It's the least I can do for Nora and her family. I've watched Nora grow up. I baptized her in this church. It was the first ceremony I performed as a priest in this parish. Nora's father was always very good to me, so I'm glad to repay the kindness to his daughter." Father Delacroix motioned to a small door off to the side of the entrance. "Come. We can use my office for the sessions. This way."

The office was roomy with a wide array of religious statues of saints, large bookshelves overflowing with religious books, and piles of boxes on the floor. Father Delacroix went to the two plain wooden chairs placed before his desk and began removing the boxes that were sitting on them.

"Sorry about that," he said, carrying a box from one chair to the corner of the room. "Sunday school textbooks just in from the publisher. I haven't had time to distribute them yet."

Once the last box had been moved out of the way, John and I were seated before a black walnut desk.

Father Delacroix took his chair behind his desk and began browsing through a small pile of papers in front of him. "I've already read through your paperwork and have set aside Saturday, September seventeenth for you on the church calendar," Father Delacroix began. He pointed to the papers on his desk. "I see here that John does not live too far from you, Nora." Father Delacroix glanced up at me. "Must be convenient," he added.

"Yes, it is," John quickly asserted. "It allows us to visit with each other as much as we can."

I found it amusing how my devout fiancé could lie so easily to a priest. Wanting to avoid a scene, I bit my lower lip and refrained from snickering.

Father Delacroix placed his folded hands on the desk. "Now, the Pre-Cana is usually coordinated by the parish priest in charge of the service and other parish laypeople come in to facilitate the sessions. A psychologist will be coming in to talk to you about communication in one session; in another, a financial counselor will give you some advice on how to set up household accounts and distribution of household funds; and we have a sexual therapist who will spend an evening going over aspects of human sexuality and health issues with you. But the time you spend with me will focus on the religious and spiritual aspects of marriage." Father Delacroix paused and collected his thoughts. "Marriage is more than a civil union according to the church; it's a religious covenant made with God, and as such cannot be broken. I hope you are entering into this marriage with an open heart and a vow to be honest and forthright with each other."

For some unknown reason, the image of Jean Marc holding me close and dancing with me in his mother's kitchen filled my head right at that moment. I could feel his muscular arms about me and smell his woody cologne. I smiled as our dance strolled across my memory.

"Nora, is there something you wish to say?" The priest's voice jolted me out of my daydream.

I felt like a cat caught with the pet canary. I stared at Father Delacroix while my mind raced with excuses. "Ah, I was just thinking about the—"

"You'll have to forgive Nora, Father," John interrupted. "All the wedding plans have got her a little flustered."

I turned to John. "I'm not flustered. I was just thinking about—"

John slapped his hand over my knee. "You weren't paying attention, dear. You were probably thinking about your wedding dress," he complained through his gritted teeth. "Now let's listen to what Father Delacroix has to say."

"I was paying attention," I insisted. "And stop interrupting me. I can speak for myself, John."

"Nora," John grumbled in a deep tone, his face turning a light shade of red. "Now is not the time to discuss this."

"Perhaps it's good that the two of you are here," Father Delacroix intervened. "Every couple has issues they need to smooth out, but just remember these sessions are to help you make your marriage stronger. Use what you learn here to help you through the rough patches together."

"Rough patches?" I almost laughed out loud. "You have no idea," I mumbled, folding my arms across my chest.

"What was that, Nora?" Father Delacroix asked.

John cleared his throat. "Nora, let's let Father Delacroix finish."

"No, John." Father Delacroix waved his hand across his desk. "It's quite all right. Perhaps there are things we can discuss tonight that can help you two get over this communication problem you seem to be having right now."

John grabbed my hand and squeezed it. "We're not having a communication problem. Nora's just tired. She gets testy when she's tired."

I flung off his hand. "I'm not tired, John. Stop making excuses for me."

Father Delacroix sat back in his chair and looked from John to me. He placed his hands before him as if praying, and then he smiled.

"I feel there are some other issues going on here," he surmised. "Most young couples I see get all caught up in the wedding, and never really think about the years of marriage that come after it. Part of Pre-Cana is planning for the changes your relationship will endure after the wedding ceremony is over." Father Delacroix focused his eyes on me. "For better or worse, it's going to be just the two of you, and you will have to learn to open up and share your thoughts and feelings." He paused. "So let's get back to the original question I asked you, Nora. When I was talking about marriage and you smiled, you were thinking of something. What was it?"

* * *

"What the hell was that about Nora?" John shouted once we were in the confines of his perpetually spotless car. "You embarrassed me in there, going on about dancing in some kitchen with a Jean Marc Gaspard. Do you know how that made me feel in front of a priest? The man probably thinks we need therapy before we can even get married."

I fought to remain calm as I spoke to him. "Father Delacroix asked me about Jean Marc and I told him the truth. He's an old family friend who has helped my uncle." I paused and frowned at him. "Why are you getting so bent out of shape about this? And stop speaking for me. I can speak for myself, damn it! I'm not your wife yet."

"What's that supposed to mean?" He briefly gawked at me and then turned back to the road. "I don't speak for you, and I certainly know you can speak for yourself and always do. All I'm saying is that tonight you spent half of our Pre-Cana session talking about Jean Marc Gaspard and Manchac. We were supposed to be discussing our marriage, not your childhood friends."

I watched as the sights of uptown New Orleans passed by my car window.

"I'm sorry," I said after an uncomfortable silence. "I guess I got carried away."

"Your mother is right. You need to forget about your uncle and those people in Manchac. This is about us, Nora."

I nodded my head. "Yes, John."

I returned my gaze to the car window. As the old mansions of the city passed quickly by, the knot in my stomach twisted tighter. Not since the death of my father had I worked so hard at hiding my emotions, and I knew it was only a matter of time before I eventually exploded. But what was beginning to weigh on my mind was who would be left in my life when the dust from my furor finally settled.

* * *

A few days later, I was in my office waiting for the head of the orthopedic department, Dr. Harris, to arrive for our quarterly medical chart review. As I sat at my desk amid a mound of patient charts, Steve ran in my office door.

"Sorry I'm late. Dr. Harris here yet?" he asked breathlessly.

"On his way," I informed him and closed the chart before me.

He moved a pile of charts from a chair in front of my desk. "Wow, you look like shit."

I glared at him. "Thanks, Steve. That's just what every woman wants to hear."

"Can your haggard appearance be attributed to pre-wedding jitters?" Steve went on as he took his chair. "Still want to marry the fine doctor, or is the fish guy making you have second thoughts?"

I threw the chart in my hands to the side of my desk. "I don't look haggard, Steve. You sound just like my mother. Everyone is saying I don't look happy, or I'm too thin, or God knows what else!"

"Hey, there." Steve jumped up and came around to my side. "This isn't like you. You always have it so together. What's wrong? This can't all be the wedding?"

"Well, most people have never had to plan a wedding with my mother. Between fending off phone calls from my mother about wanting to glue rhinestones to my wedding dress, or John calling me with another one of his plans for our future together, or trying to cram a full-time job into part-time hours, I swear I think I'm losing it."

"How long do you plan on keeping this up, Nora? If you ask me, this wedding crap is eating you alive."

I ran my hand over my forehead. "I think you're being a little overly dramatic, Steve."

"No, I'm not. For weeks I've watched you sulking around your office, losing weight, and looking as if you were carrying the world on your shoulders. This is more than just the wedding. I think your handsome fiancé and your mother are shoving you into a corner, and you're terrified of telling either one of them what you really want."

"Maybe I don't know what I really want," I whispered as I inspected my engagement ring.

"You know. You're just too afraid to go after him."

I retrieved the discarded chart from the side of my desk and opened it, trying to ignore him.

"Perhaps you should put a little space between you and the good doctor for a while. Take a little time off. Might help you sort out your feelings for both men."

"Very funny. I don't need time away from John."

Steve stood back from my desk. "I think that is exactly what you need to get a little perspective on the situation. You should take a night off from the wedding planning." He paused and placed his hands on his hips. "You could come out with me Friday night. I'll take you to one of the local karaoke bars in the Quarter and we can get stupid drunk."

"Fridays John usually works all night and—"

"Perfect." He grabbed a pen from my desk. "This is my address in the Quarter. Come about eight. We can walk from my place, and if you get too drunk you can pass out in my spare bedroom." He wrote down the address on a blue piece of paper and handed it to me.

I reluctantly took the paper from his hand. "I don't know if I'll be able to go."

"I won't take no for an answer, Nora."

I tucked the paper into my scrub suit pocket. "You're starting to sound like John."

Steve arched his gray eyebrows at me. "Girl, you need this more than I thought."

CHAPTER 14

I arrived at St. Rita's on Thursday night for our Pre-Cana meeting to find Father Delacroix working at his black walnut desk. When he saw me enter the office door, he stood from his chair.

"I tried calling you on your cell phone, Nora. John phoned ahead and said he got tied up at the emergency room."

I sighed and let my shoulders fall forward. "I'm sorry. I thought he would be on time."

He motioned to a plain wooden chair across from his desk. "Why don't you have a seat and we can talk a bit. See if John joins us later, all right?"

"Fine, Father." I headed across the office and sat down.

"I ran into Claire the other day." Father Delacroix made himself comfortable in his chair. "She seems very worried about you."

"About me?" I lightly chuckled. "I think she's more worried about what everyone thinks of my wedding, my wedding dress, what kind of food we serve at the reception, and whether or not I will have a respectable number of bridesmaids by my side."

He shook his head. "Mothers, I think, are the worst part of weddings. I've seen perfectly sane women go absolutely crazy when planning weddings. Don't be ashamed to blow off a little steam every now and then. Get away from it all. You need that."

"Do I?" I asked, surprised by his admission.

"Yes, I believe you do." He sat back in his chair and studied me for a moment. "I, ah, wanted to talk to you about our first meeting. You mentioned your childhood friend, Jean Marc Gaspard. You spoke fondly of him and how he has helped your uncle, but I'm afraid I didn't see that same appreciation in your fiancé's eyes. John seemed rather put off by the whole conversation. Was everything all right after you two left here last week?"

I glanced down at my purse in the chair beside me. "John made it quite clear that he thinks I should put my past behind me and forget about the people in Manchac."

"How do you feel about that?"

When I looked up, his large brown eyes were intently focused on me.

"You know, Nora, I've seen a lot of couples come and go through these sessions, and I'm a pretty good judge of who will make it and who won't. But there are a lot of factors to consider when discussing one's future with someone. The first thing you inevitably have to deal with is your past. You have to be willing to put it behind you in order to move on, but in your case I don't think you've done that quite yet."

"I don't understand."

"Tell me about Jean Marc Gaspard," he said in a soft voice. "How you really feel about him now that John is not here to keep you from speaking the truth."

"How I really feel?" I casually smiled, hoping to appear untroubled. "Father Delacroix, Jean Marc is an old family friend, nothing more. Other than those childhood encounters, Jean Marc and I haven't really spent any time together. With my uncle being sick, he has been helping to take care of him, and I have to admit, initially I thought him a bit a rude, but now I think we are on better terms."

"How does your uncle feel about John? I know Jack has been a pretty big influence in your life since your father died, and I was wondering what he thinks about your impending marriage."

I fidgeted in my chair as I thought of my uncle. "He doesn't like John."

"Why doesn't he like John?"

I placed my purse in my lap. "My uncle has never really gotten to know John."

Father Delacroix rested his hands on his desk and sighed. "Nora, do you love John?"

My mouth fell open. "Of course I love John. I wouldn't be going through all of this if I didn't love him."

"Yes, you would," Father Delacroix admitted with a grin. "I'm afraid you would hide your true feelings from everyone, including yourself, in order to please your mother, your stepfather, and satisfy your expectations."

I rose from my chair, clutching my purse in my hands. "I'm not hiding my feelings from anyone."

Father Delacroix stood from his chair. "Nora, all I'm asking is for you to think about this marriage. Ask yourself if this is what you want. You're doing what your mother and John want, but I don't hear your voice coming through in any of this wedding." He waved his hand at me. "I'm sorry, but I've watched you grow up in this church. I saw how much your father loved you, and I have to question if this is what he would have wanted for you."

"Whose side are you on, Father? Shouldn't you be encouraging me to be a good wife and mother instead of trying to talk me out of marrying the only man who ever...." I stopped myself.

"The only man who ever what, Nora?" He gave me an encouraging smile. "The only man who ever asked you to marry him. Is that what you were going to say?"

I placed my purse strap over my shoulder. "I should go," I mumbled.

"I've upset you and that wasn't my intention. Perhaps we should discuss something else."

"Thank you, Father, but I think I will go home now." I bolted for the office door. "If John shows up tell him I got tired and had to leave." I stopped at the door as a thought hit me. I slowly turned back to Father Delacroix. "Do you believe in happiness, Father?"

He nodded. "Yes, of course, Nora. I very much believe in happiness. That's what I want for you. I know it is what your father would have wanted, too. Do you understand?"

As I eyed Father Delacroix, standing behind his desk and wearing his black uniform of faith, the pain in my stomach eased.

"I understand. Good-bye, Father."

* * *

"You left!" John howled later that night after he got home. "Father Delacroix told me you just left. Nora, what is the matter with you?" He waved his arms about the kitchen as he stood before me, still wearing his long white coat. "I was only half an hour late, and by the time I got there you were gone. And I don't know what you said to Father Delacroix, but he was worried sick about you. He wanted me to get here right away and check on you."

I had a seat at my kitchen table. "I was very tired and he seemed to think that all the stress from the wedding was getting to me."

"So?" John shrugged. "I'm stressed about the wedding, too. But I don't go around biting everyone's head off because of it." He ran his hand through his hair. "Your mother called me today. She says you're not acting right. She wanted to talk to me about getting you some medication. She thinks you're depressed about something. Are you depressed, Nora?"

My indignation flared as I thought of my mother's desire to pump me full of happy pills. "Are you kidding me? Because my mother says I'm not acting right, you think I'm depressed? Do I look depressed to you?" I shouted.

John backed away from me. "I don't know, Nora. You've been quiet as hell, you don't want to make any decisions about the wedding, and you have lost a good bit of weight. I'm beginning to wonder if something is wrong with you."

I was about to rip into John with all the frustration I had been holding back for weeks, when a funny thing happened; I realized he was right. There was something wrong with me. I had been trying so hard to be the woman John desired and the daughter my mother desperately wanted, that I had stopped being me. I could no longer conform to everyone else's expectations. It was time for me to fulfill my desires and find the happiness that I deserved.

As quickly as it had ignited, my wrath subsided, and a comforting calm settled over me. I stood from my chair and went to John's side.

"I'm sorry. I shouldn't have yelled at you like that. I know I haven't been myself lately, but that is going to change, I promise. Nothing is wrong with me, John, and I don't need any medication. I just need some time to sort out my head."

John nodded as he let out a long sigh. "I'm glad to hear it. I know we've had a bit of a whirlwind romance, but I thought you were ready to take our relationship to the next level." He lowered his eyes to the stainless steel watch on his wrist. "I've got to get back to the hospital. I'll be home Saturday morning. We can get together and talk about all of this then."

"Sure, John. Thank you for understanding." I stood on my tiptoes and kissed his cheek.

He looked me over with his wary gray eyes. "You need to put this unpredictable behavior behind you as soon as possible, Nora. I don't like you acting this way. It's not what I planned on."

I cringed at the mention of his plans, but my stomach remained unusually still, as if my body comprehended something my mind had not yet grasped.

John gave me one last hard glance and then stomped out of my kitchen. I observed his determined gait as he headed toward the living room, and tried to imagine what kind of future I would have with the reserved Dr. Blessing. The funny thing was, I could not envision any future with John. I recalled my conversation with Father Delacroix earlier in the evening, and his words about my father suddenly resonated within me. Since this whole engagement fiasco had begun, I had never once considered what my father would have thought of it. As I pondered what kind of future my father would have wanted for me, and the kind of man he would have deemed best for me to marry, I knew he would never have approved of John. My father taught me that life was about passion. When you're passionate about something, then you know that your heart is in it for the long haul. And that, I decided was the problem with Dr. John Blessing. My heart wasn't with him; it was with someone else.

CHAPTER 15

The following night, I decided to take Steve up on his offer. Leaving the worries of the wedding behind me, I strolled along Royal Street in the French Quarter to the address Steve had given me. As I took in the old Creole cottages with their large front shutters, wrought iron gates, and quaint doorways, I tried to think back to the French Quarter of my youth, filled with so much mystery and history. But most of the area had been lost to tacky T-shirt shops and tourist-driven businesses. The old French Quarter used to be filled with friendly neighbors and small businessmen serving a close-knit Bohemian community of artists, musicians, and the generally odd. But commercialism had replaced community in this small, never-changing part of the world, and just when you thought progress could not affix itself to the brick and stucco of the Vieux Carré, it did, and something once charming and comforting became cheap and tawdry.

After ringing the doorbell at the gated entrance to 1027 Royal Street, I waited patiently for a buzzer to gain access to the narrow alleyway beyond, which would invariably lead to a courtyard. Surrounding the courtyard would be a large house that had probably been chopped into several small apartments. Many of the old homes in the French Quarter had the same basic design, allowing residents protection from all the noise that filled the Quarter day and night. Revelers who descended on the city to drink themselves into oblivion would often forget about the weary occupants of those Creole cottages. As I stood by waiting for admittance, I saw a few of those revelers pass by me, go cups in hand, and a little unsteady on their feet.

"Go Tigers!" a man yelled as he walked past me, wearing a purple and gold football jersey.

I smiled and then thanked the heavens above when the buzzer on the black gate finally rang. I pushed the heavy gate open and made my way inside.

I was immediately engulfed in darkness only broken here and there by lights placed along the bricked walls beside me. I moved slowly through a tunnel with a cement floor and rough-hewn rafters above. When I finally emerged from the darkness, I discovered a small moonlit courtyard filled with people.

Wearing long, white robes and holding candles, they were gathered near a two-tiered fountain in the center of the courtyard. They stood in a semi-circle facing a man who was wearing a crown of brown feathers. Hanging from the neck of this individual I saw a gold medallion. As I tried to make out the strange symbol on the medallion, I heard footsteps in the alleyway behind me.

"Nora," a voice said over my shoulder.

Steve came alongside me, dressed in a pair of jeans and a red T-shirt.

I motioned to the people in the courtyard. "What's going on?"

He rolled his blue eyes. "One of my wacky neighbors is having her cult meeting here tonight."

"Cult meeting?"

Steve nodded to the group. "Honey, we get all kinds in the Quarter these days. Last year my neighbor next door belonged to this vampire cult until the landlord found out they were killing chickens in his courtyard. This one is a little easier to deal with. They just drink magic juice, get high, and see spirits." He took my arm. "Let's get out of here before they try and recruit us."

But before we turned toward the alleyway that led to the street, one member of the group raised a gold chalice in her hands.

Unable to tear my eyes away, I asked, "What's going on now?"

"That's their leader." Steve pointed to the man wearing the crown of feathers and gold medallion. "He's about to drink from the cup of enlightenment, and then he falls down on the ground and claims to commune with the spirits. It's bullshit. Come on, let's go drinking." He pulled at my arm.

"No, let's see what happens."

"Are you kidding me? Honestly, you can see this on HBO any night of the week."

I directed my attention to the gold chalice that was being passed around the group. "What's in that cup?"

Steve shrugged. "I don't know. Wine, drugs, blood, take your pick. These cults seem to be into anything these days."

"Where do they get these people?"

"Nora, anyone wanting a savior is ripe for these fools. They're mostly drifters looking for a home, kids passing through town, people like that."

"So who is…?" My question died on my lips when the leader of the group faced me.

First those black eyes hit me. His dark, wavy hair fell over his right eye, highlighting the scar on his right cheek. When his eyes met mine, for a moment I could see the trepidation in them. But being the professional that he was, Henri Gaspard simply nodded to the young woman beside him, holding the chalice.

"Son of a bitch," I whispered.

"What is it?" Steve queried.

"I know their leader."

The young woman kneeled before Henri Gaspard and held up the gold chalice. Henri patted the woman's head, and then raised his eyes to me as if to say, "Look what I can do." While smirking at me, he took the cup from the woman's hands. He walked back toward the center of the courtyard and lifted the chalice to his lips. After drinking the contents, Henri slowly put the gold cup down on the edge of the fountain in front of him.

I turned to Steve. "Any idea how much your neighbor pays to belong to this group?"

"A hundred bucks a month. Why?"

Suddenly, Henri fell hard to the cement-covered ground and started convulsing.

I ran to his side as Steve followed right behind me. I could hear some of the women in the group screaming, and as I reached for Henri's head, a hand grabbed my wrist and tried to stop me.

"He must not be touched during the transfer," a tall man hollered at me with a very thick accent I could not place.

"Screw your transfer!" I wrenched the man's hand away from my wrist. "This man is having a seizure." I glanced back at Steve. "Call 911, now."

Steve pulled his cell phone from the front pocket of his jeans. As he spoke to the operator on the other end of the line, a flurry of white robes ran to and fro about the small courtyard.

"I'll go and meet the ambulance out front," Steve said as he nodded to me. "You all right with him?"

"Fine," I answered. "Go."

Steve took off down the alleyway as I held on to Henri. His body twitched and I struggled to make sure his head did not bounce on the cement beneath him.

"Shh," I whispered to him. "Easy, Henri. Nora Kehoe is here. I won't leave you." I heard his breath rattle in his throat and I prayed that he could get enough air until help arrived.

After what seemed like an eternity, I heard the sound of sirens coming closer. When I looked up, the courtyard was completely empty. By the time the medics got to me, I was still holding Henri's head, but the seizures had not stopped, and I began to wonder if they ever would.

* * *

I went with Henri in the ambulance to University Hospital. The medics were not going to allow me to ride in the front of the ambulance until they found out that I was Dr. John Blessing's fiancée.

"Nora, are you all right?" John shouted as he greeted the ambulance on our arrival at the emergency room ambulance bay. "You scared the hell out of me. I thought they were bringing you in for a second when they radioed ahead." He helped me out of the ambulance and kissed my forehead. Then he turned to one of the medics. "What have we got?"

"Non-responsive forty-year-old male," the taller of the two medics began to give his report as he pulled Henri's gurney from the back of the ambulance. "Had to bag him for half the ride. Just started breathing on his own a few minutes ago. Don't have any idea what he took. We brought the cup we found next to him. Hopefully, it has traces of the stuff he drank in it." The medic nodded at me as they approached the emergency room entrance. "She witnessed the whole thing," he added.

I saw John's gray eyes turn to me just as the automatic doors to the emergency room closed behind him. I stayed outside by the ambulance, not wanting to walk into the emergency room and face him. But moments later, John came back out the automatic doors and grabbed my arm.

"Do you know this guy?" he asked, pulling me toward the emergency room entrance.

"His name is Henri Gaspard. You know him, too. You met him at Lou's jewelry store a few weeks ago," I reminded him.

After going through the automatic doors, we stopped in a wide, white hallway.

John let go of my arm. "But why are you here with him?"

"I went to meet my secretary, Steve, at his place in the Quarter. He invited me to go to a karaoke bar for drinks. Henri was leading a cult meeting in the courtyard where Steve lives. Right after I arrived, he drank something from that cup they brought in and began seizing." I shook my head. "I told the paramedics you were my fiancé so I could come to the hospital with Henri."

John glanced down the hallway to a pair of red double doors with a sign reading "ER Trauma Room" posted above them. "I've got to get back in there and make sure he's taken care of. You'd better get his family here as soon as possible." His bleary eyes searched mine and then he said, "When things settle down, you and I will need to talk about this." John turned away and headed quickly through the red double doors.

* * *

Hoping to avoid the inevitable confrontation with John, I had turned down his offer to wait for Jean Marc in the empty doctor's lounge, and instead opted to remain among the myriad of sick and injured in the noisy emergency room waiting area.

It was well after midnight and I had been sitting on the floor next to a little girl who had broken her arm while playing in an abandoned house, when a pair of black leather shoes stepped before me.

My insides melted as my eyes beheld Jean Marc, leaning over me and wearing a tailored dark blue suit. His black hair was disheveled and his muscular body looked leaner than I remembered, but his dark brown eyes still had the same mesmerizing glow.

He reached down and helped me from the floor. "I was at the airport, getting in from a business trip, when you called. I got here as soon as I could. Where is he?"

"He's still being worked on." I surveyed the waiting area. "Where's Ms. Marie?"

"I haven't called her yet," he replied, and then lowered his gaze to my body.

I quickly realized that the blue jeans and T-shirt I had on only accentuated my weight loss. By the time his eyes returned to my face, the worry in them was riveting.

"I'll get John." But before I could turn away, Jean Marc grasped my hand.

His touch sent a shockwave up my arm. Squeezing his hand with all my might, I raised my head and our eyes locked.

"Is this the brother?" John asked, appearing beside us.

"John!" I instantly let go of Jean Marc's hand. "Ah, yes, this is Jean Marc Gaspard." I motioned to Jean Marc. "Jean Marc, this is my fiancé, Dr. John Blessing."

The two men curtly nodded at each other.

"Mr. Gaspard, your brother is being transferred to the intensive care unit," John stated in an impersonal tone. "We're still not sure what he took, but the seizures have stopped. He's still not awake, and may not be for several hours yet."

"Do you have any idea what happened?" Jean Marc questioned.

"He was leading some kind of cult in the Quarter, Jean Marc," I reported, my voice barely audible above the din of people around us.

Jean Marc's eyes flashed with fury. "A cult? So that's what he's been up to."

"That would explain the strange drugs in his system," John mumbled. "It could be a form of Peyote used by the American Indians to induce hallucinogenic trips."

Jean Marc furrowed his brow. "You mean like LSD?"

"Similar to it, but we may never know for sure," John conceded. "We had a small sample of the stuff your brother drank sent to the crime lab. But it could be weeks before we get any results."

Jean Marc ran his hands over his face. "What will happen to Henri?"

"Until he comes around, we can't determine the extent of damage his brain may have suffered because of the prolonged seizures."

"Are you saying he may have brain damage?" Jean Marc cursed and shook his head. "This is going to destroy my mother," he said under his breath.

"I would still like to know what you were doing at this little cult fest, Nora," John whispered to me as he leaned over my shoulder.

"I told you earlier. I stumbled on the meeting when I went to Steve's home in the Quarter. When I saw Henri as the head of the thing, I knew it was some sort of scam."

"Then why did you stay?" John demanded, raising his voice to me.

"I wasn't even there five minutes when he drank that stuff. Then he started seizing, and what was I supposed to do?"

Out of the corner of my eye I saw Jean Marc listening intently to our conversation.

"You are not to go on any more jaunts to the Quarter without me, Nora." John ordered.

My anger came boiling to the surface. "Don't tell me what to do!"

He pointed at the floor. "I work here, Nora. I can't afford to have people think I have a cult follower for a fiancée."

"Hey, wait a minute." Jean Marc came up to John. "Look, John, Nora is—"

"Stay out of this," John barked, turning to Jean Marc.

Jean Marc pointed at me. "Don't you speak to Nora that way!"

"Jean Marc, please," I implored, putting myself in between the two men.

John glowered at Jean Marc, expanding his chest like a proud peacock as he spoke. "She is my fiancée. Don't tell me how to talk to her."

"John, shut up," I snapped.

"Your fiancée?" Jean Marc shouted. "You treat all women like that, or only the ones you're engaged to?"

"Hey, where do you get off?" John called out.

Jean Marc motioned to me. "What have you done to Nora? For Christ's sake, look at her. She looks sick! Is that how you like your women?"

"You son of a bitch." John pulled back his arm and threw the first punch.

But Jean Marc was much quicker on his feet and ducked, avoiding John's fist. Jean Marc bounced back to his feet and was able to land an expert blow right on John's left jaw.

Someone in the waiting area shouted, "Fight," and before I knew it, an audience of at least ten people stood beside me, egging John and Jean Marc on to kill each other. By this time they were rolling around on the floor, trying to pound each other with their fists. I screamed for the two men to come to their senses, but I had seen enough fights in my life to know that once testosterone went into overdrive, all a woman could do was stand aside and watch, or find an even bigger guy to break it up.

The bigger guy came in the form of a mammoth security guard stationed in the waiting area. He immediately pulled Jean Marc off John's chest. The thick guard pinned Jean Marc to him with arms the size of small tree trunks.

"You okay, Doc?" the security guard asked as John rose from the floor.

John's left eye was already swelling and his lower lip was dripping blood on to his green scrubs. I noticed that Jean Marc did not have a scratch on him.

John held his hand to his lip. "Let him go, Vincent. It was just a misunderstanding."

I was scrambling to think of something to say when a uniformed police officer stepped out from behind John. He was a scrawny man with a long, pointy face and intense green eyes.

"I'm Sergeant Yeager of the NOPD, Homicide Division," the policeman announced as he spied John's bloody lip. "You Henri Gaspard's brother?" he inquired, turning to Jean Marc.

Jean Marc stepped forward "Yeah. What is it? Am I under arrest for hitting a doctor?"

"No. Not my department." Sergeant Yeager smirked. "I need to speak with you about your brother, and if you knew of any relationship he had with a…." Sergeant Yeager glanced down at a notepad in his hands. "Carrie Ann Wendell."

"Who?" I asked.

"The girl I told you about," John stated, while wiping his bloody lip with the back of his hand. "The one with the muscles cut away around her eyes that came into the ER last month. She was wearing a white robe and medallion like Henri's. She was admitted in almost the same drug induced state as Henri."

"Except she died," Sergeant Yeager chimed in. "We think your brother may have had something to do with her death."

"Ah, goddamn it," Jean Marc muttered.

"Do you know anything, Mr. Gaspard?" Sergeant Yeager probed.

"No, my brother and I haven't spoken for years. I didn't learn about this cult business until tonight."

Sergeant Yeager nodded and then turned to John. "We'll need to talk to him when he comes around. I've got your statement. Thanks, Doc." He looked over at Jean Marc. "We'll be in and out while your brother is here. If you think of anything, let us know." He quickly walked away.

John leveled his gray eyes on me. "You need to go home, Nora. We'll talk later."

Jean Marc came up to my side. "Nora, I'd like you to stay."

As my gaze drifted from Jean Marc's dazzling, dark eyes to John's expressionless face, I heard my mother's voice in my head, begging me to make the right decision. But what was the right decision? Did I listen to my heart or my head? Then I recalled the thrill of dancing in Jean Marc's arms, and my indecision rapidly evaporated.

"I'll stay, Jean Marc," I declared.

John gave me one last outraged scowl and walked out of the emergency room waiting area. My eyes followed his tall figure as he passed through a pair of electric glass doors and disappeared into a sea of people dressed in green scrubs.

Somewhere in the deepest reaches of my soul, I knew I had made an inalterable choice regarding my future that night. I just didn't realize at the time how monumental that decision would turn out to be.

CHAPTER 16

Henri spent the night in the intensive care unit, and on Saturday morning his eyes opened. Jean Marc and I were waiting in the family lounge next to the ICU, along with Ms. Marie and my Uncle Jack, when a short, fat neurologist in a dirty white coat came to tell us the miracle had finally happened.

"Now he's awake," the neurologist, a man called Binder, explained as he sat with the four of us in a corner of the family lounge. "But his motor skills are not where they should be," Dr Binder confided as he sighed and lowered his eyes to the blue carpet beneath his chair.

"What does that mean?" Ms. Marie asked as she held on to Uncle Jack's hand.

Dr. Binder sighed again. "It means we may have a long haul before us. I think your son, Mrs. Gaspard, may have some brain damage from the effects of the seizures. His speech is very slow, and he has some right-sided weakness in his hand and foot that may resolve with therapy. As of right now he remembers nothing about the night of the incident."

"Nothing at all?" Jean Marc questioned.

"He doesn't remember what brought him to the hospital to begin with." Dr. Binder went on. "But he is aware of being in a hospital, and the year, and recalls a lot of details about his life. That's good news. It means most of his memory is intact, which would just leave us the physical difficulties to deal with."

Ms. Marie stared at Dr. Binder. "When can my boy come home?"

"We will transfer him out of the ICU tomorrow and start him on physical therapy to see what kind of level we can get him up to," Dr. Binder evasively responded. "But your son will have to go home with special care, Mrs. Gaspard. There will be therapy and nursing visits to help him get his strength back." Dr. Binder sighed yet again, a habit I was finding quite annoying. "But whether your son will ever be as he was before the seizures, I cannot say. Only time will tell." He stood from his chair. "I wish I could be more hopeful, but we will just have to wait and see."

Jean Marc stood up next to the physician and held out his hand to the short man. "Thank you, Dr. Binder."

After Dr. Binder left, Jean Marc's eyes went from me to his mother, who was still sitting in her chair, holding on to Uncle Jack's hand.

"Come on, Ms. Marie," I said, leaning over her. "I'll take you back to my house so you can rest."

"Good idea," Jean Marc affirmed. "I'll stay here and see if anything new develops." Jean Marc eyed Uncle Jack. "Why don't you go, too, Jack? You look exhausted."

Uncle Jack let go of Ms. Marie's hand and stood up next to Jean Marc. "Perhaps I'd best be gettin' back to Manchac, Jean Marc. Sounds like I'll have things to do to get ready for when Henri comes home." He glanced over to Ms. Marie. "We'll have to move a bedroom downstairs, and make a wheelchair ramp for him."

I watched my uncle's face as he went through a list of changes needed for Henri's return home. Then I remembered how Uncle Jack had nursed Aunt Elise through the last two years of her life after her stroke. He knew better than Ms. Marie and Jean Marc what was ahead for all of them.

"Jack, why don't you take Momma home to Manchac with you?" Jean Marc suggested. Ms. Marie opened her mouth to protest, but Jean Marc stopped her. "Momma, there is nothing more you can do here today. I'll call you if there's any change."

Ms. Marie stood defiantly from her chair. "I must be with my son."

Jean Marc's eyes pivoted to me, pleading for help.

I rested my hand on her arm. "Ms. Marie, Jean Marc is right. Tomorrow when Henri is out of the ICU and settled in his hospital room, you can visit with him. You should go home with Uncle Jack and rest."

"You need to save up your strength, Marie," Uncle Jack assured her. "When that boy comes home, he'll need lots of help. We should get ready for that." He took her hand. "You come home with me, and we'll plan Henri a new bedroom in the small parlor downstairs, close to the bathroom. You come help me get everythin' ready, all right?"

Ms. Marie slowly nodded her head.

"Take care of Jean Marc," she whispered to me. "Don't let him work himself into a state."

After kissing her son on the cheek, Ms. Marie took my uncle's arm and left the family lounge.

"Thanks, Nora." Jean Marc turned to me. "She means well, but where my brother is concerned she can see no wrong in him. I don't want her around when I beat the living crap out of him." He shook his head. "What happens if it turns out he did hurt that girl? What will Momma do if Henri is a murderer?"

"I can't see Henri killing anybody. John told me someone with the skills of a surgeon had worked on that girl's eyes. Henri is no surgeon."

Jean Marc put his hands in the front pockets of his blue suit pants. "Yeah, you're right." He paused for a moment and grinned. "I never did apologize for beating up your fiancé last night, did I?"

I smiled for him. "No, but you're forgiven. Considering the circumstances, I understand."

"When I first saw you in the ER, you looked so thin and pale. Then when John started letting into you, I just lost it." He rubbed the heavy, dark stubble across his chin. "I guess I'm still that stringy fourteen-year-old boy chasing you all over the docks."

"You sure didn't fight like a stringy fourteen-year-old boy. Where did you learn to fight like that?"

"Here and there. I've seen my share of scrapes over the years."

"Well, thanks for sticking up for me." I took in Jean Marc's wrinkled white dress shirt, tousled hair, and thick beard. "Look, it will be some time before Henri is ready for visitors, so why don't you come back to my place? You can shower and I'll cook us something to eat."

"Nah, I should stay."

"Please, Jean Marc."

"Please?" He raised one dark eyebrow to me.

"Please take a shower."

He chuckled. "Are you telling me I smell?"

I grinned as I reached for my purse. "What are friends for?"

He leaned over and whispered, "You're much more than a friend to me, Nora."

My heart plunged in my chest as I gripped my purse. "I know, Jean Marc, but I'm engaged to John."

"We both know that won't last." He reached for his suit jacket on a nearby chair. "All right, let's get out of here. I'm starving."

* * *

An hour later, Jean Marc was in the shower while I prepared eggs, bacon, and grits in my kitchen. I puttered around, happy to be behaving so domestically for Jean Marc, something I realized I had never really liked doing before with John.

"That smells great," a deep voice called from my bathroom down the hall.

"Ready in ten minutes."

I heard what sounded like a key in my front door and then the thud of the heavy oak door shutting. I placed my spatula down on the cooktop and went to the living room.

John was standing by the table next to my front door, wearing his green scrubs and two different beepers around his white coat lapel. He had a noticeable black bruise under his left eye, and his lower lip was still slightly swollen.

"John!" I exclaimed as I immediately thought of the man in my bathroom. "Why are you here?"

He gave me a quizzical look. "I thought I still called this place home, or has something changed between us?" He deposited his keys on the table by the door.

"I just thought after the fight last night…."

He came toward me. "Yeah, about that. I was out of line. I should not have started a fight with your friend." He paused and removed his white coat. "I stopped in and saw his brother in the ICU before I left. He's looking better."

"John, I need—"

Jean Marc came out of the bathroom, dripping wet, barefoot, and dressed only in his blue suit pants.

He walked into the living room still toweling off his wet hair. "Ah, I'm sorry," he said when he saw John standing in my living room.

"What's he doing here?" John roared, throwing his white coat on my green couch.

"John, stop it. He's here getting a shower and some food."

John's gray eyes turned to me. "In my house?"

I stomped my foot on the floor. "It's my house!"

"That's just great, Nora. Did you sleep with him, too?"

"No, John," Jean Marc protested as he came forward. "It's not like that. I just needed a shower. I'm here because of my brother, that's all. When he goes back to Manchac, I'll be out of Nora's hair."

John's body relaxed, and then he shook his head. "Yeah, I know," he grudgingly admitted. "I guess I just didn't expect to find you here like that." He waved at Jean Marc's bare chest.

"I understand." Jean Marc turned to me. "I'll go."

I went to Jean Marc's side. "At least eat something before you go back to the hospital."

"Yes," John agreed. "You don't have to leave because of me."

"Thanks." Jean Marc looked down at his half-naked body. "I'll just finish dressing." He quickly departed the room.

"I thought we might need to talk," John clarified as soon as he saw Jean Marc leave the living room.

I folded my arms over my chest. "Maybe you need to apologize."

He threw his hands in the air. "For what?"

"For over-reacting." I proceeded down the hall to the kitchen.

"What was I suppose to think, Nora?" John followed me into the kitchen. "I walk into the ER waiting area and see you holding hands with the same man you went on and on about to Father Delacroix. Then I find him here, half-naked, in your living room."

I went back to the cooktop and picked up my spatula. "He's my friend. Am I not allowed to have any male friends once I become your wife?"

"No, you're not," John affirmed as he stood by the breakfast table. "You're going to be my wife. What would you need to associate with another man for?"

I pointed the spatula at him. "I never realized it until now, but you're an asshole, John Blessing."

Jean Marc entered the kitchen right at that moment. He had put on his white dress shirt and black shoes. He glanced nervously from me to John. "Smells good," he commented as he clapped his hands together.

I motioned to the breakfast table with the spatula. "Have a seat."

Both Jean Marc and John sat down at the same time, facing each other. I turned back to the cooktop and began piling scrambled eggs, bacon, grits and toast on two plates. After I had crammed each plate with food, I carried them to the table.

"Thank you, Nora," Jean Marc commented as I placed his plate before him.

"Yes, it looks great, Nora." John examined his plate. "Nora's a great cook," he enthusiastically added.

Each man picked up a fork and began eating. I stood by the table and watched the ballet unfold. They filled their forks, and as they were about to place the utensils into their mouths, they glared at each other.

"How's the eye?" Jean Marc inquired as he chewed on his eggs.

"Better," John replied. "You pack quite a punch."

"You learn how on the bayou, especially with a brother like Henri." Jean Marc shrugged. "We were always fighting."

John picked up a slice of toast. "What did Binder say?"

I relaxed, somewhat confident that the two men were not going to lunge at each other from across the breakfast table. I went back to the cooktop and picked up a piece of bacon from the plate of leftovers.

"He says he's going to start him on physical therapy, and then we can take him home. But he will need more care once he's back in Manchac, nurses, and a therapist to help him recover." Jean Marc paused as he swallowed his eggs. "The police are still waiting for the toxicology reports. In the meantime, I've called the family attorney to handle things from a legal standpoint."

"A lot of work ahead for you and your family," John remarked as he began to butter his toast. "Nora knows some nurses. Maybe she can find someone to help with your brother."

Jean Marc's eyes scrutinized John. Then for a split second I thought I saw something resembling a smirk crawl across the man's thin lips. "Actually, Nora has already volunteered to come to Manchac and help with Henri after he's discharged from the hospital," Jean Marc announced as he sat back from the table.

John almost dropped his knife. "Has she?" His eyes immediately flew to me.

I put my bacon down on the plate and wiped my fingers on a nearby towel. "I'm not sure yet if—"

"But we have a wedding to plan, Nora," John cut in. "We have things to do here in New Orleans. How can you spend all of your time in Manchac?"

"It's only forty minutes away," Jean Marc argued.

John hesitated for a moment and then he asked, "What about your job at the hospital?"

I folded my arms and scowled at John. "I thought you wanted me to give up my job at the hospital."

"Nora, that's not what I said." John's tone of voice dropped as if he were disciplining a child.

Jean Marc picked up his fork again. "See, she's going to take some time off, just like you wanted."

"You just can't go off to Manchac, Nora. I will not—" John was interrupted by the page of his beeper in the living room. "Aw, hell," he muttered and got up from his chair. He went down the hall to the living room.

I glared at Jean Marc. "That was dirty. I never said anything to you about going to Manchac, and you know it. Are you purposefully trying to destroy my relationship with John?"

He gave me a cocky grin. "That idea had crossed my mind." He looked me up and down as I stood by the cooktop. "Are you sure you want to marry this guy?"

When John returned from the living room, he was wearing his white coat.

"I've got to get back. One of the residents called in sick, and I need to cover until eleven tonight."

I walked up to him. "All right."

"See you later, John," Jean Marc called from the table. "Thanks for everything."

John took my hand and dragged me from the kitchen. We made our way down the hallway to the living room.

"He will be gone when I come back tonight, right?" John demanded.

I nodded. "Absolutely."

When we reached the front door, he let go of my hand. "We need to talk about this Manchac business, Nora. I think it is time we straighten out a few things between us."

"Like what?"

"We'll talk about it later." He leaned over and kissed my forehead.

But before he could pull away, I put my hands about his face and pulled him back to me.

"What are you doing, Nora?"

"Just kiss me, John."

He pressed his lips against mine, and in an instant he was done. Putting his fingers to his swollen lip, he headed out the front door and down the walkway to his pristine automobile, waiting by the curb.

"I bet if I was a fine German road machine, I'd get a better kiss than that," I mumbled as I watched him climb into his car.

When I stepped back into the kitchen, I found Jean Marc still sitting at the table, picking at his food.

I leaned against the kitchen doorway and pointed to his plate. "I thought you were hungry?"

"I am, but you're a lousy cook, Nora." He laughed as he stood from the table and brought his plate to the sink.

I frowned at him. "Thanks a lot."

"He really likes your cooking?"

I nonchalantly shrugged. "He's never complained about it."

"He has a key to your place?" Jean Marc probed without looking up from the sink.

"Yes."

"He stays here at night?"

"I'm not a nun, Jean Marc," I defended from the doorway.

He turned to me. "You're not in love with him, either." He snapped his fingers together in the air. "No spark, Nora."

I took a step into the kitchen. "So what? He's dependable, practical, and he's a doctor, for Pete's sake."

"He's also an arrogant ass who is definitely wrong for you."

"And who is right for me, Jean Marc. You?"

Jean Marc came across the room and halted before me. "Admit it, Nora; I'm the one with the spark," he whispered next to my cheek.

The warmth of his breath against my skin sent a chill down to my toes.

"Just remember that," he added, and then he walked down the hall toward my guest bedroom. I jumped when I heard the bedroom door slam.

I grabbed the doorframe and tried to steady myself against the onslaught of emotions bombarding my mind. When my head finally cleared, I glimpsed the mess of dishes in my kitchen. While heading to the sink, it struck me that the disarray in my kitchen mirrored the chaos beginning to envelop my life. Unfortunately, a little warm water and soap was not going to put my life back in order. I would need a deep cleanser to purge my growing feelings for Jean Marc from my heart, but I was not sure if I wanted to be rid of those emotions just yet. Perhaps I needed some time to discover if he was the man for me, and to get away from John, my mother, and the burdens of my life in the city. I recalled Jean Marc's comment about my volunteering to go to Manchac to care for Henri, and as I considered the idea, a speck of sunlight from my kitchen window made the diamond on my left hand shine.

"Oh, crap," I murmured as I peered down at my engagement ring. "John is going to be so pissed."

CHAPTER 17

"You can't go to Manchac!" John roared four days later as he stood in my bedroom. "You call me out of the blue and tell me you're going to Manchac for two weeks. I couldn't believe what I was hearing. I walked out of the ER and came right home to talk to you about this."

"You didn't have to leave work," I calmly assured him as I packed some underwear in my suitcase.

"What did you expect me to do? You can't go running off to Manchac just because the Gaspards need your help." He began pacing back and forth in my bedroom. "Nora, I thought we already discussed this, and you promised you would talk to me before you made up your mind about going."

"I don't have much of a choice. Jean Marc called and told me Henri is going to be discharged tomorrow morning. The hospital has only arranged for a physical therapist to check on Henri three days a week. The rest of the time the Gaspards would be left to care for Henri without assistance. Someone needs to be there to help out day and night. Ms. Marie and Uncle Jack aren't exactly young, and they may not be able to handle Henri."

He stopped pacing. "What about Jean Marc? He can care for his brother."

"He has to run Gaspard Fisheries." I took in John's angry countenance and sighed. "John, I owe him. He bailed my uncle out of trouble; he gave him a job at the house when he could no longer work as a shrimper. I can't say no."

"We still have to get married in September," John insisted as he sat on my bed. "I will not postpone the wedding because of Henri Gaspard. Do you understand, Nora?"

I smiled weakly for him. "We won't postpone, John. It's only for two weeks. After that Jean Marc's cousin Ethel can help out. She'll be back from her cruise by then."

"What about your job at the hospital?"

I picked up a T-shirt by my suitcase and began folding it. "I told them I had a family emergency and needed to take two weeks of vacation time."

"What about your mother?" he asked, raising his eyebrows.

I turned back to my suitcase. "I'll call her from Manchac."

John shook his head. "All right, Nora. I can't stop you, but do me one favor. Be careful. I don't like what I have heard from the police about Henri, and I don't want you near that Jean Marc character."

"Why, because he got in a lucky punch?"

"No." He paused for a moment and lowered his head. "The way he looks at you. It's like he owns you or something. I don't like it."

I raised his head with my hand. "No one owns me, John. No one ever will."

He removed my hand from beneath his chin and inspected the engagement ring on my finger.

"When you're my wife, will you still feel the same way?"

I took my hand from his. "Marriage is not about ownership, John. When I give myself to you as a wife, it's as a partner and not a piece of property."

"Of course, Nora." He leaned back on my bed and glared at me. "But when you get back from Manchac, you are to be completely mine. I will not share you with anyone. And I will never allow you to leave me, ever again."

The acid inside my stomach began to churn.

He stood from the bed. "I have to get back to the hospital."

As his prized BMW pulled away from the curb, I began to dread the moment when I would have to return from Manchac to my life with John. To come back to the chaos of our wedding and to the life he had planned for us. For the first time, I began to wonder why I was marrying a man who made me feel so anxious. Then, I thought of Jean Marc and the possibility of seeing him everyday for two weeks. Instantly, the unsettling sensation within me receded.

After I shut my front door, I rested my forehead against the cool wood. "Steve was right. You're in trouble, Nora Theresa Kehoe. Big trouble."

* * *

The following morning I was heading down the interstate with the rising sun shining through the numerous bald cypress trees in the swamps surrounding me. The water glistened with the early morning light while elegant white cranes and blue herons, perched along the expressway railings, searched for their morning meal in the water below. The air was warm and filled with all the promise of another ruthless summer day in the swamp, but I did not care. Feeling in tune with the hum of the life around me, it was as if I belonged among the cypress stumps and stagnant water. The world was alive with possibilities as I sped toward Manchac, eager to leave my cares behind me.

I pulled into the driveway of Gaspard House and heard the howl of the two old Catahoula hounds as they ran up and greeted my car. I climbed out of my little Honda and stretched my back. Napoleon and Nelson were all over me, eager for a friendly pat on the head. Once they were appeased, they happily trotted away. I took in the Spanish moss-laden oaks and smelled the rich scent of magnolia in the air. Everything appeared so much greener in the swamps, a sort of living green a painter could never hope to recreate on canvas. I felt the tension inside me disintegrate as I wrapped my arms about my body.

"You made it," a man's smooth voice called out.

Then I noticed Jean Marc standing a few feet away from me.

"I didn't see you there," I admitted with a nervous smile.

He moved closer to me. "I was just heading to the house when I saw your car pull up."

I searched the long driveway for another car, but did not see one. "Where did you come from?"

"My house." Jean Marc pointed to a narrow path in the brush. "The old caretaker's cottage we used to play in when we were kids. I fixed it up after I moved back from Texas. I live there now."

"Why don't you live in the main house?"

He shrugged as he looked down at his brown loafers. "A lot of reasons, the main one being Henri. He and I could never stand to be together under the same roof, so I moved into the cottage when I came home. Been there ever since."

"I didn't realize Henri stayed here that much. He gave me the impression New Orleans was his home." I walked to the back of my car and opened the trunk.

"It was, but now he'll be here for a while. Mother called me at the cottage. She said Henri arrived about twenty minutes ago," he added as he came up beside me. He grabbed my suitcase from the trunk.

"I can carry my own suitcase, Jean Marc," I insisted.

"I've got it. I'll take it into the house for you."

I shut the trunk. "Thanks."

"Save your thanks until after you've spent a few days with my brother, Nora. You've got your work cut out for you."

I sighed as I remembered Henri seizing in my arms. "I don't think Henri is going to give me any problems, Jean Marc. He's never going to be quite the man he once was."

"Don't let his docile behavior fool you. A dangerous tiger still lurks inside him. It always will. It would take more than a near death experience to change Henri." He directed his gaze toward the house. "I owe you one, Nora. You don't know how much this means to my family…and to me. It will be nice having you around."

A zing of excitement quickened my heart. "I'm happy I could help."

He smirked at me. "Are you?"

I smiled back at him. "Yes, Jean Marc. I am."

*   *   *

After greeting Uncle Jack and Ms. Marie, I immediately went to check on my patient. I entered Henri's makeshift bedroom in the small parlor and found a frail man sitting on a hospital bed. His round, dark eyes were almost hollow as they stared out the window next to him. His cheekbones protruded from under his sickly, yellow skin, emphasizing his gaunt appearance. He was wearing a blue knit short-sleeved shirt that revealed numerous bruises up and down both of his forearms. His baggy khaki pants only enhanced his sudden weight loss, and he seemed to be but a shadow of the man I had seen in Lou's store just a few weeks earlier.

"Henri?" I walked up to his bed. "Henri, it's Nora Kehoe."

A thin smile eased its way across his pale lips, but he never said a word.

"Why don't we get you out of those clothes and into some pajamas?" I suggested.

I went to the chest of drawers beside the bed and began searching for his pajamas. Most of the furniture had been removed from the room, and except for the bed, chest of drawers, nightstand, and a pale blue high back chair, the only things left from the original décor were the assorted paintings of boats hanging on the pale blue walls.

"Why?" a weak voice asked from the bed behind me.

I turned from the chest of drawers and faced Henri.

"Why you…here?" Henri went on, struggling with the words.

I sat down next to him on the bed and patted his left hand. "I'm here to help you. You're not completely well yet, and I thought I would come by and help you until you get better."

"You…can't help…me."

"Henri, you will get better. You cannot give up. You have to work at this. I've seen patients do amazing things after going through what you've been through. You'll recover, just be patient."

His eyes curiously explored my face. "You were…there. You saw. I re…member."

"I thought you told the doctors you couldn't remember, Henri?"

He kept his black eyes on me. "Silly…Nora. I'm sm…smart." He nodded slowly to the parlor doors. "They…know about…me? The…family?"

"Yes, your mother and Jean Marc know. The police know as well, Henri."

He grinned, looking thoroughly amused. "My…brother must…be…pi…." With a grunt of frustration, he punched his left hand into his left thigh. "Pi…pissed about every…thing."

I placed my hand over his fist. "No, Henri. Jean Marc is worried about you."

Henri shook his head slightly. "Not him. He…hates me. I…hate him…ever since…." His voice faded.

I glimpsed the long scar down his right cheek. "Jean Marc is your brother. You should not say such things, Henri. He does not hate you."

"Old…habits…die hard."

Not wanting to pursue the subject further, I stood from the bed and returned to the chest of drawers.

"Let's get you changed and then see what your mother has made for you in the kitchen. She's glad to have you home, Henri. Everyone is glad you're here."

Henri just snickered, but said nothing else to me the remainder of the morning.

* * *

My first day at Gaspard House was spent getting Henri settled and meeting with the physical therapist who was sent to evaluate him for the home health portion of his recovery.

Ms. Marie wandered in and out of the bedroom, helping me dress and feed Henri as best she could. But the sight of her son so debilitated took its toll. She could not spend much time in his room before her eyes began brimming with the tears, and I would have to shoo her away to find some other project about the house to occupy her mind.

Uncle Jack was much more help to me, especially when it came to getting Henri's tall body in and out of the bed. But I could tell by the discomfort in his blue eyes that such duties were reawakening painful memories, so I tried to do as much as I could on my own.

Jean Marc, on the other hand, never made an appearance in his brother's bedroom. By the time nightfall came and Ms. Marie brought Henri's supper to the room, I decided to inquire about the missing member of the Gaspard family.

"He's been at the business all day, child," Ms. Marie explained as she fed Henri small spoonfuls of jambalaya. "Dealin' with budgets or some such thing. I've never had a head for the family business."

"Yes, I'm sure he's been too busy to visit," I reasoned, feeling slightly disappointed that Jean Marc had not come to see me.

"Why don't you take a break and get some fresh air?" Ms. Marie proposed. "I'll sit with him a while."

"You're sure?" I asked, remembering her crying bouts throughout the day.

"I'm all right now." She nodded. "Oh, I almost forgot. Your fiancé called the house earlier. He said your cell phone was off and wants you to call him." She turned back and gently stroked her son's cheek. "You run on, Nora T. We'll be fine."

I left Ms. Marie with Henri and went upstairs to my bedroom to unpack. While climbing the steps on the wide oak staircase, I decided I would call John after Henri was asleep, wanting to postpone the inevitable argument that I was sure would take place.

My spacious second-floor bedroom had three long windows situated in the east corner of the house, ready-made for taking in the early morning sun. The room was also filled with a slew of antiques. There was a hand carved praying stool in one corner and a dark oak dresser set next to the bathroom door. On the wall were assorted portraits of people long since dead. Men with thin moustaches and ladies in high lace collars stared back at me.

My suitcase was sitting on the antique four-poster bed where I assumed Jean Marc had left it, but when I opened it, I discovered all my clothes were gone. I went to the intricately carved oak armoire next to my bed and found that all my shirts, jeans and a pair of black casual pants had been ironed and were hanging on linen-wrapped hangers. My extra pair of tennis shoes was on the bottom of the armoire. Across the room in the oak dresser, all my T-shirts, socks and underwear had also been neatly put away.

"She spent the mornin' doin' that," a familiar voice said from the doorway of my room.

I saw Uncle Jack standing by the door, dressed in his worn blue jean overalls with his blue cap on his head.

"She wanted to make sure your things were hung up proper." He waved at the open armoire. "I think she was just preparin' herself to go spend time with her son."

"She seemed awfully upset earlier today," I commented as I closed the dresser drawer.

"Yeah, she cried like a bébé this mornin', but then I think her instincts took over." Uncle Jack moved inside the doorway. "I saw her down there feedin' him. She'll be fine."

"I guess she just needed some time to adjust."

"What about you, Nora T? Are you adjusted yet? 'Bout gettin' married and all?"

I glanced down at the ring on my left hand and my emotions gushed to the surface. "Oh, I don't know what I'm going to do, Uncle Jack."

"That be the first step, girl. At least you're admittin' that you don't know." He nodded to the windows in my room. "Perhaps you should go and take a walk outside in the evenin' air. You could go see Jean Marc's place right down the path. He could use some company." He stepped back through the doorway.

I smiled at my uncle's suggestion. "That sounds like a great idea."

CHAPTER 18

The path to Jean Marc's cottage was located between clumps of trees and green brush that led to Owl Bayou. I had not been down that path since I was a little girl, but somehow I remembered places along the way as I walked. There was a tree where I had swung from an old rope or the spot where I had caught my first turtle. Memories came pouring into my head, like water from a long dried-up spring. I was six years old again and the world was one big playground.

Over the trees, the roof of the caretaker's cottage came quickly into view. The faded terra cotta tiles, just like the ones on the main house, glowed in the light from the setting sun. Around me buzzed dragonflies, mosquitoes, and assorted black bugs the swamp seemed to produce in abundance. I quickened my step, not wanting to be a tasty morsel for the man-eating insects that were quickly swarming about my flesh. I was jogging by the time I reached the clearing in front of the house, and then I stopped, overtaken by the beauty of the cottage I remembered only as a run down hovel.

It had been built as a smaller replica of Gaspard House, but it did not have the thick columns in front, and there was a screen-covered porch that wrapped around the entire first floor. Long, white french windows decorated the façade, while a red-bricked chimney rose from the side of the home. Bald cypress trees dotted the surrounding property, and their unique feather-like branches cast eerie shadows along the plaster-covered walls of the two-story structure. Owl Bayou flowed behind the raised cottage, and a small pier could be seen connecting the back porch with the dark water.

The sting of a mosquito on my arm quickly distracted me. I slapped the pesky bug away and took off at a run for the safety of the screened porch.

After I darted inside, the screen door smacked shut behind me while the old porch planks moaned beneath my feet.

"Who's there?" I heard Jean Marc brusquely demand from behind the white cypress front door.

Instantly, he was standing in the doorway, wearing only a pair of faded jeans. His bare chest glistened with sweat in the late afternoon light and his dark hair was tossed about his head as if he had just tumbled out of bed. Then, I spotted the .9mm pistol in his hand.

"Is something wrong?" he asked, his intense brown eyes filled with alarm.

I stared at the gun in his hand. "No, everything is fine. I left your mother with Henri."

He glanced down at the gun. "Sorry." He placed the pistol on a table near the front door. "Sometimes you have to be a little cautious out here."

I set my eyes on the planks beneath me, wanting to avoid staring at his naked chest. "I just thought I would get out and stretch my legs."

He came closer. "Picked a fine time. You know better than to go traipsing around the swamp at sunset. You would have been eaten alive out there."

"Very nearly was." I scratched my arm where the mosquito had bitten me.

He stepped back against the open front door and waved me inside. "Come in. I'll see if I have something for that bite."

I walked in the door, making sure to keep enough space between his bare chest and my body as I passed him.

Once inside the cottage, the rough planks on the porch turned into fine, highly buffed wood floors. A red Oriental rug covered the floor in an expansive living area just beyond the entrance. Atop the rug, a deep red leather couch and a rustic oak coffee table faced a massive red-bricked fireplace with a thick cypress mantle. Along the wall next to the fireplace was an entertainment center with a flat screen television, satellite receiver, and DVD player. Behind the living area, a straight polished oak staircase led to the second story.

To the left of the stairs I could see into a wide gourmet kitchen with a built-in refrigerator, gas cooktop, and double ovens. In front of the kitchen was a small dining area with a walnut dining table and four high back, intricately carved walnut chairs. Another blue Oriental rug sat beneath the dining table, while a brass chandelier hung from the cypress-paneled ceiling above.

"This is exquisite, Jean Marc. You really have turned this place around. I remember how it was falling apart when I was a little girl."

Jean Marc shut the front door with a bang. "Yeah, I put enough money into it. Cost me a small fortune to get this place into shape." He walked past me to the oak coffee table. Spread out on the table were several stacks of papers and an array of manila folders. Jean Marc sat down on the couch and picked up a beer that had been sitting on the coffee table.

"I've got a lot of work to do, Nora. Feel free to browse around on your own." He took a sip from his beer.

"Mighty neighborly of you," I said, sarcastically.

He motioned to the papers in front of him. "You would feel the same staring at this mess all day."

I ambled over to the fireplace and inspected the flowers, roses, and long intertwining vines carved into the mantle. Above the mantle were assorted pictures in silver frames. One caught my eye right away.

In the picture a tall, older man held a small girl with pigtails in his arms, and beside the pair, a young man with black, wavy hair stood watching them. The older man was my father, happy and healthy years before his diagnosis of cancer. I could not have been more than six or seven at the time the photograph was taken.

"That's my favorite," Jean Marc declared behind me. "We were on Jack's boat. Jack took the picture. I remember watching you and your father and feeling so lucky just to be around the two of you."

I gazed at my father holding me in the photograph. "I cut off my pigtails when I turned twelve, thinking them childish. Now I wish I hadn't."

Jean Marc chuckled. "Yeah, I still miss those pigtails."

I turned to him, holding the picture in my hands. "You used to always tease me about my pigtails. You were either pulling at them, or threatening to cut them off with your big knife."

Jean Marc sat back on the couch with a mischievous glint in his eyes. "You remember that?"

"I remember that you were always mean to me."

"Not mean. I was just trying to make sure you didn't turn into one of those sissy girls I hated from school." He took another swig from his beer. "I wanted to make you tough. I'd say I was pretty successful."

I returned the picture to the mantle. "Maybe too successful."

"Why do you say that?"

I turned back to Jean Marc. "Nothing." I pointed at the beer in his hand. "Can I have one of those?"

"No. You're on duty."

"No, I'm not."

"Well, then, you're too young."

"Jean Marc, I'm thirty."

He raised his dark eyebrows at me. "You're that old!"

"Just give me the damn beer."

"My God, you're still bossy." He waved to the kitchen. "In the fridge, top shelf."

I went to the kitchen and opened the refrigerator door. To my surprise, the entire top shelf was stocked with Heineken Beer. I grabbed one of the green longnecks, found the opener hanging from a rope on the refrigerator door handle, and opened the bottle. I walked back to the couch and sat down next to Jean Marc.

"You must really like beer," I commented.

He put his beer down and picked up a folder from the table. "I relax at night with a beer."

"How many?" I took a sip from my beer.

He gave me a perturbed side-glance. "You're very nosy all of a sudden."

"Haven't seen that much beer in one fridge since college. I think you have more than one."

"Enough about the beer." He directed his attention to the yellow manila folder in his hands.

I noticed the word "Crawfish" scribbled across the top of the folder. "What's that?" I asked, nodding to the folder in his hands.

"Nora, you're being a pest."

"All right. I could go back to talking about the obscene amount of beer you have in that refrigerator."

He sighed and shook his head. "It's a quarterly report on the crawfish farm. Happy?"

"What does the report say?" I tried to lean over his shoulder and grab a peek.

"I don't know; I haven't read it yet," he curtly replied.

Jean Marc put the folder down on the coffee table, making sure to close it so I could not see the contents. "Nora, I have a lot to do. You've had your beer and seen the cottage; you can go back to the house and leave me to my work."

"What about my mosquito bite?" I complained, holding up my arm to him. "You said you had something for it?"

"What, are you six again?"

"Only around you." I perused the folders on his coffee table. "Seriously, Jean Marc, what is this stuff? Maybe I can help."

"How can you help me, Nora?"

I put my beer down on the coffee table. "I have to do my own budgets at the hospital. I know how to read a balance sheet and a P&L."

"Where did you learn how to read a profit and loss report?" he asked, eyeing me with a dubious smirk.

"Dad taught me. I also used to help Lou during the summers at his store. He taught me the ins and outs of business." I paused and playfully elbowed him. "Let me see if I can help."

Jean Marc took a moment, as if trying to make up his mind. "All right, here." He picked up the folder marked "Crawfish" from the coffee table and handed it me. "What do you make of that?"

Inside the folder I found a profit and loss statement for the first two quarters of the year. I gleaned over the actual versus projected sales, and then I reviewed the expenditures from the previous quarters. After several minutes I gazed up at Jean Marc.

"You're in deep trouble here."

"That's one way of putting it." He sighed. "What do you recommend?"

I leaned in closer to his naked chest, acutely aware of the proximity of him, and I pointed at some figures on the report.

"Your expenditures are too high, for one. Your health care and worker's compensation fees have tripled in two years. So, there are a few options here. First…." And then I began going through the long list of options Jean Marc could implement to save his struggling crawfish farm.

* * *

Two hours later Jean Marc and I were still sitting on the couch. We had finished four beers between us, and the shade of night had unknowingly descended over the cottage windows.

He scratched his head and glanced up from the legal pad he had been writing on. "You really do know your stuff. Any one of your suggestions would help cut the expenditures for a lot of the business. I could actually make a profit."

"You just have to rearrange some of your benefit and insurance plans," I informed him, while moving a beer bottle out of the way of the notepad in front of me.

Jean Marc's eyes seemed to dance in the light of the living room lamps. "Then I could move out of the trawler business and go into farming shrimp, crawfish, and catfish full-time. That's where the real money is. Trawlers have become too expensive.

Between gas, upkeep, and insurance, the boats are getting impossible to keep going."

"What about the men who run those trawlers?" I questioned, knowing what Jean Marc had in mind would leave dozens of families without a breadwinner.

"I plan on reeducating them. Teach them how to run the farms, harvest the farmed fish and shellfish. Maybe even let them get into sales. They would be a little resistant at first. All Cajuns hate change, but then when they see the potential profit for them and their families, they would be persuaded."

The enthusiasm in his voice was contagious, and I wished I could take part in his dreams, but I doubted that would ever happen. I had another's plans to consider. "I think that's a fine idea. I hope it all works out for you, Jean Marc."

Then, quite unexpectedly, Jean Marc leaned over and gently kissed me on the cheek. "Thank you, Nora." He quickly turned his attention to the french window overlooking the front porch. "It must be late. I'll walk you back to the house."

Unhinged by his kiss, I quickly rose from the couch. "I can find my way."

Jean Marc stood up beside me. "No, I'll take you back; but do you think you could come over tomorrow night? I would like your opinion on a couple of other ideas I have."

"Sure," I said, trying to conceal my excitement.

He glanced down at his bare chest, as if suddenly realizing he was half-naked. "Let me just get a shirt." He went around me and quickly bounded up the stairs two at a time.

I listened as he rummaged around upstairs and within seconds he was back down the steps.

He motioned to the door as he shrugged a pale blue, long-sleeved shirt around his broad shoulders. "Let's go."

I stepped on to the porch and was shocked by the intensity of the night around us. It was pitch black, and I could not make out any of the landmarks I had passed on my way to the cottage.

Jean Marc reached for my left hand. "Here, hold my hand." He led me down the porch steps to the soft ground. "You'll get lost if you don't hold on," he softly insisted.

I kept a firm grasp on his hand as we started down the path to the main house. There was no moon out and the darkness pervaded every crack in the landscape.

"I can't see a thing," I murmured.

Jean Marc hand tightened around mine. "Helpless at last."

"I've taken self defense classes buster, so watch it."

His warm breath stirred against my face as his fingers fondled my engagement ring. "Why don't you just beat me over the head with that rock on your hand, or sick that overprotective fiancé of yours on me?"

"John is far from overprotective," I asserted, feeling his body close to mine.

He sighed next to me. "Then he doesn't deserve you."

"Maybe it's the other way around. I don't deserve him."

"Nora, you don't have to…never mind." He moved away from me. "Let's just get you back to the house."

When the lights of the main house finally broke through the darkness, Jean Marc stopped.

"You can make it the rest of the way by yourself." He let go of my hand and a sudden coolness came between us.

"What time do you want me to come over tomorrow night?"

"After Henri goes to sleep." He stepped away. "And Nora?"

"Yes, Jean Marc."

"Leave that damn ring on the dresser when you come over."

"Why?" I laughed, thinking he was joking with me.

"Just do it," he harshly ordered. Then I heard the sound of his feet crushing the grass beneath him as he walked away.

CHAPTER 19

The next morning I was up with the sun, seeing to Henri and helping Ms. Marie set up a schedule for her son. We went over therapy sessions and medication times. I wrote the whole week out on a chart for Ms. Marie and Henri to see and posted it on the wall by his bed.

"What did he…pay you…to come here?" Henri asked me later that day after his therapy session. He was lying tucked into his hospital bed, watching me.

"Who?" I inquired while I folded some sheets for his bed.

"My brother."

"He didn't pay me." I put the sheet down and faced Henri. "I told you, I wanted to come."

"For…me?"

I nodded my head. "Yes."

"Liar." He tried to smirk at me, but it appeared more like a grimace.

"No, I'm not lying. I came to help you and your mother."

"And Jean Marc." He looked out the window next to his bed. "He has…always wanted…you."

"Jean Marc loves me like a sister, Henri. You once said I've always been like a sister to the two of you."

"Not…to Jean Marc. I could always…tell. So could…your uncle."

I pulled back the tight blankets Ms. Marie had buried Henri under. "Now I know you're feeling better. You're starting to egg me on like you used to when we were kids. You were always so damned cocky."

"You…loved it."

I shook my head. "Lord, this is going to be a long two weeks."

* * *

After I had put Henri to bed for the night, I went to my bedroom to prepare for my evening with Jean Marc. I tried to convince myself that our time together was merely for discussing business, but I could not quell my nervous energy. I dressed in my casual black slacks and a long-sleeved shirt before heading to the bathroom to apply my make up. I was standing in front of the bathroom mirror and putting on my lipstick, when I saw a shadow cross my open bedroom door.

"You look nice. You goin' out?" Uncle Jack inquired as he came in and sat down on my bed.

I shrugged, trying to appear casual. "No, I'm just going over to help Jean Marc with the company books."

"You need lipstick for that?"

I turned from the bathroom mirror and scowled at my uncle. I put the lipstick back in my make up bag and exited the bathroom.

"You leadin' that boy on?" he asked.

"Who?"

"Jean Marc." He nodded to my left hand. "You're engaged to that doctor. If you're goin' to sport with Jean Marc and marry that doctor, you'll break poor Jean Marc's heart, and I couldn't stand to let you do that. I love that boy. You do too. Just don't know it yet." He stood from the bed.

"Is that why you came up here, Uncle Jack? To tell me that?"

He shook his head. "Your mama called my cell phone. She wants a word with you."

I waited until Uncle Jack had left my bedroom before I retrieved my cell phone from my purse. Mother answered after the first ring.

"You went to Manchac to care for that good for nothing Henri? Are you insane, Nora?" Mother began, shouting at me. "You leave your fiancé and run off to those godforsaken swamps to care for a suspected murderer. You have a wedding to plan. I've got over three hundred people on the guest list already, your dress is not fitted yet, your china has not been picked out, you haven't even decided on a band for the reception, and you're playing nurse to that white trash snake."

"Did John tell you I was here?"

"Of course he did!" she hollered. "He's worried sick about you. He told me he has tried your cell phone repeatedly and only gets your voice mail. He has called the house three times, and Marie always tells him you're busy."

I swore silently to myself. "It was not his place to say anything to you, Mother."

"What's wrong with him telling me? He's going to be my son-in-law, Nora, and he thought I should know the whereabouts of my daughter."

"I was going to call you when I was ready, Mother."

"Ready!" Her voice broke under the tension. "Nora Theresa Kehoe, do you not give a damn about your fiancé, about me, about your future? I'm at the end of my rope. Since the beginning, planning this wedding has been like pulling teeth with you. I don't understand you anymore."

"Did you ever understand me, Mother?" I sighed as I looked down at the engagement ring on my finger.

There was an uncharacteristic moment of silence over the phone. I could still hear Mother's teeth grinding, so I knew she had not yet hung up on me.

"What in the hell is the matter with you?" she questioned, trying to keep her voice steady. "You have a handsome doctor who wants to marry you. Then you run off and leave him hanging for some low class bum and his worthless family."

I stared at my cell phone as that familiar nagging burn flared in the pit of my stomach. "I'll be back in two weeks. Why don't you just forget about the wedding for a while? Take a vacation." I pulled the phone away from my ear. "You sound like you could use it." Without another thought, I hung up.

I headed out the back door of Gaspard House and found myself almost running toward the path that led to Jean Marc's cottage. My mother's words kept circling around my head like tornado. Three hundred wedding guests, the dress fittings, the band for the reception, all the things she wanted done. All the things she felt were important for me. Then, I began to think of John and about his demands, his timetable for our life, and all the things he thought were necessary for us. As I made my way along the path, the wall of trees on either side of me began closing in, choking off my breath and stifling my voice. I picked up my pace, jogging quickly, then running, and before I knew where I was heading, I broke free of the trees and I was standing in the clearing in front of Jean Marc's cottage.

I stopped and bent over, grabbing my knees and trying to catch my breath, but I couldn't. The wall of trees closing in around me was gone, but the feeling of panic was still ricocheting within my chest. My heart was pounding and I was breathing in short, fast gasps, as if there was not enough air to satisfy me.

"Stop…this," I wheezed, trying to halt the anxiety coursing through me.

"Nora!" a man's voice cried out, sounding far away across the clearing.

I glanced up from the ground to see Jean Marc standing on the steps of his cottage.

I tried to call to him, but my lips could not form the words. All I could do was stand there, fighting for breath and wishing the world would swallow me up.

I thought I could make out Jean Marc rushing down the steps toward me, but the little black spots forming before my eyes were making it difficult to see.

"Nora!" I heard his voice coming closer.

I forced my lips to obey my commands, but the words only sounded garbled and unintelligible.

"Nora!" His voice sounded close by, but by this time I could not tell if it was truly him, or some figment of my imagination.

Blurry spots and flashes of light were zooming around before my eyes, and then, just when I tried to stand up, everything went black.

* * *

I woke up spread out on Jean Marc's red leather couch inside the little cottage, not entirely sure how I got there. As I tried to sit up, the dizziness hit me.

"Whoa, there. Take it easy, Nora." Jean Marc kneeled next to the couch and gently guided me to a sitting position.

"What happened?" I asked as I placed my hands on either side of my head.

"You were hyperventilating like hell when I got to you. Next thing I know, you went out like a light. I carried you in here and put you on the couch." He reached to the coffee table behind him and grabbed a mug. "Here. It's chicken soup."

I frowned at the mug in his hand. "I don't have the flu, Jean Marc."

"Well, I didn't know what to do. I'm not the doctor, Nora." He put the mug back on the coffee table.

"Do you have any Valium, Xanax, or Ativan?"

He shook his head, half-laughing. "No, of course not."

"Then how about a beer?" I closed my eyes, hoping to ease the throbbing in my head.

"Yeah, I got beer."

I listened as his feet padded across the hardwood floor to the kitchen, and then heard the clink of two bottles coming together. When I opened my eyes, Jean Marc was standing by the couch, holding out a cold longneck to me. After greedily taking the bottle from him, I poured the liquid into my mouth.

Jean Marc had a seat on the coffee table across from me and watched me quickly down three gulps of beer. "So what happened out there?"

"I had an anxiety attack," I told him, after swallowing the cool alcohol. "A pretty bad one."

"Anxiety attack? You? That's something new." He raised his bottle of beer to his lips.

"I haven't had one in years. After Dad died, I used to have them quite a bit."

He leaned in closer to me. "I don't understand. Why were you having anxiety attacks?"

"Mother was spending a lot of money. Money we didn't have. I remember phone calls from bill collectors, and people showing up at the house looking for money. I thought we were going to end up on the streets; living in a cardboard box, with Baccarat crystal and Royal Worcester china, but living in a box, nonetheless."

He placed his bottle on the coffee table. "Why didn't you call me? You could have talked to me, Nora. Even come here to stay, you know that."

"Mother would never have allowed that. You know how she feels about your family. Anyway, you were in Texas at the time. You couldn't have helped." I took another swig from my beer.

"I didn't leave you, Nora," he softly said.

I lowered my eyes to the green bottle in my hand as I remembered back to the time right after Jean Marc went off to college. "For a long time I thought you did leave me. I was really mad at you for leaving. I remember crying into my pillow every night for days after you left for college. When I grew up, I realized you probably needed to get away for one reason or another. I thought perhaps I would hear from you. You were gone twelve years, Jean Marc. That's a long time."

He placed his hand under my chin and raised my eyes to his. "Before I went off to school, you asked me to marry you. You thought maybe that would make me stay."

I removed his hand from my chin. "I was eight and you were eighteen. It would never have worked out."

"You even gave me a ring made from aluminum foil. You had painted it gold, and glued rhinestones on it."

I laughed and put my drink on the coffee table. "I had forgotten about that ring. I stole the rhinestones from one of Mother's dresses. She about killed me when she found that dress."

"I still have that ring," he disclosed.

My heart skipped a beat as his eyes stared into mine. A nerve-racking silence settled between us. I looked away and fidgeted on the couch, pretending to get comfortable.

He picked up his beer from the table. "What brought on tonight's anxiety attack?"

I took a deep breath. "I had a fight with my mother. She yelled, I listened and then I hung up on her. Never have hung up on her before."

"Let me guess. She's mad because you're here and not in New Orleans planning your wedding. Is that what brought on the attack?"

"No, her telling me about the three hundred people she has on her guest list. That's what did it."

He lightly chuckled. "I'm sure my name is not on that list." He took another sip from his longneck.

"I will be adding your family to my list."

"Thanks, but I have no intention of watching you throw your life away at an expensively catered affair." He pointed down at my left hand. "I thought I told you not to wear that ring tonight."

"Yeah, I wore it, so what?" I jumped from the couch. "Stop treating me like a child, Jean Marc; and while you're at it, you can stop acting like a child, as well."

"Me?" He slammed his bottle of beer on the coffee table. "You're the child here, Nora. Letting people boss you around, having an anxiety attack because you hung up on your mother." He stood up next to me.

"I did not have an anxiety attack because of that. I had one because…." I stopped and turned away. "I have to get out of here," I mumbled, and started for the front door.

"Oh, no." Jean Marc was behind me, racing me to the door. "You're not leaving here just when things start to get interesting." He leapt in front of the door, blocking my escape.

"Get out of my way!"

"Why, Nora? Why are you running from me? What are you so afraid of?"

"I'm not afraid of anything, especially not you. Now let me out of here." I reached for the door handle.

"Not until you tell me what has upset you?" He grabbed my arms, pinning them to my sides.

"I can't do this," I whispered as the fight faded within me. "I thought if I came here and saw you…but I can't just throw everything away for you."

He moved his face closer to mine. "Do you have feelings for me, Nora?" He grinned, a cruel grin. "Maybe you had a panic attack because tonight you realized you can't marry John."

"I have to marry John!"

"You don't love him, Nora!"

"I care for him," I insisted in a quivering voice.

"Admit it." His lips hovered over mine. "You're in love with me."

My knees began caving in. "I'm not in love with you."

He wrapped me in his arms. "Yes, you are. You've always been in love with me, Nora. Just like I've always been in love with you."

His lips came down ruthlessly on mine just as my legs gave way. He pressed my body to his and a rush of passion consumed me. I was overwhelmed by his kiss, overcome by the force and desire behind it. I wanted to pull away, but then again I did not want it to stop.

His kissed my cheek and forehead. "How do you feel now?"

"I'm not sure," I admitted as his lips burned against my skin.

Suddenly, he let me go. "What am I doing?" He turned away from me. "Go back to the house, Nora." He opened the front door. "I don't want to compete with another man. I've done it before and I really don't want to go down that road again. If you want me and just me, you know where to find me."

I examined Jean Marc's profile as he stood beside the open door. I noticed how his straight nose sloped down perfectly to his upper lip, the strong line of his jaw, and the way his jaw muscles were flexing under his cheek.

"You're right." I sighed and took a step toward the door. "I can't have both of you."

I ran from the house and across the clearing just as the last gasps of sunlight were fading behind the trees.

CHAPTER 20

For the next three days I stayed inside Gaspard House and never ventured beyond the back porch. I took care of Henri, helped Ms. Marie with chores, and when I wasn't needed for anything, I sat on my bed, thinking.

I kept running the conversation with Jean Marc over in my mind. He had said he loved me, and it had not been because it was the right moment or time to define our relationship. His declaration had been spontaneous, passionate, and completely unexpected. Or was it? That was what really bothered me. I guess I had always known how he felt, but never wanted to confront it.

For years I had believed that I was impervious to my mother's toxic tirades against the Gaspard family, but looking back, I had to question if some of her venom had not found its way under my skin. Perhaps if she had been more accepting of them, I would have been more receptive to Jean Marc. All my life I thought I had been ignoring my mother's constant nagging, only to discover I had been listening all along.

As I deliberated on my growing feelings for Jean Marc, my thoughts eventually turned to John. The practical Dr. Blessing had never made me feel the way Jean Marc had. His timetable of how to proceed with our relationship had cut me off from my emotions. But Jean Marc had awakened those dormant emotions. With him I was empowered, alive, and ready to conquer the world. With John, I simply wanted to disappear into a hole and never again face the sunshine.

I placed my head in my hands and sighed. "Mother is going to have a stroke."

* * *

The following afternoon I had just put Henri in bed for a nap after one of his physical therapy sessions when I joined Ms. Marie in the kitchen. Henri was making progress and was able to stand and walk without assistance, but his right foot still dragged behind him and his right hand was still too weak to hold on to objects such as a spoon or fork. Ms. Marie, on the other hand, believed that every day brought new miracles of recovery.

"Don't he look wonderful?" she happily declared as I sat at the kitchen table. "I think every day he gets better and better. Why, soon he'll be gettin' 'round like his ole self again."

"It may take some time, Ms. Marie," I insisted, feeling Henri's miraculous recovery may have reached a plateau. "His physical abilities may not improve much more. He will get stronger, but he may always have some problems with his right foot and hand."

"Nonsense," the doting mother responded as she refilled my mug of coffee. "My boy will recover just fine. He'll get that hand back, and soon he'll be runnin' 'bout the place just like when he was mon p'tit'boug."

"I hope so, Ms. Marie," I said, picking up the mug of coffee.

"Why don't you let me cook you somethin', child? You're so thin, and I don't think you've been eatin' enough since you came here. I'm worried about you, Nora T."

"I'm fine, Ms. Marie." I eagerly sipped my hot coffee.

"Miss your fiancé, I 'spect." She walked across the kitchen and put the coffee pot on the warmer.

I peered down into my black coffee as the guilt swirled within me. "It's hard being away from him."

"Is that why you stopped wearin' your ring?"

I struggled to come up with some plausible explanation. "I didn't want to damage it," I eventually told her.

Ms. Marie came back to the table. "I saw it settin' on your night table. I thought perhaps there was another reason."

"No, there's no other reason," I assured her and then quickly took another gulp of coffee.

"Have you been to see Jean Marc's house?"

I put my mug down on the table, avoiding her inquisitive gaze. "Yes, it's quite beautiful."

"Mais oui." She took a seat in the chair next to me. "When he first came back from Texas I fretted 'bout him. That girl over there, you know the one he married…."

"Cynthia," I inserted.

"That bonne a rienne, good for nothing woman. She broke his heart so I thought it would never heal. Then he started fixin' up that cottage. Started workin' with his papa at the company, and slowly he seemed to get back to his ole self. But somethin' was still missin' in him. I never could put my finger on it, until the other day at the hospital I realized what it was."

I smiled at her. "Really? What was that?"

"It was you."

My heart trembled and my jittery hand reached for my mug of coffee.

"You know, Nora T, I've watched you and Jean Marc ever since you were little, tearin' 'round in the bushes, chasin' mouche a mielle, what you say…bumble bees. All you ever had to do was call his name and he came a runnin' to you. There was no one could make my Jean Marc smile like you could. I saw it again at the hospital; you walked in the room and my Jean Marc came alive. He's been in love with you ever since you first came to Gaspard House, but somehow I 'spect you already knew that."

I raised my head and confidently confronted her warm brown eyes. "Ms. Marie, I am marrying John Blessing. You're right, I love Jean Marc, but as a friend, as a podna."

She sat for a moment just staring at me, and I squirmed under the weight of her eyes. She stood from her chair and went to the sink.

"Did I ever tell you 'bout the time your Uncle Jacques asked me to the prom?" she inquired as she looked out the window behind the kitchen sink.

"I remember hearing something about it," I admitted, not sure of where this conversation was headed.

Her oval face sobered and her eyes became touched with sadness. "I went with Emile Gaspard to the prom and turned your Uncle Jacques down. But do you know why I went with Emile?"

"No." I took another swig of coffee.

"I was a very silly pet't' fille, Nora T." She turned to me. "You must understand, I grew up poor and the Gaspards were the wealthiest family in Manchac. When Emile Gaspard even noticed me, I used to get motier faux…half crazy. Somethin' your Uncle Jacques never liked. Your uncle, he was my beau in school. We even planned on marryin' one day." She gently stroked the deep umber granite countertop with her slender fingers. "Then Emile Gaspard came along. When my papa found out a Gaspard fancied me, he ordered me to drop Jacques Mouton and go to the prom with Emile. Said I had to do it for mon famile."

"You and Uncle Jack?"

She nodded, smiling, "When I told Jacques 'bout what my papa had said, he understood and told me to go with Emile. Eight months later, Emile asked me to marry him and I agreed, but on one condition. I made Emile promise to give Jacques a job at Gaspard Fisheries. Jacques' family was so poor. I wanted to make sure they'd always be taken care of, and workin' for Gaspard Fisheries meant you were set for life in Manchac."

"Did you love him?" I asked, wrapping my hands around my warm mug.

"Emile? I grew to love him, and two years later when my Henri and Jean Marc came, it was easier. I put Jacques out of my mind." She sighed and looked away. "But then Elise Caldwell came to work as a secretary for Emile. She met Jacques, and I watched them fall in love, even went to their weddin'. Leavin' the man you love is hard enough, child, but watchin' him find love with another is a cruel reminder of what you gave away."

"I never knew. Did my mother know about you and Uncle Jack?"

"Absolument." She laughed, a light tinkling kind of laugh "Claire was madder than a tahyo when she heard I was marryin' Emile Gaspard. Everyone in town knew she had eyes for the Gaspard family fortune. Not long after I married Emile, she set her sights on his brother Etienne, and she got him."

"Did you ever tell Uncle Jack about this?"

"No need to, child. He always knew why I married Emile."

"But now you two have a second chance. Aunt Elise and Mr. Gaspard are gone. You can start over."

"There's no second chances at love, Nora T. It's either always there, shinin' bright, or it dims out and fades away. The love I had for your uncle, I still have, but Jacques…." Her lower lip trembled. "He loved his Elise. Broke his heart when she passed on; broke my heart when I realized at her funeral that he'd found true love with another."

I stared into my half-empty mug of coffee for a few moments, finding the nerve to say what was on my mind.

"Why are you telling me this, Ms. Marie?"

"Jean Marc, of course. You love him, don't you, mon p'tit'? So don't waste the rest of your life wonderin'. Marryin' that doctor would make your mama happy, but you would regret it sooner or later." She smiled as she took in my shocked face. "Parents are the burden to their children, Nora T, not the other way 'round. We try to make them happy, but in the end we're the ones who suffer. My papa pushed me into marryin' Emile, just like your mama is pushin' you into marryin' that doctor. Don't make my mistake. Don't settle for somethin' you never really wanted in the first place."

"Do you regret marrying Emile Gaspard?"

"I regret not takin' a chance with Jacques Mouton. I was content with Emile and he was good to me, but perhaps Jacques could have made me somethin' better."

I put my mug on the table. "I think you and Uncle Jack still have a chance, Ms. Marie."

She winked at me. "You and Jean Marc still have a chance, too."

CHAPTER 21

After the house had settled down for the night, I went to the back porch and looked out in the direction of Jean Marc's cottage. Through the trees I could see the glow of his lights. As a warm summer breeze drifted by, I entertained the idea of a life with Jean Marc. I thought of the way his body felt next to mine, the touch of his hands against my skin, and the passion his kisses awakened in me. A sudden rush of something unfamiliar overtook me. It was an overwhelming realization that this thing between us, this energy, was right. No acid churning in my stomach, no more twisted anger deep within the pit of my being. There was just a pure sense of bliss.

I bounded down the porch steps and headed across the clearing behind the house. Like a moth eager to find guidance in the night, I set out in the direction of those cottage lights, determined to find out if what I felt for Jean Marc could last a lifetime.

When I arrived at his porch steps, I heard voices coming from behind the cottage. I slipped around the side of the house, trying my best not to make a sound. After I crept around the corner, I could see Jean Marc and another man loading boxes on to a small flatboat tied up to his dock.

"You know where to go, Pierre?" Jean Marc asked.

"Oui, past Owl Bayou to North Pass. The usual drop off point," the other man said in a raspy voice.

"Come back here when you're done." Jean Marc paused. "You have your gun, Pierre?"

Pierre patted the butt of a gun sticking out from the waistband of his dirty jeans. "Loaded and ready, Jean Marc, but I ain't 'spectin' no trouble." He climbed into the boat and started the engine.

"Just keep your eyes open," Jean Marc warned over the sound of the engine.

Pierre maneuvered the flatboat, piled high with boxes, away from the dock and into the swamp. After Pierre's boat had disappeared behind a veil of darkness, Jean Marc marched down the dock and through the back door of his house. When I heard the back screen door slam closed, my heart rose in my throat. Suddenly, all of my mother's ramblings about Jean Marc and his shady past came hurtling to the forefront of my thoughts. I slowly backed away from the side of the house, keeping my eyes on the empty dock. When I came around the corner of the front porch, I heard the sound of something moving behind me.

"Care to tell me what you're doing out here?"

I twisted around to see Jean Marc with his .9mm pistol in his hand, glaring at me.

He grabbed my arm. "What did you see, Nora?"

"What the hell is going on, Jean Marc? What was all that about on the dock?"

He pulled me to the screen door on the front porch.

"You shouldn't have been sneaking around like that. I could have shot you." He dragged me inside the house and slammed the old cypress front door closed with his foot.

He let go of my arm. "What are you doing here, Nora?" he gruffly demanded as he placed the gun on a table by the door.

"Oh, no. You're going to tell me what that was all about on the dock back there."

"What do you think it was?" he asked, his voice peppered with anger.

"It looked like you were smuggling stuff through the swamps."

He chuckled. "What would you know about smuggling?"

"I know what I saw, Jean Marc."

He raised his dark eyebrows. "What you saw? Maybe I was shipping goods to another business, transporting shellfish or parts." He walked toward the kitchen. "I never figured you to be the kind to spy on people, Nora," he added over his shoulder.

I followed him to the kitchen. "I wasn't spying. I came here looking for you."

He removed two beers from his refrigerator. "Why?"

"I wanted to talk to you."

He picked up the opener and popped the tops off both of the bottles. "I think we said just about all there is to say between us the other day. You're going to marry that idiot doctor no matter my feelings for you. What else do you have to add?" He came up to me and handed me a beer.

I took the green bottle from his hand. "First, tell me what that was on the dock?"

He took a sip from his beer and moved toward the couch. "You're not going to like hearing it."

"But I would rather hear the truth from you than a lie."

He had a seat on the couch. "You've seen my books. You know what a deep financial hole my company is in. How do you think I'm able to keep Gaspard Fisheries going?"

I approached the couch. "I know your family history. I've heard the stories. You've gone back to smuggling, haven't you?" I took a drink of beer.

"You're letting your imagination run away with you." He scowled and then his features softened as his eyes studied me. "What would you think of me if I told you that I was smuggling?" he asked.

I sat down next to him. "Nothing would change between us, Jean Marc."

"Are you sure about that?"

"How long has this been going on?"

He sat back on the couch, letting an unseen weight press him down into the soft leather. "Five years." He glanced down at the bottle in his hand. "Twelve years ago when I returned from Texas, I tried, really tried, to make a go of the business. I sank all the money I had into the fisheries, but it wasn't working. Finally, the money ran out and I had to go back to what I knew best. One run a month became five, and the money started pouring in. I've cut back in the past two years, and I have other men, men I can trust who need the money, making the runs now."

"What are you smuggling?"

He shrugged as he evaded my eyes. "Electronics, booze, exotic animals, whatever is needed. I draw the line at drugs. I've never done that, and I never will. Smuggling is dangerous enough without adding drugs into the mix."

"Is that why your man in the boat needed a gun?"

He nodded. "One can never be too careful."

I knew I should have hurried out of that cottage, but I couldn't. Something inside me refused to give up on Jean Marc. My father had always taught me that one should never judge a man because of what he has done without first looking at why he has done it.

"You need to get out of this business, Jean Marc," I finally said as I placed my beer on the coffee table.

"I know, and I have been trying to do just that. There are other things I want to do with my life besides sleep with a gun under my pillow." He swallowed back a long swig of the alcohol.

"What other things?"

He kept his eyes peeled on the coffee table before him. "Now that you know my dirty little secret, perhaps it would be best if you just tell me why you came here. Then you can head back to the house and never come here again. When cousin Ethel arrives next week, you can go back to your life in New Orleans."

"I don't want to go back to my life in New Orleans."

He raised his eyes to me. "I find that hard to believe. I thought you were bound and determined to marry that doctor of yours."

I edged closer to him. "I thought I wanted to marry John, but then I realized you were right."

He grinned at me. "I was right? Right about what?"

I shrugged. "John. I can't marry him. How can I marry one man when I really belong to another?"

His face became like stone. "Who do you belong to, Nora?"

"You," I casually stated as I nodded to him.

He put his beer down on the coffee table next to mine. "What does dear Dr. John have to say about this?"

"I haven't told him yet. I wanted to see what you thought of my idea first."

Jean Marc's face softened and he leaned toward me. "Are you sure? Considering what you have just learned about me, you might want to go right back to John."

My heart began to beat furiously. My toes tingled and my stomach danced with butterflies. "I must admit, your smuggling activities do pose a problem."

He moved closer to me. "Then I'll quit, starting right now. I'll find a way to make the business work."

I placed my hand on his chest. "You will give it up, just like that?"

He positioned his lips right above mine. "Just like that."

"I don't believe you."

"Try," he whispered, and then he kissed me.

An electric charge rushed through my body when he kissed me. I opened my mouth, accepting him, and he wrapped his brawny arms about my waist. As I eased into him, all the apprehension I felt about leaving John and disappointing my mother instantly vanished.

He pulled away. "I can think of a thousand reasons to tell you to get the hell out of here right now, Nora." He stood from the couch and helped me to my feet.

I slipped my arms about his neck. "I'm not going anywhere, Jean Marc."

He stared into my eyes. "Ever since I came back from Texas and saw you all grown-up, I have done nothing but think about you. I want you, Nora. I've always wanted you."

"Perhaps that's why I was always so mean to you. I was afraid to admit that I wanted you, too."

He unclasped my arms from about his neck and led me toward the stairs. When he reached the foot of the steps, he stopped and placed his hands about my face. "Are you sure? I don't want to rush you into this."

I slowly began undoing the buttons of his long-sleeved blue shirt as I gave him a seductive smile. "We've waited long enough, Jean Marc."

He took my hand and quickly pulled me up the stairs. When we reached the second floor landing, he lifted me into his arms and carried me down a short hallway to his bedroom door.

I bit down hard on his right nipple as he pushed the bedroom door open.

"You're killing me, Nora," he groaned as he took me to a large mahogany sleigh bed waiting in the center of the dimly lit room.

I giggled against him. "I thought that was the idea."

Kissing my lips, he lowered me on to the dark green bedspread. He stood back from the bed and removed his shirt. "Two can play at that game," he declared as he threw his shirt to the floor and climbed onto the bed.

He immediately began easing me out of my T-shirt and bra. His fingertips gently caressed my breasts and when he pinched my nipples, I moaned.

Aroused by his touch, I pressed my body against his warm flesh and reached down to the fly of his jeans. But when I began fumbling with the buttons, a pang of uncertainty gripped me as I remembered my encounters with John.

"What do you want me to do?" I asked breathlessly.

Jean Marc stopped and looked at me. "Do?"

My face flushed. "Is there someway you want me to be, or certain things you want me to do?"

He stroked my left cheek. "I just want you to be you, Nora."

"I'm sorry, but John used to always tell me—"

He placed his finger against my lips. "Forget about him." He traced his lips up the side of my neck to my earlobe, "Just do whatever feels right," he whispered.

His lips felt like warm silk against my skin. "I don't think I ever knew how to do that," I admitted.

"I'll show you. Making love is like a dance, darlin'. We must learn to move together as one." He placed my hands above my head. "Just relax."

I tried to relax my body against the bed, but when Jean Marc's teeth scraped the nape of my neck, I shuddered.

"Move with me, Nora." He reached for my jeans and slowly pushed them down over my hips. After he tossed my underwear aside, Jean Marc ran his hand along the inside of my thighs, urging my legs apart. When his hand came to rest on my delicate folds, I closed my eyes. His lips teased my throat as his fingers slid inside me.

I gasped against his cheek

"Give in to what you are feeling," he said as he drove his fingers into me.

I gripped the comforter and arched my body against the bed.

"That's it," he whispered as he started slowly moving his fingers in and out of me. "Now you're learning how to dance."

The tension in my body began to build and I yearned for him to go deeper. A swell of pleasure took over my senses until I thought I could not stand it any longer. When the orgasm erupted, I buried my head in his chest as I bucked against him.

Just as I began to catch my breath, Jean Marc wriggled beside me. When I opened my eyes, he was lying naked next to me. I rolled over and let my fingertips traverse the outline of the thick muscles in his chest, shoulders and arms.

Jean Marc leaned away from me and reached over to a small nightstand next to the bed.

"What are you doing?" I asked while my hands explored his round butt.

He kissed my cheek as he removed something from the drawer. "Just taking precautions."

Jean Marc spread my legs wide apart and pulled my hips to his. He kissed my breasts, and then teased my right nipple with his teeth as his fingers stroked my sensitive flesh.

I wrapped my legs about him and looked up into his dark eyes. "Yes, Jean Marc."

He kept his eyes on mine as he entered me in one slow thrust.

Enfolding me in his arms, he began to move inside me. I pushed my hips against his, urging him deeper. He responded by driving harder into me. My hips rocked back and forth with every powerful penetration. I clung to him, and soon we were moving together as one. My body tingled as the climax quickly spiraled up my spine. I bit down into his shoulder as the spasms of quivering rolled through me. When the passion overwhelmed me, I threw my head back and cried out his name.

Jean Marc's arms tightened around me as he began to arch his back, slamming his hips faster into mine.

I held him against me as the last waves of his climax rolled through him. When he finally settled his head against my shoulder, he turned his face to me and kissed my cheek.

"Now you're mine," he softly said.

I ran my hands through his wavy hair and whispered, "I've never done that before."

"What?" he murmured against my skin.

My cheeks burned, but I said nothing.

"What? Tell me, Nora."

I shook my head. "I've never…you know. I always had to fake it before. I never had one when I was with a man."

He sat up slightly. "Even with John?"

I nodded.

He removed a strand of blond hair from my face. "Why would you want to marry a man who didn't please you in every way?"

"Because he was there. He wanted me. I figured if no one else wanted me, why not marry him?"

"But I wanted you," Jean Marc asserted.

"I thought you didn't like me. You were always so abrupt with me whenever we saw each other."

Jean Marc's deep laugh filled the bedroom. "Nora, I was abrupt because I was frustrated as hell every time I saw you. It was driving me crazy, and I didn't know how to get through to you."

"You could have just asked me out on a date," I suggested and sat up in the bed.

Jean Marc sat up next to me. "If I had asked, would you have gone out on a date with me?"

I studied his rugged features and frowned. "Probably not."

He shook his head. "See my point."

"I guess." I curled my body into his broad chest. "Can I ask you a question?"

His strong arms enveloped me. "Can I stop you?"

"Why did you marry Cynthia?"

Jean Marc rested his head against mine. "She reminded me of you. She was smart, funny, asked a lot of questions, and seemed filled with an innocent enthusiasm for the world around her. After we were married, I realized she was a poor substitute for the woman I really wanted. I began to pull away, and she turned to someone else for comfort."

"When I was a little girl, I always dreamed that one day we would be together. Then you went off to college and I figured it was time to give up on my dream. But somewhere in the back of my mind, I never could forget about you."

"I'm glad to see your head has finally accepted what your heart knew all along."

I smiled as I thought of the years we had wasted. "Why do you think it took us so long to finally get here?"

Jean Marc sighed as he settled his body against mine. "Sometimes you have to discover what you don't want in order to appreciate what it is you really need. Once you have lived, only then can you truly love."

As Jean Marc held me, I mulled over his words. Maybe we have to suffer through the bad to appreciate the good in our lives. If John had not come along, I might not have discovered my feelings for Jean Marc. The dark trials of life had a way of making the special moments shine a little bit brighter for all of us. Maybe it was not so much that we had to first live before we found love, but that we had to first love before we truly started living.

CHAPTER 22

I awoke in the middle of the night to find Jean Marc gone from the king-sized bed. I scanned the darkened bedroom, and fumbled to find a lamp on the nightstand by the bed. When I turned the switch, the small bedroom was flooded in a warm light. I took in the plain oak chest of drawers next to the bed and the round nightstand with the white porcelain lamp on top. I spotted the small drawer in the nightstand Jean Marc had reached into earlier that night. After pulling the drawer open, I peaked inside and found a few packages of condoms, and a hammerless .32 caliber handgun. I picked up the gun and felt its weight. I thought back to the .9mm pistol I had seen Jean Marc carrying in his hand earlier that evening. With all I had learned about him, I wasn't too surprised to discover another gun in Jean Marc's home. I replaced the revolver in the drawer and climbed out of the bed. To the right of the bedroom was a blue and white-tiled bathroom, but Jean Marc was not in there. Then, through the silence of the night, I heard the sound of a boat motor. A few seconds later, the slap of the screen door broke through the quiet of the house, and I listened as someone came running up the stairs.

"You're up," Jean Marc commented as he stopped in front of the bedroom door.

He had on his jeans, but had not buttoned up his rumpled long-sleeved blue shirt, and his muscular chest peeked out from behind the fabric.

I stepped from the bathroom doorway. "Where did you go?"

His eyes hungrily took in my naked body. "I had to take care of some business." He shrugged off his shirt and hung it on a green wing chair by the door.

I spied the .9mm pistol in the waistband of his jeans. "I heard the boat motor outside. Want to tell me what you were doing?"

He took the gun from his waistband and put it on the chest of drawers. "I had to meet with my man after his run."

"Was there a problem?" I asked, staring at the gun.

He came up to me. "No. He was just letting me know how it went. Forget about that. Right now I have other matters to concern myself with."

I stroked my hands up and down his thick chest. "Other matters?"

He slid his arm around my back. "Yeah, like keeping you satisfied."

I reached for the fly on his jeans and began to slowly undo the buttons one by one. "Satisfied?" I grinned. "Who said I was satisfied?" I eased the jeans down from around his hips.

He stepped out of his jeans and kicked them away. "That is something I will have to work on," he mumbled as he kissed my shoulder.

"Then you better get cracking, buddy," I teased as I slapped his firm backside.

Jean Marc picked me up in his arms and carried me to the bed.

"I'm going to spend the rest of my life making you happy, Nora Theresa Kehoe," he whispered, lowering me on to the bed.

I placed my hands about his wide shoulders. "I'm already happy, Jean Marc."

He kissed me and I wrapped my legs around his hips, eager for more of him.

His fingers traveled down my stomach until they came to the mound of flesh in between my legs. "Happy, but not satisfied…yet."

* * *

The tinkle of the raindrops against the window behind Jean Marc's sleigh bed roused me from a deep sleep. His thick arms were draped about me, and I could feel his naked body spooned against my back. I listened to the rhythm of his breathing and felt the rise and fall of his chest. It was the most comforting sensation I had ever known.

I slowly wrestled free of Jean Marc's embrace, trying all the while not to wake him. When I was finally able to climb from the bed, I quickly searched for something to stave off the early morning chill. I found his blue long-sleeved shirt on the wing back chair by the door and slipped it on. The cotton shirt still had his scent on it, and I breathed in the aroma of him as I wrapped it around my body. When I looked back to the bed, I saw his face scrunched against his pillow, looking like a little boy dreaming of cowboys and Indians. Somewhere deep inside me a yearning began. I wanted to spend every morning for the rest of my life gazing down at that handsome face and watching Jean Marc Gaspard dream.

I tiptoed down the creaky stairway to the first floor landing. In the darkness, I fumbled my way toward the kitchen, desperately looking for something to eat. As I trudged along the floor, feeling my way with my bare feet, I heard the grumble of my stomach.

"Serves you right," I scolded. "I haven't had a workout like that since playing on the high school volleyball team." I smiled, remembering the feel of Jean Marc's hands on my skin, his mouth kissing my flesh, the weight of his body on mine, and the way he moved inside me.

I silently cursed. "Get a grip, Nora." I wiped a film of sweat from my forehead. "John never did this to me."

I opened the refrigerator door and began fanning myself, trying desperately to cool my ardor.

"You'll catch a cold doing that."

I jumped as Jean Marc entered the kitchen, dressed only in his blue jeans.

"You scared me." I nodded to the refrigerator. "I was hungry."

"You came down here to raid my fridge, or are you using it as an air conditioner?" He came toward me. "I woke up, and thought you had left."

I inspected the contents of the refrigerator. "Where was I going to go?"

"You could have gone back to the house, or back to John."

"There will be no going back to John," I proclaimed.

"No regrets?"

"Regrets?" I stood from the refrigerator and smiled. "'Regrets only show up in the rearview mirror of life,' my dad used to always say. The way to avoid them is not to bother looking back." I reached out and touched the dark stubble on his chin. "I'm only looking ahead from now on."

"I'm happy to hear it." He peered into the open refrigerator door. "I'm afraid the only thing in here is eggs, a package of shredded cheddar cheese and…." He reached in and grabbed some foreign looking green object wrapped in plastic. "This," he added.

"What is that?"

"I'm not sure." He turned it over in his hand. "It's either a very old green pepper, or something that is not of this earth." He tossed the green moldy thing into the nearby trash. "I'll make us some omelets."

"You never get to the store much," I remarked as he retrieved the eggs and cheese.

He stepped in front of the cooktop. "Never have time." He placed the eggs and cheese on the black granite countertop next to him. "When I'm not out of town, I usually pick up something on the way home for dinner. Lunch, I always eat out." He reached for a large frying pan in a light oak cabinet above his head.

"How often do you have to go out of town?"

He placed the pan on the cooktop. "Usually once a month for the business."

"Doing what?"

"Dealing with clients," he coolly replied as he pulled out a glass bowl from another cabinet to his left.

"Do you have a lot of out of town clients?"

He nodded as he put the bowl on the counter. "Quite a few."

"Really?" I folded my arms across my chest. "Like where?"

He sighed and reached for the eggs. “Nora, do you want me to cook for you or do you want to interrogate me?”

“Sorry. I was just curious.” I waved to the bowl on the counter. “You really don’t have to cook. We could sneak over to the house and grab something to eat. Your mother made a big pot of gumbo yesterday.”

He shook his head. “Henri’s home. I won’t go near the place if I have to look at him.”

I stared at him, slightly taken aback by his comment. “After everything Henri has been through, how you can’t still feel such animosity toward him?”

Jean Marc snorted as he broke some eggs into the glass bowl. “There has never been anything emotionally between us. Ever since we were children, we have been distant.” He beat the eggs with a fork. “As far as what my brother has been through,” he added some shredded cheddar to the eggs, “it’s nothing less than he deserves.”

I leaned my hip against the counter next to him. “Don’t you think you’re being a little hard on him?”

“Nora, don’t try and make me look through that rearview mirror of yours when it comes to my brother.” He mixed the eggs and cheese together. “My family is filled with nothing but regrets about Henri. My father bailed him out of a lot of fights, a few pregnant girlfriends who needed abortions, and even a jail sentence or two. I think that’s what drove my father to an early grave. Now it’s my turn to be my brother’s keeper.”

“What do you mean?”

He poured the eggs and cheese into the large frying pan. “Who do you think is paying for all that fancy health care he’s getting at the house? Henri had no insurance. I had to shell out a bundle for the hospital and the doctors.”

“But why are you paying his bills?”

“Mother asked me to. She thought it would help mend fences between Henri and me. She has been trying to get us to make up for years.”

“Make up? I don’t understand, Jean Marc.”

"When I came back from Texas, Henri was supposedly helping our father run Gaspard Fisheries, except I found out Henri was stealing from the company, and was using the trawlers for running drugs through the swamps for some associates of his. Father was ill by this time and I didn't want to make things worse for him, so I confronted Henri, privately."

"What happened?"

He shrugged. "We fought, like always. It got physical and I finally convinced him to leave Gaspard Fisheries and my parents alone."

I raised my eyebrows skeptically. "You convinced him?"

"That scar down his right cheek." He traced a finger down his right cheek. "A reminder of our bargain. He has never forgiven me for taking over the business, and I have never forgiven him for almost bankrupting our family." He placed his arm about my waist and pulled me next to him. "So, don't feel too sorry for my brother." He paused for a moment and then frowned. "I want you to consider yourself on notice as far as Henri is concerned. Next week, when cousin Ethel arrives, you are to move in here with me."

I was stunned by his proposal. "Move in here? And do what?"

"Help me run Gaspard Fisheries, of course. We can build our little empire."

"What about my life, my job, my home back in the city?"

"To hell with all of it." He flipped the omelet gracefully over in the pan and then moved toward the cabinet to the right of the sink. "Your place is going to be here with me."

As I watched Jean Marc searching for a plate, the certainty of last night returned to me. No feelings of doubt ate at me. My stomach was quiet and the only burning I felt was my hunger for food. The inner depths of my being were calm.

"Maybe you should call John right now and tell him of your change in plans," Jean Marc suggested as he slid the omelet on to a large blue plate. "Better to get the bad stuff over with early."

"It's still dark outside." I said, looking out the kitchen window to the bayou.

"When are you going to tell him?"

"I don't know. Perhaps I should wait a bit."

"Perhaps I should call him," Jean Marc grumbled, his merciless eyes probing mine.

"I get the message. I'll call him today and tell him it's over. I hope he doesn't come here to try and talk me out of it." I paused and thought for a moment. "Maybe I should just wait and go back to New Orleans to tell him."

Jean Marc shook his head as he placed the plate in front of me. "Not a good idea." He handed me fork. "What if he calls you before you confront him? Are you going to lie and pretend everything is fine between you two?"

I took the fork and shrugged. "He's already called, but I've been busy with Henri. I could just be busy when he calls."

"He'll know something is wrong, Nora. Any man would." Jean Marc turned away to put the frying pan in the sink.

"I think he already knows something is wrong." I sighed as I broke a piece off the omelet with my fork. "But John won't be the real problem."

"Claire?" Jean Marc asked, turning back to me.

"When she finds out I'm canceling her dream wedding, she'll kill me."

"Well, she'll have to go through me first, darlin'." He stepped to my side and kissed my cheek. "And your Uncle Jack."

"What do we tell Uncle Jack and your mother?"

"Mother will be overjoyed. As for Jack?" Jean Marc winked at me. "I think he already suspects. Once you get rid of that fiancé of yours, we can tell everyone, officially. Then, we will deal with Claire."

"You will deal with Claire." I made the sign of the cross over him with my fork. "And may God have mercy on your soul."

* * *

After the sun came up, I returned to the main house. When I opened the back door and stepped into the kitchen, a wave of smoke accosted me. At first, I thought something was burning, but then I saw the culprit sitting by the kitchen table smoking a cigarette.

"You're sleeping with him," Henri clearly pronounced as the smoke billowed around his head.

He was grinning at me with the cigarette smoldering in his left hand while his right hand was still curled up, useless, against his side.

I walked slowly over to the table. "Look who's made a miraculous recovery."

"Only for you, dear Nora." He took another puff on his cigarette. "As far as the rest of the house is concerned, I'm still weak and feeble Henri, all right?"

"What makes you think I would go along with that?" I asked, taking the cigarette from his hand.

"You're screwing my brother while still engaged to another man." He waved his good hand at me. "So don't pass judgment on me, little one. Besides, what would your mother say? Claire would die if she thought you were involved with Jean Marc. You know how she hates all of us Gaspards."

"Why show me this?" I put the cigarette out in the ashtray on the table.

"I need you to play along with my little disability." He pulled at his right hand. "At least some of it is true, but up here…." He tapped at his head with his left hand. "That's intact."

"Why should I play along?"

"You know how Jean Marc feels about me. First sign I can be on my own, he'll pitch me out of here faster than a pelican can snag a fish from the water. I need to stay a while longer, get stronger, and collect some funds. You can help me. Keep Jean Marc distracted while I get ready."

I placed my hand on my hip and stared at him. "Did you have something to do with that girl's death?"

"You know Henri ain't no murderer. I like the ladies, Nora. I don't kill them. But the men I owe, they're the ones that sliced her up."

"The men you owe?"

"My backers." He paused and then chuckled at me. "Nora, you've lived in New Orleans all your life, but you have no idea what really goes on inside of the French Quarter. The cults that exist there are a powerful attractant to the weak-minded. There are a few men that organize those cults, collect dues from the followers, and recruit new initiates from the homeless teenagers that flock to the city thanks to Anne Rice and her vampire novels. Kids come to New Orleans seeking vampires and voodoo. These guys I work for give it to them."

I took a wary step back from him. "What are you talking about?"

"My backers are the ones who set me up in my group. They brought me some of my members and spread the word around town that I was something special. I made them a lot of money, and got them boys or girls for their other interests."

"What the hell are you involved with, Henri?"

"Can you see why I need to hide out here? I'll eventually have to get out of town, but I need to stay here until I'm ready. I don't want to hurt anyone, but if the men I work for think I'm like Jell-O, then I'm safe. As soon as anyone finds out I have all my wits about me and can talk, I'll be killed."

"But what about the stuff you drank and the seizures you had? You couldn't have faked that."

"A simple miscalculation on my part. I was supposed to appear enlightened for my followers. I was even going to tell them you were an evil spirit and chase you out of our meeting that night." He scratched his head. "In the right amounts that little drug I'm supplied with can make you seem very omnipotent."

"What is it?"

"I'm not sure. The men I work for get it from some old Indian in New Mexico."

I looked over at Henri; my head was still reeling from the information he had just given me. "The girl, the one who died. She drank that stuff?"

He nodded reluctantly. "Yeah. My backers use it to break in new additions to their stables; if the boy or girl rebels too much, the doctor cuts them up."

"The doctor? Jesus, Henri, from what I heard a precision surgeon mutilated that girl. Who are these people you work for?"

"Men who will kill anyone who gets in their way." He struggled to get out of his chair, and then with his good hand he pulled himself to a standing position. "Now you know my secret and I know yours. Keep Jean Marc occupied for another week, help me collect some money, and keep your mouth shut about this. If my brother finds out, he'll just call the cops and I'll be hauled away. Mother will be devastated and eventually my associates will find me…and kill me. So you see, I have to keep up this act until I can get away. All right?"

"I don't know, Henri." I examined the long scar along his right cheek and thought of what Jean Marc had told me.

He saw me starring at the scar and quickly turned from me. "The resemblance between me and my brother is rather uncanny, isn't it, Nora? Imagine if someone came here not knowing I had a twin. What would they do to Jean Marc if they thought he was me?" He paused for a moment and then added, "I suggest you think about this."

That burning knot returned to my stomach with a vengeance. I stood riveted to my spot as Henri made his way out of the kitchen, dragging his right foot alongside him. I listened as he slowly shuffled down the hall to his bedroom in the parlor.

"Apparently, the dangerous tiger has awakened," I mumbled, remembering Jean Marc's warning. "And he's going to eat us all alive."

CHAPTER 23

Four hours later, I walked into Henri's room to find Ms. Marie ladling gumbo down his throat. I almost burst into laughter when I saw the napkin secured as a bib around Henri's neck as his mother lovingly spooned mouthfuls of seafood gumbo to her son.

"Ah, he's looking much better today, Nora T," Ms. Marie cooed as she gave the last spoonful of gumbo to Henri. "His color, she is back."

"Yes, he does appear full of it this morning," I commented, giving Henri a sly smile.

Ms. Marie cleared the soup bowl and the bib out of Henri's way. "I'll leave you two to do your therapy." She turned to Henri and kissed his cheek. "Mind Nora T, Henri." Then she placed the soup bowl on a large wooden tray and carried it out of the room.

I waited until the parlor doors were securely closed before I approached Henri's hospital bed.

"Enjoying yourself?"

"Immensely," he replied and wiped his left hand across his mouth. "Mother hasn't paid this much attention to me since I was seven and had the chicken pox."

"You'll break that poor woman's heart when you leave here and she finds out you were never as sick as you pretended. She may never forgive you."

"Mother?" He snickered as he sat up in his bed and made himself comfortable. "She'd forgive the devil himself."

"What about Jean Marc?"

"Now, he could pose something of a problem for me." He arched an eyebrow at me. "Thought about our little situation anymore?"

"Of course." I sat down on the edge of the bed next to him. "Can't think of anything else. But before I agree to your scheme, I want some guarantees, or I swear I'll turn you into the cops myself."

"Oh my, little Nora Kehoe has grown some balls." The smile faded from his thin lips. "What do you want?"

"That when you leave you will never return to Gaspard House, Manchac, or the state of Louisiana. I want to know that your family is free of you forever. No one will ever hear from you or see you again. Agreed?"

He looked me over with his cold eyes for a moment and his smile returned. "You drive a hard bargain, girl. This is my birthright, my land; I may want to bring my children back to this place one day."

"I could throw in your having a vasectomy as part of our agreement, but I think it's safe to say that any woman ever knocked up by the likes of you will never want you around to raise children."

"I could change."

"Do we have a deal or not?" I asked, raising my voice to him.

He hesitated for a moment and then nodded his head. "You're just like Jean Marc. He tried to keep me away."

"Yes, I know about that." I pointed to his right cheek. "If you ever cross me, Henri, I'll be just as ruthless as your brother. I will tell the cops everything, and then I'll find out who you've been working for and I tell them everything, too."

"Vindictive little bitch, aren't you?" He rubbed his right hand with his left. "Is my brother worth all this?"

"I'm protecting him and your mother." I paused and grinned. "You're just like all the stories I've heard about your Uncle Etienne, Henri. Bad to the bone, and you don't give a rat's ass about anyone else but yourself."

He leaned back on his bed and folded his arms across his chest, looking smug. "I guess that means you're gonna help me."

"Yes, Henri, I will help you. But once you leave town, I never want to see you again."

He snorted with disgust. "Trust me, once I'm out of here I'll never come back. Let Jean Marc keep this hellhole."

I opened the parlor doors. "Your therapist should be here shortly. I'll check back with you," I stated loud enough for the rest of the house to hear.

I returned to my room and took a few moments to cool down from my conversation with Henri. Thinking ahead to my next uncomfortable confrontation, I flopped down on the bed. I groaned as I reached for my purse on the night table next to me. I retrieved my cell phone and stared at it, dreading what was about to happen.

"Oh, to hell with it." I dialed the number to John's cell phone.

"Nora!" he shouted into the phone. "Where in the hell have you been? Why haven't you called me? It's been two days since I've talked to you. Do you know how worried I've been?"

"Yes, John, I know it's been a while since we have talked, but I've been busy."

"Busy? Do you know what I have been going through these past few days? Worrying about you taking care of that murder suspect in that house with only an old man to protect you?"

"Jean Marc's around," I assured him.

"Is that supposed to make me feel better? When are you going to come home? I need you here with me. We have things to plan. Father Delacroix has called me three times wanting to schedule the rest of our Pre-Cana sessions. The dress maker needs another fitting, and your mother is screaming about the guest list."

"Yes, I heard." I sighed, sensing the difficulty of the task ahead. "John, I already spoke to Mother. I know about all the wedding stuff, and to tell you the truth…." I held my breath for a moment. "I really don't care."

"You don't care? What is it you don't care about, Nora? Is it the wedding, or is it something else, like me? Is that what you're saying?" He paused. "Or is it someone else? It's that Jean Marc asshole, right? Is he talking you out of the wedding? Goddamn it! I told you that man wanted you, and then you go up there and put yourself at his mercy."

"I'm not at his mercy," I asserted. "For one thing, I've known Jean Marc a hell of a lot longer than you. He's my friend, and I'm fed up with hearing from you and my mother about who I should associate with."

"What in the hell is wrong with you? Why are you snapping at me? I knew I should never have let you go up there."

My grip tightened on my cell phone. "Never let me come up here? John, I don't need your permission to do anything. I'm a grown woman who knows what she wants and what she doesn't want. And the one thing I don't want right now is your bullshit!"

"Nora, do not speak to me in that manner. You're not being rational! I'm coming to get you."

"No, John, I don't want you here, and I am being rational. For the first time in a long time, I'm speaking my mind! This is the real me."

There was a tense silence on the other end of the line. "Nora, I know you have been under a lot of stress lately, and I figured some time away would help you, but—"

"John, didn't you hear what I said? It's not the stress, it's not the wedding, it's me." I paused and summoned my courage. "I can't marry you," I proclaimed.

"Can't or won't?" he quickly asked.

"Does it matter?"

"Think very carefully about this, Nora," John warned, his voice seething with rage. "I'm willing to give you time to sort things out. You get over whatever is going on with you while you're in Manchac, but when you come home all of this erratic behavior better be out of your system. I will not change our plans. We either get married in September, or we do not get married at all."

"Then we don't get married at all," I calmly affirmed.

"I will not accept that as your final answer. You need some time to think about this," he growled.

"I've made my decision, John. I'm sorry, I really am, but I don't want to marry you. I don't want to live by your plans anymore. I just want to live. Good-bye, John." I hung up my cell phone.

Naturally, the phone started ringing again immediately after I hung up. I checked the caller ID and found it no surprise that the number shown was John's. I shook my head, turned off my phone, and returned it to my purse.

I sat on my bed, enjoying the uplifting sensation of being free of John and unburdened of all the silly wedding plans. My thoughts then drifted to the reason why I had canceled my wedding, and to the man I had turned my life upside down for; or perhaps turned my life right side up for.

Jean Marc's face and body filled my mind, and just when my memories of our night together began to get really interesting, a knock on my bedroom door startled me.

"Nora T," Uncle Jack called out from the other side of the heavy cypress door. "Your mama's on the house phone."

When I opened the door, I found Uncle Jack holding his blue cap in his hands, frowning at me.

"She sounds tres boudé. She keeps yellin' at me in French."

"I'm sure she is mad. I just told John that the wedding is off. He's probably already been on the phone to her."

Uncle Jack smiled at me, but his blue eyes still had a hint of uncertainty in them. "You wanna tell me why you called off the weddin'?"

"I think you know the answer to that, Uncle Jack."

"Jean Marc, he knows about the weddin'?"

"He knows." I stepped into the hallway. "He's the reason the wedding is off."

Uncle Jack placed the blue cap back on his head. "Guess I'll get started on them trellises Ms. Marie wants for her rose garden." He stepped over to the stairway behind him. "I 'spect you'll be stayin' on here instead of goin' back to the city."

I nodded. "I'll be staying."

"Well then. I'll just go and tell your mama that you're too busy to come to the phone."

"Thanks, Uncle Jack."

He turned and winked at me. "You made the right decision, girl. You'll be happy now." Uncle Jack made his way down the steps to the first floor.

As I stood on the landing and listened to my uncle's heavy boots treading along the wood floors to the kitchen, I realized he was right. I was happy, because for the first time in a long time, I was myself. Not the busy woman I had been prior to John's appearance, but I was once again the little girl who had been passionate for all life had to offer. Jean Marc had taken that passion with him when he went to Texas all those years ago. Last night he had put that missing puzzle piece of me back into place, and I was complete.

Suddenly, a loud crash, followed by a lot of expletives, came from the downstairs parlor. I quickly ran down the stairs, heading toward the ruckus. I made it to Henri's bedroom and threw open the old cypress doors.

Before me was a rather buxom woman dressed in blue scrubs and pinned to the floor beneath Henri. He had his arms about her, and for a brief second it looked as if his good hand was trying to go up the poor woman's scrub shirt.

"Should I come back later?" I joked.

"Oh, Ms. Nora." The young woman struggled to her feet. "I was trying to show Mr. Gaspard how to use his new cane when we took a nosedive to the floor."

"I…fell." Henri laughed and his black eyes glowed with mischief.

I glared at him. "Yes, I can see that. You need to be careful, Henri; not all women like to be on the bottom."

He grinned and then he placed his head against the floor, as if he was trying to hide his true response to my comment.

"Let's get you up, Romeo." I struggled to get Henri back on his feet and over to the nearby pale blue chair.

"I'm so sorry, Ms. Nora." The young chestnut-haired therapist kneeled before Henri and began checking his arms for injury. "I thought he was strong enough for a cane," she explained as she lifted his blue T-shirt and examined his chest.

"Oh, he is, Margie. Don't worry. It's not your fault. I think Henri just bit off more than he could chew today." I shook my finger at Henri. "I told you not to push too hard."

"Sorry," he said, sulking in the chair like a punished child.

"Perhaps I should take him in for x-rays," Margie fretted as she slowly began groping her way up Henri's left pant leg. "I want to make sure he didn't hurt himself," she added.

I noticed the way Henri was smiling as he watched Margie's progress up his leg. I quickly grabbed her hands. "Stop, Margie, he's fine. Probably just tired from all the exercise we did yesterday." I let go of her hands and stepped back.

Henri gave me a dirty look.

"Yes, perhaps that's it," Margie agreed as she stood up next to Henri's chair.

"Why don't you call it a day?" I suggested.

"If you think that's best." She nodded and her pretty blue eyes worriedly scanned Henri's face. "You're sure you're all right, Mr. Gaspard?"

Henri grinned for Margie. "Fine," he answered.

Margie nodded to me. "I'll just get my bag."

"I'll see you out," I told her.

After I got the overly compassionate Margie on to her next appointment, I went back into Henri's room to find him still sitting in the chair where I had left him.

"What in the hell were you trying to do to that poor girl?" I whispered as I shut the parlor doors.

He waved toward the doors with his good hand. "The silly cow tripped me. It's not my fault."

I went to his chair. "No, but it sure looked like you were taking advantage of the situation once you had the girl pinned beneath you."

"Can I help it if she finds stupid men attractive? She's been hot for me ever since she arrived here."

"Shut up, Henri. Get up and get back in your bed."

He struggled to rise from his chair, but then once on his feet he walked slowly to his hospital bed. I listened as his tennis shoes squeaked along the hardwood floor as his right foot dragged alongside him. When Henri sat down on the edge of the bed, he held out his arms to me.

"Are you going to inspect me all over for bruises? I know where you can start." He playfully raised his eyebrows and then let his eyes travel down to his crotch.

"Spare me." I folded my arms over my chest and kept my distance from the bed. "Don't go molesting the therapists. If you do that again, they will want to put you away in a psychiatric facility."

"You would love to see that happen, wouldn't you? Sorry, Nora, but I'll be out of here before any more horny therapists try to have another roll on the floor with me."

"When exactly did you plan on leaving?"

"I figured by next Wednesday, Thursday at the latest, my foot will be good enough to drive. If not, I'll use my left and just steal automatics."

"Can you use your foot?" I inquired as I stepped a little closer to the bed.

He raised his right leg and bent the foot about forty-five degrees up and down.

He winced slightly as he lowered his leg. "I figure that's good enough for driving. Another few days and it will be stronger."

I pointed to his right hand. "What about the hand?"

He held his right hand up but I did not see any movement.

"This is as good as it gets, I'm afraid. I'll just have to become a lefty from now on." He cupped his right hand with his left, then his eyes returned to me. "So, now you know my plans, what are yours?"

"What do you mean?"

"What are you going to do about Jean Marc and that fiancé back in New Orleans?"

"Ex-fiancé. I've already called John and canceled the wedding."

Henri cocked his head to the side. "Giving him back that rock?"

I nodded warily.

"Why don't you give it to me?" He smiled, or should I say leered. "I could use that to make my way out of the state."

"What about your money? I would have thought being an enlightened leader of a cult would have been a lucrative venture?"

"It was, but by now the gentlemen who set me up in the spiritual business have raided my apartment on Royal Street, taken all the cash I had hidden away, and made off with the best of my clothes, jewelry, and anything else that might have struck their fancy. Besides, if I go back they will know my memory has come around, and I can't have that."

"What if I try to get you some money?"

He stared at me, his black eyes filled with doubt. "Why would you do that? Just give me your ring. I can hock it at a place I know outside of Baton Rouge."

"I can't give you my engagement ring. It belongs to John, not me."

He shrugged his bony shoulders. "Just tell John I stole it. Once I'm gone, who cares what happens?"

"I care, Henri." I shook my head and turned away from him. "I'm not going to hurt people who have been good to me. I'm not like you."

"Maybe not one-hundred-percent like me, but I'd swear there's a little of me in you. Only dirty angels ever make deals with the devil." He snickered behind me.

"I'm no angel, Henri," I assured him as I reached for the parlor doors. "I would kiss the devil himself, if it would get you out of my life."

I quietly shut the doors behind me and then let out a long sigh. This was going to be harder than I thought.

CHAPTER 24

That evening, while Ms. Marie's church friends came by to read the bible to Henri, I went to the back porch to see if Jean Marc's cottage lights were on. The hot, humid air engulfed me as my eyes peered through the thick brush.

"He's home all right," Uncle Jack called from around the side of the porch. "I saw his truck drive down the lane to his place about thirty minutes ago."

"You should have told me you were there, Uncle Jack."

He came up to my side. "I didn't know what you were doin' out here at first. Then I saw where you were lookin'. Why don't you go on over? I'm sure he'll be just as anxious to see you."

"I've got to get Henri ready for bed after Ms. Marie's friends leave."

"I'll tell Ms. Marie you decided to take a walk before it got dark. I can help her get Henri ready for bed." He nodded toward the cottage. "You go on. But don't be keepin' that boy up too late. I'll be by early in the mornin' to take him crabbin'."

"Thanks, Uncle Jack." I kissed his grizzled cheek and then took off toward the cottage.

When I arrived in the clearing in front of Jean Marc's, I was surprised to find the cottage blanketed in darkness. Wondering why Jean Marc had not turned on any lights, I climbed the porch steps and pulled the screen door open. The old cypress floorboards on the porch moaned beneath my feet as I made my way to the front door. I lightly knocked and then tried the doorknob. The door had been left open, and I eased my way inside.

The lights were out in the living room and kitchen, except for a faint glow emanating from the upstairs hall.

"Jean Marc?" I called from the bottom of the stairs.

"Nora, I'm up here." I heard his voice coming from somewhere on the second floor. "Make sure you lock the front door before you come up."

After I secured the deadbolt on the front door, I made my way up the stairs. I followed the light to a door across from his bedroom. When I stepped inside, I found Jean Marc sitting in a high back black leather chair behind an old mahogany desk. The long desk had intricate designs of swirls and crowns carved into it.

"Hey, darlin'," he said, glancing up from a letter in his hand.

I slowly approached the desk. "What are you doing?"

He dropped the letter on top of a small pile of papers in front of him. "Just going over some paperwork." He watched as I traced a large swirl carved in the wood with my fingers. "Beautiful isn't it?" He motioned to the desk. "It was my father's; belonged to his grandfather, who shipped it over from France." He ran his fingers reverently over the edge of the desk. "I brought it from the house. I didn't want to take it to my office at the warehouse, it's too grand." He looked up at me. "I thought you would be coming by later, but I left the front door open just in case."

"Uncle Jack offered to take over bedtime duties with Henri," I explained as I eyed the papers on his the desk.

"I take it he knows about us?"

I nodded. "Your mother suspects, too." I hesitated for a moment before I went on. "I called John today and told him everything was off. He blames you. He always thought you were after me."

He rested his hands on the top of the desk. "He was right. Male intuition."

"God only knows what my mother thinks by now. John called her right after I hung up on him."

Jean Marc knitted his dark brows. "I don't really care what Claire or John thinks about us." He cast his eyes to the papers on his desk. "At least Henri will never realize anything, and if he did, I doubt he would care."

"Oh, you would be surprised what he can do," I mumbled, rubbing my hand across my forehead.

He leaned back in his chair, observing me. "Is he recovering?"

Wanting to avoid his intrusive gaze, I directed my eyes to his desk. "Henri's improving," I told him. Desperate to change the subject, I motioned to the papers before him. "What is all this, Jean Marc?"

He stood from his chair. "Faxes and e-mails from several insurance companies. I took your advice and started getting quotes on different insurance plans for the business." He came around the desk to my side. "I also went grocery shopping on the way home; thought I would cook us something really great for dinner."

I slipped my arms about his waist. "What?"

"Chinese."

"You can cook Chinese?" I asked, somewhat surprised.

He nibbled at my earlobe. "No, but I can put it in a microwave and warm it up."

"Sounds wonderful," I murmured as his lips inched their way down my neck.

"For dessert, I have something really special," he whispered against my skin.

"Mmm. What?"

His teeth grazed the nape of my neck. "Me."

I leaned back and grinned. "Well, then to hell with dinner, let's get right to the dessert."

"Excellent choice."

He picked me up in his arms and deposited me on top of the pile of papers on his desk. His hand went straight to the zipper on my shorts.

I glanced down at the papers underneath me. "But this is your father's desk."

He stood back from me and pulled at the buttons on his shirt. "Yeah, wouldn't Dad be proud."

He threw his shirt to the floor and reached for my legs. Pulling my hips to the edge of the desk, he quickly removed my shorts and underwear. He ran his callused hands up and down my thighs, making my skin prickle with excitement.

I tossed my T-shirt and bra to the floor and then began to explore the curves of his broad chest. I kissed his neck gently at first, but then I started teasing him with my teeth, leaving little kisses down his neck and chest until I sank my teeth into his left nipple.

"Oh, you little…" He reached his hands under my thighs and pulled my hips high in the air.

My body fell back against the desk. Before I could wiggle free of his grip, his teeth began nipping their way down my inner thigh. I reached my hands behind me and gripped the edge of the desk as his mouth closed over my sensitive folds. I moaned with pleasure as his tongue began to tease my flesh.

"Oh, God, Jean Marc," I cried out.

My back arched and my insides ached with need as my climax drew near. Jean Marc's tongue made me feel as if I would explode if he did not stop. My nails dug into the edge of the old desk, my body began to pulsate and soon I lost all sense of the world outside his office door. I screamed when the orgasm overwhelmed me.

Relaxing on the desk, I tried to catch my breath, and then I felt the press of a stapler against my back. I sat up and was about to grab at the stapler, when Jean Marc pulled my hips to his.

"Don't get too comfortable, darlin'. I'm just getting started." He lowered his lips over my right nipple and his teeth clamped down hard on my tender skin.

Then I heard the distinct sound of his zipper being lowered on his black trousers. He wrapped my legs about his waist as his pants and briefs fell to the floor. He stopped teasing my right nipple and he looked into my eyes.

"It's my turn," he whispered as he eased slowly inside me.

I sighed with pleasure when he entered me. He pulled completely out and then pushed his way into me once more. I raked my nails along his chest as he began to increase the speed of his thrusting. Jean Marc groaned and slammed his hips harder into mine, going deeper than before. Grabbing at the papers around me, I struggled to raise my hips higher to satiate the frenzy taking over my body. I closed my eyes as my climax came barreling up from my groin. He thrust again and again, bringing me to the edge. Then, my whole body began to tremble as the orgasm rocked every inch of me. His breath came hard and fast against my neck as he arched his body and grunted into my neck.

I went limp against the desk and he relaxed on top of me.

"You're driving me crazy," he mumbled, catching his breath.

I giggled. "I know the feeling."

His body tensed. "Damn."

"What is it?"

He sat up and his deep brown eyes gazed worriedly into mine. "I didn't use a condom. I guess I got so carried away, I forgot."

I traced my fingertips over the red marks on his wide chest. "I forgot, too. I guess that means we're both in trouble."

His features darkened, but his eyes shone in the light of the room. "Are we?"

I nodded. "Could be."

His fingers stroked the valley between my breasts. "I'd love to get you pregnant. Then we would have to marry right away."

"I wouldn't force you to marry me if I got pregnant, Jean Marc."

He eagerly embraced me with his strong arms. "You wouldn't be forcing me, Nora. You would be saving me."

I ran my fingers along the outline of his wide shoulders. "Maybe we can do it once more without the condom. What could it hurt?"

He nuzzled my cheek. "I like the way you think, Mrs. Gaspard."

"Jean Marc—" But his hungry kiss silenced me, and my growing desire for him quickly swept all my doubts away.

* * *

The following morning I awoke in Jean Marc's arms again and delighted in the feel of his warm body next to mine. But the peace in the bedroom was soon disrupted by the grating "beep, beep, beep" of the alarm clock next to the bed. Jean Marc rolled away from me and shut the alarm off with a slap of his hand.

He turned back over and wrapped me in his arms. "I don't want to get up."

I cuddled against his chest. "What's the alarm for?"

"Jack's taking me out to pull crab traps from the lake this morning; he wants to get an early start."

"Then I should get going." I made an attempt to get out of bed, but he only dragged me back to his side.

"Five more minutes," he begged. "Better yet, I'll cancel."

"No. Don't let Uncle Jack down. I'll be at the house when you get back."

"It's Sunday, and Momma will be off to church early. You'll be on your own with Henri." He sat up in bed. "Will you be all right?"

"I'll be fine." I nestled back into his arms.

He pulled me close and sighed into my hair. "About last night, I meant what I said about marrying you." He kissed my cheek and then he whispered, "I love you, Nora. I always have."

At that moment, I knew all the animosity I thought I had harbored for Jean Marc through the years had simply been love hiding behind my fear. There was no great flash of light, no angelic choirs from above to signal my epiphany; there was only a profound sense of contentment permeating my soul. Odd, how you could know someone all your life and then, without warning, what you thought had been friendship turns out to be love.

I traced the dark stubble over his chin as my heart soared with happiness. "As long as it is a quick ceremony and there is no fancy reception, bridesmaids, or long guest lists." I rolled my eyes. "I can't go through that again."

"Here at the house, family, close friends, and, of course, your mother."

"She'll hate it. But it sounds perfect."

He let me go and threw his covers aside. "We need to make this official," Jean Marc proclaimed, jumping from the bed. He went to his chest of drawers, and after removing something from the middle drawer, darted back to the bed.

"What is it?" I asked as he sat down next to me.

He took my left hand and slipped something over my third finger.

"This will have to do until I can get you a proper ring," he told me.

On my finger was the gold-painted aluminum ring covered with rhinestones that I had given Jean Marc all those years ago. The ring appeared so crude and childlike on my hand, but the emotion it instilled in me at that moment made it the most precious thing I had ever owned.

I lovingly caressed the rhinestones. "You really did keep it."

"How could I throw it away? You made it for me."

I leaned over and kissed his lips. Instantly, his arms flew about me and he pulled me down on the bed.

I pushed him away. "What about Uncle Jack?"

"You're right." He slapped my thigh. "You'd better get out of here before Jack shows up, or else I will have to marry you with his shotgun at my back before sunset." He stood from the bed. "Tonight, we can make some plans."

I climbed out of the bed. "I like the sound of that." I paused for a moment and reached for his long-sleeved shirt strewn over the footboard of the sleigh bed. "Why is it when you talk about making plans, I don't feel sick to my stomach?" I shrugged his white shirt over my shoulders.

"Sick? What do you mean?" He walked to his closet by the bathroom door.

"Whenever John talked about making plans for us, I would always get this burning feeling in my stomach."

He opened the closet door. "That's because you never really loved John, Nora. That was pretty obvious to everyone who knows you."

"I tried to love him. I really did. I kept thinking he was good for me, that we would be good together, but it wasn't enough."

He removed an old pair of blue jeans from his closet. "I kept telling myself the same thing when I was with Cynthia, hoping it would be enough to keep our marriage going." He tossed the jeans to the bed. "When I found out she was sleeping with someone else, I wasn't angry, I was relieved." He stepped over to his chest of drawers.

"You never told her how you felt, just like I never told John." I eased up next to him. "Promise from this point on we will never keep anything hidden between us."

His body stiffened and he turned to the chest of drawers.

"Jean Marc? What is it?"

He opened the top drawer, keeping his back to me as he spoke. "I've done things I'm not proud of, and one day that past may catch up with me."

"Are you talking about the smuggling?"

He lifted a white T-shirt from the drawer and faced me. "I'm not like my brother, Nora, but I am not what you think."

"I know what you've done. I know you smuggled goods through the swamps to keep your family business going. You did what you had to. I will never think any less of you because of it."

He threw the T-shirt on the bed behind me. "You don't know everything. There are things I need to tell you."

I patted my hand reassuringly on his chest, convinced that there was nothing more he could disclose to me about his business dealings. "Tonight you can tell me all about your smuggling secrets, and then we will make plans."

His deep brown eyes anxiously searched mine. "You might not feel the same way about me after I tell you of my past, Nora."

I shook my head. "None of it can ever change how I see you. To me you will always be that adorable boy chasing after me on the docks. The boy I fell in love with because he believed in me before I believed in myself. "

"You may despise that boy after tonight," he warned with a frown.

"I won't change my mind, Jean Marc. I promise I never will."

He pulled me into his arms. "I hope so, Nora. I truly hope so."

I knew no matter what he told me, it would never lessen my love for him. My faith had taught me that true love could forgive a multitude of sins. I had never believed in such absolution prior to that moment, but my feelings for Jean Marc had opened my heart to such possibilities. After all, our souls are not judged by the sins we accumulate in life, but by the love we take with us after our life has ebbed away.

CHAPTER 26

I had just stepped up to the back door of the main house when I heard Uncle Jack's truck heading toward Jean Marc's cottage. The sun was coming up over the horizon and the house was still. When I entered the kitchen I expected to see Henri, but instead I found his half-full ashtray on the kitchen table. I walked over to the coffee machine and started filling the coffee chamber with the aromatic coffee and chicory blend so many of us in the South had grown addicted to. I turned the machine on, then stood by the counter and waited impatiently for those first few drops of the dirt-colored liquid to appear in the pot.

"Damn things always take forever," a hard-hearted voice said behind me.

I turned to see Henri standing in the kitchen doorway, wearing his robe over his pajamas and leaning heavily on the cane the physical therapist had given him the day before.

"Using the cane, I see." I pulled out two coffee mugs from the cabinet above me.

"It's easier for getting around," he admitted as he came toward the kitchen table and eased himself into the closest chair.

I placed a mug in front of him. "You'll be ready to travel soon."

He rested his cane against his chair. "A few more days."

"How about today, Henri?"

"Why should I do that, Nora? I'm not quite ready yet, and I still have to get some cash."

I took a deep breath. "I'll give you my engagement ring and the keys to my car if you leave today."

He sat back in his chair and eyed me for a moment. "Things must be progressing nicely with my brother for you to want me out of the picture so quickly. Did he ask you to move in with him already?"

I said nothing to confirm or deny his suspicions. His eyes went to the gold-painted ring on the third finger of my left hand and then he grinned.

"Jean Marc wants to marry you. You do work fast. Haven't even dumped fiancé number one and you've got number two all lined up. Like mother, like daughter."

I slapped him hard across the face.

He did nothing. He did not even flinch when I hit him. He kept his soulless eyes on mine. Then he gave me a cold sneer and raised his left hand to rub his red cheek.

"Was it something I said?" he quipped.

I glared at him. "It's no business of yours what happens between me and Jean Marc." I returned to the coffee machine on the counter.

"Far be it from me to stand in the way of true love, Nora. But you must admit it gives one pause how quickly you fall in and out of love. First with the nice doctor, and now with my brother; some people might wonder what you're after, girl."

I wheeled around. "What I'm after? I'm not after anything, Henri. I'm in love with your brother and he loves me. There is nothing else."

"Love? With Jean Marc?" He chuckled and reached for his cane. "That man doesn't know how to love."

"What do you know about love, Henri? You're so wrapped up in yourself that there can never be room in your heart for another person. You can't love; all you can do is destroy. That way you don't feel so alone and so empty inside."

"You think you have me all figured out with your psychobabble." He looked down at the ring on my finger. "Let me tell you something, love tarnishes. I've seen it a hundred times. It starts out great, but after a while the luster fades and the polish wears away. Then all you're left with is a cheap piece of tin, and you wonder what in the hell you ever found so appealing to begin with." He leaned on his cane and slowly stood from his chair. "I'm not the kind of man who goes around filling a woman's head with promises of white picket fences and wedded bliss, because I know it doesn't exist. Such happiness is a myth, the golden grail of life. If you set out searching for it, all you will ever find is sorrow." He paused as he caught his breath for a moment, leaning heavily on his cane. "Take some advice, Nora. Go back to your doctor and be content with that, because you will never have happiness with my brother."

I held up my head defiantly to him. "You're the one who has always carried unhappiness around with you like an all-consuming plague. You have no idea what happiness is, what love is, and you hate the idea that Jean Marc and I could ever be happy."

"Oh, yes, try and be happy with the untouchable, cool, and always perfect Jean Marc." He wavered on his feet. "You've never had to grow up in the shadow of a sibling, Nora. To be compared day in and day out to the better half of your biological self. I'm sick of hearing from everyone how great and dedicated dear, sweet Jean Marc is. You'll never know everything about him; all the bad things he has done. God help you if you ever learn the truth." He slowly made his way out of the kitchen, leaning on the cane as he went.

I stared out the window behind the sink as I waited for Henri's shuffling to fade away. The red light of the coffee pot beside me started to blink, signaling the brewing phase was complete. But I did not feel like coffee anymore; the fight with Henri had ruined my happy mood.

I tried to relax my shoulders and let all the tension his words had created leave my body. But as I replayed the conversation over in my head, one thing he said ate at me.

"God help you if you ever learn the truth," I repeated the words he had used as I inspected the full coffee pot next to me. "What truth?" I asked out loud.

"Oh, Nora T, you're up," Ms. Marie's cheerful voice came from the kitchen doorway. "And you have made the coffee. Ca c'est bon."

The dainty woman was dressed in her Sunday best. Her plain, white cotton dress was dotted with yellow daises, and her pale yellow shoes matched perfectly with her yellow handbag.

"You look very pretty," I commented, admiring her outfit.

"Thank you, child." She came forward and placed her handbag on the kitchen table. "Was that Henri I heard shuffling about?" she asked as she reached for the empty coffee mug on the table.

"Yes, he was awake so we have been practicing walking with his new cane. He's doing well with it."

"Oh, that's wonderful." She brought the mug to the sink and then pulled out another mug from the cabinet beside her. "I want him to get out of that room. Maybe we could take him out this afternoon, get him some sunshine."

"That would be good for him," I concurred.

She turned to me, holding her mug in her hands. "I don't know what we would have done without you these past few days, Nora T. Havin' a nurse 'round here would have broken my Jean Marc. The therapists were expensive enough, but I can't imagine how—"

"What do you mean 'broken Jean Marc,' Ms. Marie?" I interrupted.

"Jean Marc pays for everythin' 'round here, child; has ever since he came back from Texas. He's spent a fortune fixin' up this house and his cottage, and then havin' to pay all of Henri's medical bills on top of everythin' must be costin' him. I know my boys haven't spoken in years, and I would never have asked Jean Marc to spend any of his money on his brother, but I had no choice."

"His money? I don't understand."

"Money from his accounts," she replied, smiling. "From the money he made in Texas." She reached for the coffee pot. "Investments, or somethin' like that." She poured the coffee into her mug. "I can never remember," she added.

"Texas?" I asked, feeling an uncomfortable twinge in my gut.

"Oui, he made a lot of money in Texas. When he came home, he took over the business from Emile. Henri and Jean Marc were supposed to take it over together, but they had a fallin' out and Henri left." She replaced the coffee pot on the warmer.

"Ms. Marie, this is very important. Do you know what these investments were?"

She shook her head and frowned. "But Henri knew. Shame Henri can't remember. He could have said more 'bout it."

My happiness disintegrated as the bite of bile rose in the back of my throat. I left Ms. Marie and went down the narrow beige hall toward the parlor. I tore open the doors to Henri's bedroom and caught sight of him by his hospital bed, wearing only his pajama bottoms and struggling to pull his blue T-shirt over his head.

"How did Jean Marc make his money in Texas?" I questioned as I entered the room. I quickly shut the doors behind me.

Henri peered out from under his T-shirt. With his good left hand he pulled the T-shirt off his head and then threw it on the bed.

"Mother ran her mouth, I suspect." He shifted his weight and leaned on the bed next to him. "She always had a bad habit of talking too much."

I marched up to the bed and stood before him. "What happened when Jean Marc came home from Texas?"

He sat down on the bed and rubbed his left hand across his thin, pale chest. "The question is, dear girl, what didn't happen? You never would have guessed it by looking at my brother, but he is a very shrewd businessman, Nora. Do you know what I mean?"

I shook my head, waiting with a sickening impatience for his next words.

"I'm sure you know about the history of my fine family. Smugglers and thieves, that's what we have been for almost two hundred years, and in many ways what we still are." He paused, looked down at the sheets on his bed, and picked at a piece of lint with his left hand. "Granddad taught my uncle and father all about the business of swamp running, and in turn, my father taught Jean Marc and me." He raised his head. "The real family business, you could say. Trawling has always been something of a cover for the Gaspard family…sort of an alternative career."

"Jean Marc told me you ran drugs," I confessed.

He nodded. "Yeah, drugs, small arms, whatever was needed. Father had many clients, and I picked up the business from him."

"And Jean Marc?"

"Oh, he started out like me, running stuff occasionally through the swamps for Dad. But he never really had a taste for it. He found his true calling when he went to Texas."

My gut tightened. "Why Texas?"

"He met his father-in-law, Lawrence Castille, when he was in school there. Castille was one of the best smugglers in the world. He took Jean Marc under his wing and taught him all about the art of smuggling. He became a real asset to Castille, even married his daughter. My brother ran everything from antiquities out of Egypt, to illegal arms into North Korea. He made a lot of money doing it."

A wave of nausea rolled in my stomach. "I can't believe this."

"Believe it, Nora. Jean Marc was never crazy about the business, but he sure did like the money. Tried not to get into it, even got a regular job after he graduated from college to support his wife, but that soon failed and he eventually succumbed, like we all do. The money is too damn good to walk away from."

"Why did he walk away from it?"

"Castille was killed in a raid on one of his compounds in Texas. Jean Marc was on a run for him at the time, out of the country. When Jean Marc came back to the States, he decided to come home and put his money into expanding Gaspard Fisheries. But when he found out I was still smuggling, he decided it was time to go straight and cut the family business off from our other enterprises. I tried to talk him out of it." He grazed his hand down the scar on his right cheek. "Unsuccessfully. So, I left and went out on my own."

I leaned over the bed. "Why didn't you want to go straight, Henri? You could have worked with Jean Marc to build up the business."

"The last thing my brother wanted was having me around to spy on him. Jean Marc doesn't like anyone knowing his dirty little secret. But I heard about it from a few associates I know. They said that he was a real pro in Texas, a cool customer with a ruthless reputation and some very powerful connections. When I heard he had returned to his former ways, I wasn't surprised."

I shook my head, feeling confused. "What former ways?"

"His smuggling ways, of course. Rumor around the swamps is that Jean Marc Gaspard never left the business."

I sighed with relief. "I already know about his smuggling activities, Henri. When I went over to his place the other day, I saw him loading up a boat with boxes to take into the swamps. I confronted him about it, and he told me everything."

Henri rolled his eyes and laughed at me. It was a harsh and evil sound that reverberated throughout the small parlor. "You think I'm talking about swamp smuggling, girl? Lord, Nora, you really are innocent, aren't you? You can't make enough off smuggling junk through the swamps to pay all of the bills my brother has racked up through the years. No, I'm talking about high-end smuggling; taking stuff across borders and into other countries. Dangerous stuff that can get you killed, like gems, weapons, money, antiquities, even secrets. My brother is still an international smuggler, Nora. He's considered one of the best in the business. His clients are some of the wealthiest men on the planet. That's how he has been able to pay for everything around here since he came home from Texas."

I thought of Jean Marc's frequent business trips, the guns in his home, and his sudden desire to tell me everything about his past. The blood drained from my head and I wobbled on my feet.

"What's the matter, Nora? Shocked by my little disclosure about my brother? Still think you could be happy as my brother's wife?"

I stared into his icy, black eyes. "I have to talk to Jean Marc." I turned to go.

"Whoa, wait a minute, Nora." Henri stood up and grabbed my arm. "You can't tell Jean Marc anything I've just told you."

I shook off his arm. "Why not?"

"If he finds out I talked, that I've made him vulnerable, he'll kill me."

"Jean Marc wouldn't hurt you," I assured him as I headed for the parlor doors.

"Jean Marc will protect himself, Nora," he stated behind me. "He couldn't give a damn about me. As far as he's concerned, I'm a liability. Just like Uncle Etienne was a problem for my father, until he was finally gotten rid of."

I stopped at the doors and then slowly turned back to Henri. "Are you saying Etienne was killed?"

He shrugged. "Of course. My father was furious about Etienne's marriage to your mother. Claire was a smart woman, like you. Father felt she would learn about the secret family business sooner or later. He pressured Etienne to end the marriage, but my uncle refused. He loved your mother." Henri paused and shook his head. "Even when Claire left Etienne for Kehoe, he still refused to divorce her. So my father found another way to get Claire out of our lives. He set up the accident, and told everyone that Etienne had shot himself because he could not handle losing his wife."

My knees began giving way. "Why are you telling me all of this, Henri?"

"I'm tired of living with all the lies. When I told you I wanted to get out of here, it was the truth. I want out of this business. I want to start over." He sneered at me. "You're here because Jean Marc wanted to keep an eye on me. He knew that you would tell him everything about my progress. That's why he let you take care of me. But he didn't bargain on you finding out everything about him. It would destroy his whole plan for your future together."

"Christ, Henri, I can't believe—" The sudden sound of the doorbell interrupted me.

Henri grabbed his T-shirt off the bed. "My mother probably has more of her idiot friends from the church coming over. Go and see who it is." He stood from the bed and started pushing me toward the parlor doors.

"Are you kidding me, Henri?" I balked as I threw off his hand.

He slung his T-shirt over his shoulder. "Nora, now that you know everything, you must keep it together. I need you to play along until I can get out of here. Just go and see who it is, and then send them away."

I took in a calming breath and let it out slowly, hoping to settle my frazzled nerves. "All right, but this has to end, Henri. I can't keep lying to Jean Marc for you. If you're not gone in three days, I'll tell him everything."

He nodded and pointed to the parlor doors. "Deal. Now go and get the damned door."

I headed out of the parlor and walked down the narrow beige hall to the living room, where I found Ms. Marie already at the dark red front door.

She was speaking with three men, standing on the porch outside. The man in front was dressed in a tailored black suit with a cream-colored tie. He was tall, skinny, and had dark hair sprinkled with gray. His face was long and he had deep-set, bright green eyes. He was holding up a bible in his left hand as he smiled warmly at Ms. Marie. The two men flanking him were thick, muscular, and bald. Each was dressed in casual dark slacks with white, long-sleeved shirts. One of the men had a thick, white scar down the left side of his face, running from beneath his eye to his upper lip. When he smiled at Ms. Marie, his upper lip crinkled, looking more like a sneer than a smile. A rush of anxiety gripped me as Ms. Marie waved the men inside. The man with the scar refused Ms. Marie's invitation and remained outside as the two other men entered the home.

I knew from the steady flow of Ms. Marie's friends who had been coming and going over the past few days that these three men were not from her church. If anything, the sight of them made the hairs on the back of my neck stand up.

I ducked out of the living room before I was spotted and headed back to the parlor. When I opened the parlor doors, Henri was already in his bed, dressed in his pajamas and pretending to be asleep.

"Henri, get up. There are three men here and something is not right about them."

Henri rolled over in the bed and looked at me. "What are you talking about?"

"Two of the men came inside when Ms. Marie invited them in, but one man stayed on the porch. He had this scar down the side of his face and—"

"What scar?" Henri sat up in the bed.

"It ran from underneath his eye to his lip." I watched the color drain from Henri's face. "What is it, Henri?"

Just then a knock came from outside of the parlor doors.

"Coming," I called as Henri stood from the bed.

Ms. Marie opened the parlor doors and peeked inside. She smiled at Henri. "Henri, some nice men are here to see you. They're friends from your church in the city. I put them in the livin' room and told them you'd be out shortly."

"I'll help him get ready," I assured her.

"See, Henri," Ms. Marie said to her son. "People care about you. And you told me you didn't have any friends in New Orleans. You shouldn't be telling your mama such fibs." Ms. Marie shifted her eyes to me. "I'll just be off to church, Nora. But make sure those nice men get some refreshments, all right?"

I nodded at Ms. Marie. "Of course. I'll take care of it. You go on. You don't want to be late for church."

Ms Marie waved good-bye to her son, and I waited until she had closed the parlor doors behind her before I spoke.

"Who is here, Henri?"

He quickly moved from the bed to the parlor doors and I was shocked by the effortless grace of his movements. I figured he had been hiding his true physical abilities from me all along. I wondered what else he had kept from me.

Henri listened at the door as the tap of his mother's shoes on the hardwood floor headed down the hallway toward the kitchen. He turned to me. "It seems my associates from the city have come to see how bad off I really am."

My heart fell to the floor.

Henri, however, remained cool and collected. "Go to the cottage and get Jean Marc."

"But he went crabbing with Uncle Jack."

Henri cursed under his breath. He gazed about the room and then his black eyes returned to me. "Go to the cottage. Call his cell phone. He takes it everywhere with him. Tell him what's going on."

"What about you?" I asked, feeling the nervous beads of sweat begin to collect on my upper lip.

He went to the foot of the bed and picked up his robe. "I'll stay here and talk to them. Try and convince them that I'm as stupid as they need me to be. But if they aren't convinced…." Henri slipped the robe over his shoulders. "Looks like you might get your wish after all, Nora. As soon as I can get rid of these guys, I will have to leave. I can't stay here anymore." He nodded to the door. "Take the back door from the kitchen to Jean Marc's. Now go."

Before I pulled the parlor doors open, I glanced back at Henri.

"Go get my brother," he urged with a wave of his left hand. "He'll know exactly what to do."

Chapter 27

I took off down the hall and headed toward the kitchen. I didn't see any sign of Ms. Marie, and prayed that she was on her way to church and out of harm's way.

I rushed out the back door and down the porch steps. As soon as my feet hit the soft, green grass, I took off running toward the path that led to Jean Marc's.

I reached the clearing in front of Jean Marc's cottage and recognized my uncle's blue pick up truck parked under a nearby oak tree. As I approached the screened front porch, I heard raised voices coming from the back of the cottage. I ran around the side of the house and noticed two men leaning over the back of a green flatboat tied up to the dock.

"Check the sparkplug again," Jean Marc's voice barked as I ran up to the dock.

"I already did that. She ain't the problem," Uncle Jack replied as he turned from the back of the boat and saw me.

My uncle nudged Jean Marc next to him as I hurriedly approached the boat.

Jean Marc stood up in the boat. "Is something wrong?"

"There are men at the house for Henri," I explained as I tried to catch my breath.

My uncle looked from me to Jean Marc.

"Men?" Jean Marc scowled. "Policemen?"

I shook my head and took another few quick breaths. "They showed up at the front door and your mother let them in. They said they were friends from his church, but Henri told me they are his former associates, the ones who set him up in all of that cult business." Jean Marc climbed out of the boat. "He sent me to get you. He said you would know what to do," I related as he came up to my side.

Uncle Jack followed Jean Marc onto the dock.

Jean Marc ran his hands over his face. "Where's my mother?"

"She went to church," I informed him.

"You sure 'bout that?" Uncle Jack demanded.

I nodded. "She wasn't in the house when I left."

"How many men?" Jean Marc questioned.

"Three," I answered. "One stayed outside on the front porch, and the other two were in the living room waiting for Henri."

He turned to Uncle Jack. "You got your shotgun?"

Uncle Jack nodded. "In my truck, loaded and ready to go."

Jean Marc motioned to the house. "Meet me out front."

Uncle Jack hurried down the dock and headed around the side of the cottage.

I turned to Jean Marc. "What are you going to do?"

Jean Marc started for the back door of the cottage. "The only thing we can do. Go over there and make sure nothing happens to Henri."

I followed him to the back door. "You can't just walk in the door, guns at the ready, and shoot everyone."

Jean Marc stopped at the door and faced me. "Nora, if these men are as Henri said then we have no other choice. They came here for one thing and one thing only; to make sure Henri can't talk and incriminate them in any way. It won't matter to them if he can remember any of his dealings with them or not."

"But he can remember everything, Jean Marc. Mentally he's still the same Henri, and has been for some time."

Jean Marc grabbed my arm. "How long have you known this?"

"Since yesterday morning when I returned to the house. I walked into the kitchen and found him smoking a cigarette. That's when I learned the truth about his recovery." I dropped my gaze from his outraged eyes to his hand, clutching my arm.

He let go of me and shook his head. "You should have said something to me last night. I could have kicked his sorry ass out of the house and avoided this mess." He opened the back screen door and waved me inside.

We stepped through to the rear of the kitchen and then headed for the living room. I followed behind him as he went to the table by the front door and retrieved the .9mm pistol from a drawer. He pulled out the magazine, checked it, and then slammed it back into the gun.

"Are you going to kill those men, Jean Marc?"

"Possibly."

"Have you ever killed a man before?"

He stared at me as if trying to understand why I had asked such a question.

"Henri told me about you. He said you're considered one of the best in your profession. How long have you been an international smuggler?"

Jean Marc uttered a heaving sigh. "Fifteen years. I was going to tell you about all of it, tonight. I would have said something earlier, but I was afraid of losing you." He dropped his eyes to the gun in his hand. "Am I going to lose you, Nora?"

The front door flew open and my uncle came bounding into the cottage. In his hand was a double-barreled shotgun.

"You ready?" he asked, nodding to Jean Marc.

Jean Marc moved toward my uncle.

I reached for his arm. "What about the police? Shouldn't we call them?"

Jean Marc pulled his cell phone from the front pocket of his jeans and handed it to me. "Mel Cadeaux is on my call list. He's the local police chief. Tell him what's going on and to get out here right away."

I took the phone from him. "What do you want me to do?"

Jean Marc took a step closer to me. "Stay here. I can't protect you if things get dicey up at the house. Promise me you will stay here until the police arrive."

"Please be careful," I whispered to him.

He kissed my cheek. "Don't worry about me, Nora. I'll be fine." He stood back from me and winked.

I looked to my uncle, who offered me a reassuring nod, and then the men headed down the porch steps. I watched from the cottage doorway as Jean Marc's tall figure disappeared into the brush.

I peered down at the cell phone in my hand and began scrolling through Jean Marc's long list of contacts, until I came across the name Mel Cadeaux. After four rings a man's gritty voice picked up on the other end.

"Gaspard, you old son of a bitch."

"This isn't Jean Marc, Mr. Cadeaux. It's Nora Kehoe. There's trouble at Gaspard House. Three men have shown up and are threatening to harm Henri. Jean Marc wanted me to call you right away."

"You're Claire Mouton's girl. I remember you, Nora," Mel Cadeaux said into the speaker of the phone. "Tell Jean Marc I'm on my way."

I hung up the cell phone and placed it on the table by the door. I stepped on to the screened porch beyond the front door and waited. As the minutes ticked by, I began to pace back and forth on the noisy porch planks. I felt helpless waiting there. I was worried about Jean Marc, about my uncle, and even about Henri. I silently prayed to the heavens above for a peaceful resolution to this mess. Unable to stand it any longer, I decided to slowly make my way to the main house and see if I could detect any activity from the brush just beyond the back door. But I knew I could not just go traipsing over there without some form of protection. Then I remembered the hammerless .32 revolver Jean Marc kept in the drawer of his nightstand.

I flew back into the house, and when I reached his bedroom, I pulled the gun from the drawer of the nightstand. While checking to make sure the gun was loaded, two loud pops echoed from outside. My heart stopped and my stomach shrank with dread. I ran from the bedroom, down the stairs and out to the porch. Once outside, I heard the frantic barking of Napoleon and Nelson coming from the rear of Gaspard House.

I clicked off the safety on the gun, and then immediately started down the porch steps. I had to find out what was going on.

Sticking close to the green brush along the way, I ran toward the house. By the time I sighted the terra cotta roof shingles of Gaspard House glowing in the late morning sun, my heart was pounding. I stayed close to the brush as I came around the back of the house. Only the occasional chirp of a bird broke through the eerie stillness of the morning air, and then I heard the distinct sound of growling coming from just behind the back porch.

I moved as fast as I could while trying to remain hidden in the brush. When I came around the edge of a small cleared area beyond the back of the house, I saw Napoleon and Nelson growling menacingly at something on the ground near them. As I stepped from the cover of the brush, I noticed the blood; deep red and pooling in the bright green grass on the ground in front of me. Then, the reason for the blood became evident. Lying face up in the grass was the tall man dressed in a black suit, and in his hand a .38 snub-nosed revolver. His dull green eyes were staring into the sky. In the middle of his chest, two spots of blood on his white dress shirt were slowly expanding. Not far from his side was an open bible. The center of the bible had been hollowed out like a box. I walked over to Nelson and patted his thick neck as the two dogs kept a vigilant watch over the dead man.

"Nora?"

Henri emerged from the open back door of the house. His robe and pajama's were stained with blood. He was holding a .9mm pistol in his left hand.

I ran up to his side and examined his body for a wound.

"It's not mine," he insisted, placing his arm about my shoulders and pulling me inside.

I glanced down at the old bricked kitchen floor and saw a trail of blood leading across the room to the hallway.

"Where are Jean Marc and Uncle Jack?" I asked as we hurried across the kitchen.

"Jack's around front. He's got the other two guys on the ground with his shotgun on them," Henri clarified as we made our way quickly into the narrow hall.

"Who was that man, Henri?"

"Dr. Max Morgan, a New Orleans physician and the man I worked for," Henri explained next to me. "I chased him into the kitchen. Took two bullets to bring him down."

"Where's Jean Marc?"

He stopped at the entrance to the living room. "I was coming to get you," Henri said, and then his eyes anxiously peered into the room.

When I followed Henri's eyes to the center of the dark green living room, my heart shattered into a million pieces. Lying on a cream-colored rug, and surrounded by a pool of blood, was my Jean Marc.

I ran to Jean Marc's side and fell to my knees, tossing the gun from my hand. I immediately began to apply pressure to the bleeding bullet wound in his right upper leg.

Henri stood beside me. "Max pulled a gun out of that bible of his and shot him when Jean Marc told him to get out." His voice became fraught with panic. "I didn't know what to do and I was—"

"Quick, get me something to make a tourniquet! The bullet has hit an artery," I shouted at him.

He removed the belt from his robe and handed it to me. "What about this?"

I grabbed the belt and tied it above the wound on Jean Marc's right thigh.

I examined Jean Marc's face. He was so pale. His lips were white and his eyes were glazed over. When I touch his cheek, he turned to me.

"Nora," he barely whispered. "I wanted to see you one more...." His head fell slightly to the side and then he was perfectly still.

"Jean Marc!" I cried out. "Jean Marc, stay with me. Don't you leave me!"

As I knelt beside him, begging for him to come back to me, the sound of sirens could be heard approaching from the main road.

EPILOGUE

I sat at my oak desk and skimmed through the invoices that had been piling up since the previous day. Easing back in my leather chair, I let my eyes wander to the large window next to me and marveled at the way the early summer sun shimmered on the waters of Lake Pontchartrain.

"You have a visitor." Steve Seville's voice came through the intercom on my desk. "And she ain't friendly," he added.

I pressed a button on the intercom. "Send her in, Steve."

A few moments later Steve entered my office with a comical frown on his face. Right behind him walked my mother. She was newly dyed blonde and dressed in her best blue designer suit, blue leather Prada shoes, and an expensive array of gold and diamond jewelry covering every piece of exposed skin.

I sighed as I leaned forward in my chair. "Hello, Mother."

She glared over her shoulder at Steve.

Steve just smiled at her and nodded to me. "Can I get you ladies anything?" he sweetly asked.

"No thanks, Steve," I answered.

Mother waited until Steve had closed the door to my office before she turned to me.

"Why did you have to hire that man to work for you?"

"I wanted Steve to join me, Mother. He's a good secretary and a good friend." I shuffled some papers around on my desk. "Why are you here? You always swore you would never return to Manchac."

She took in my compact, wood-paneled office at Gaspard Fisheries and threw her hands up. "I can't believe you actually want to run this place. I did not raise you to be a fish farmer, Nora."

"I doubt any of us actually set out to be what we end up becoming. But circumstance tends to overpower even the best of intentions. Besides, who else is going to help run Gaspard Fisheries?"

My mother came toward my desk, her brown eyes blazing. "You should come back to New Orleans. You can stay with me and Lou, at least until you're married, then we can decide what—"

"Forget it, Mother." I sat back in my chair.

Mother's lower lip trembled as she took a seat in the red leather chair in front of my desk. She opened her handbag, pulled out a newspaper clipping, and then gingerly placed the clipping on the desk in front of me.

"I thought you should see this, before you heard about it from anyone else."

I picked up the paper and gleaned over the small article on the page. It was a wedding announcement for Dr. and Mrs. John Blessing. I smiled as I looked at the picture of the woman in John's arms. She was petite, had long flowing hair, and was very pretty. I put the clipping back down on my desk.

"That could have been you," Mother professed, pointing at the clipping.

I lightly chuckled. "Thank God, it wasn't."

She stood from her chair and waved her hand around the office. "You think this is better? Running a bunch of fish farms, living at that old cottage, and raising his bastard child?"

"Children, Mother," I corrected her. "They're twins, you know."

"I know; God, how I know!" She turned to the large window overlooking the lake. "You have no idea what I have had to go through since word got out about you and Jean Marc. I had to practically beg Father Delacroix to preside over the children's baptism next month. Why you won't let me plan a proper reception for the boys at my house is beyond me, Nora. Even Father Delacroix said it would look better for the boys if they were introduced properly to society, considering the circumstances of their birth."

"Father Delacroix said that?" I tried to picture my mother and our parish priest discussing the indelicacies of my out of wedlock conception.

A ray of sunlight on the water outside my window illuminated my mother's angry face, making her appear older than I remembered. As she stood there, silently staring at me, I could see the redness retreating from her cheeks. Then her eyes drifted to a framed picture of the boys on the shelf behind my desk.

"Lou told me about what you went through during the delivery. How difficult it was." She shook her head. "I should have been there. I'm sorry, Nora."

"Lou was there for both of you," I assured her.

"He said you named the boys after their grandfathers and my brother."

I nodded. "Jacques Clayton and Emile Louis."

"Lou was so pleased you thought of him." Her face softened and her voice wavered with emotion. "Your father would have been very proud of you."

I leaned forward in my chair, fascinated by the change in her expression. "Were you happy with Daddy?"

She fiddled with one of her diamond rings. "It was the best time of my life. Lou is…well, Lou is very good to me. But your father, he was magic. With him, I was happy."

"That's why I stay here, Mother."

She frowned. "Despite everything he did, everything he was?"

A glimmer of the sunlight caught the edge of a silver frame on the corner of my desk. I glanced at the picture of my father and Jean Marc standing on Uncle Jack's boat when they were both so young and so happy. "Everyone has a past. It's whether they want a future or not that matters."

"What kind of future did he give you?" Mother shouted, sounding like her old self. "A future filled with misery, wondering if those two boys will grow up to be like their father, or worse, like that criminal Henri. Oh, Nora, you have no idea what you are in for."

"Yes, Mother." I sat back in my chair, grinning at her concern.

"So, where are my grandsons?"

"At the house, with Aunt Marie and Uncle Jack."

"Nora, don't call her that. It's bad enough Marie Gaspard has become my sister-in-law, yet again." She rolled her big brown eyes at me. "How could you leave those two boys in the hands of that nitwit and my alcoholic brother?"

"Uncle Jack gave up drinking, Mother."

"My brother, give up drinking? That won't last and you know it," she snorted. "If you're not careful those boys will grow up to be just like Jacques. They will need better examples in their lives, if you want them to—"

"Why don't you go over to the house and see them?" I suggested.

She straightened her back and held her head up to me. "Yes, I would like that." She walked to the door, but as she reached for the door handle, she stopped. "Do you think one day, Nora, you might come back to New Orleans?"

"I'll be back in a few weeks for Henri's trial."

She showed me her profile. "They should have gone after him for murder one," mother stated emphatically.

"He didn't kill that girl, Mother. Henri shot the real murderer at the house that day, but the DA still wants to go after him for being an accessory."

"And when the trial is over?" she persisted.

I shook my head. "My life is here."

She faced me, and her features became uncharacteristically somber. "I know what you must think of me, but I have only wanted the best for you. I always pushed you because I had to make sure you never ended up like me."

All the guilt she had instilled in me through the years came pouring out of my soul like water breaking through a dam. I was not completely absolved, but I knew my life was no longer going to be guided by my mother's expectations.

"I understand, Mom. Without you, I would not be the woman I am. You've always been the voice inside my head. Thank you for pushing me, and for believing in me."

My mother quietly opened my office door. "I'm glad you're happy, Nora. You deserve to be happy," she softly said, and quickly stepped into the bright light of the warehouse beyond.

Not two seconds later, Steve was in my office doorway, examining me with his piercing blue eyes.

"Honey, they heard her yelling all the way in Baton Rouge." He frowned. "Was it bad?"

"Better than I expected. She came to see the boys."

He snickered. "'Bout damn time. They're three months already and she has never set eyes on them. I'm amazed Claire volunteered to plan the christening."

"Well, the past year has been a bit too much for her. She had to have time to adjust to everything."

He moved toward my desk. "What about you, Nora? It's been a hell of a year for you, as well."

"It has. But I'm still here, Steve. I survived."

"I guess in your case every dark cloud does have a silver lining." He raised his eyes to the clock on the wall behind me. "Well, it's almost time for lunch, and I want to get a good view of all those buff and tanned fisherman coming down the dock for their lunch break." He clapped his hands together and winked at me. "The highlight of a gay man's day." He sauntered out of the office and closed the door behind him.

A twinkling of light from my desk distracted me. I turned to see the sunlight dancing on the picture of Jean Marc and my father. I reached out and touched the image of Jean Marc's young face.

"Nora!" a man's velvety voice called from the other side of my office door.

A tall, muscular man with wavy, gray-speckled black hair and fiery, dark brown eyes limped into my office.

"Did you put those orders in for the new bilge pumps?" he bellowed.

I smiled up at him. "Yes, Jean Marc. Two days ago."

He had a seat in the red leather chair in front of my desk. "I saw Claire storming out of here. What did she say?"

"She came to see the boys. She's mortified that we aren't married, and wants me to come home to New Orleans."

Jean Marc sat back in his chair and rubbed his right leg. "I've asked you a dozen times to marry me, but you keep putting me off."

"I wasn't about to marry you when you were lying in a hospital bed, and then by the time you were strong enough to walk, I was already five months pregnant with the boys."

Jean Marc got up from his chair, wincing slightly as he stood. "In a few more weeks I'll be done with therapy for my leg, and perhaps then we should plan our wedding." He came around to my side, took my hand, and pulled me from my chair. "Marry me, Nora. Before our sons are old enough to give you away."

I straightened the bent collar on his crisp white shirt. "Perhaps in the fall, after shrimping season, when it's cooler. We can have a small ceremony outside at the house, like we planned."

He reached his arms about my waist. "When we are married, you will have to waltz with me in front of all our family and friends." He started to slowly step back and forth as he held on to me.

I laughed as I remembered the steps. "The Acadian Waltz, like when we were children."

"We will marry, and dance, and then I will make you mine all over again."

I rested my head against his chest as we danced beneath the bright fluorescent lights. "I've always been yours, Jean Marc."

"I know, my love. I have always known."

I gazed into his brilliant eyes. "Even when we were little, chasing each other around the docks?"

He held me close. "Even then."

"How did you know?" I questioned.

"Every Cajun knows that you can only dance the waltz with your true love. Because you can never master the steps, until someone touches your heart."

The End

ABOUT THE AUTHOR

Alexandrea Weis is a registered nurse from New Orleans who has been writing novels and screenplays for over twenty years. Her first novel, To My Senses, was a finalist for commercial fiction in Eric Hofer Book Awards, a finalist for romance in the Foreword Magazine Book of the Year awards, and a finalist for romance in the USA Book Awards. Her second novel, Recovery, was ranked #1 on the Amazon top rated for romantic suspense in kindle books. Buyer Group International, an independent production company in Austin, has optioned the motion picture rights for Recovery.

Ms. Weis is also a permitted wildlife rehabber with the Louisiana Wildlife and Fisheries and when she is not writing, Ms. Weis is rescuing orphaned and injured wildlife. She lives outside of New Orleans with her husband and a menagerie of pets.

Made in the USA
San Bernardino, CA
03 April 2014